M000303952

DREAM KEEPER

DREAM KEEPER

A Novel of
Myth and
Destiny in the
Pacific
Northwest

MORRIE RUVINSKY

SASQUATCH BOOKS
SEATTLE

Copyright ©2000 by Morrie Ruvinsky
All rights reserved. No portion of this book may be reproduced or utilized
in any form, or by any electronic, mechanical, or other means without the
prior written permission of the publisher.

Printed in the United States of America
Distributed in Canada by Raincoast Books, Ltd.
04 03 02 01 00   5 4 3 2 1

Cover illustration: Simona Bortis
Cover design: Karen Schober
Interior design: Dan McComb

Library of Congress Cataloging in Publication Data

Ruvinsky, Morrie.
        Dream keeper : a novel of myth and destiny in the Pacific
Northwest / Morrie Ruvinsky.
             p. cm.
        1. Northwest, Pacific—Fiction. 2. Reincarnation—Fiction. I. Title.
PS3568.U85 D74 2000
813'.54—dc21
                                        99-054196

Sasquatch Books
615 Second Avenue
Seattle, Washington 98104
(206) 467-4300
www.SasquatchBooks.com
books@SasquatchBooks.com

For my wife, Alicia, who walked with me

from first word to last

And our daughter, Jessica,

who brightens every step of the way.

Oh, the Sisters of Mercy
They are not departed or gone.

—Leonard Cohen, "Sisters of Mercy"

PROLOGUE

It seemed a singular honor to Dzarilaw when the Thunderbird came to him in a dream. He was just a young warrior then, long before his great potlatch, long before he ever saw his first white man.

In the dream Dzarilaw follows a grizzly bear along a river, up through the high mountains and great forests to a gleaming glacial lake. Preparing camp he hears a noise so terrible that it makes the trees tremble and shake.

He becomes aware of a man standing alone on the opposite shore. "Who are you?" Dzarilaw calls out, but the man doesn't answer.

This is Kwakiutl land and the stranger has no right to be here, so Dzarilaw gets into his canoe and paddles across the lake to kill him. When he reaches the far shore, the stranger has become an old hag cooking over an open hearth. Dzarilaw points out that she has no fire, and the logs immediately burst into flame.

"You have no right to haul me into your dreams," the woman reproaches him. "Can't you cook for yourself?" She hands him a bowl and fills it with fresh blubber. He cannot imagine how she comes by whale fat so high up in these mountains, but it is the best he has ever tasted. When he's done he thanks her and asks about the man he had seen earlier.

"There are no Men here," she says, "not even you, Dzarilaw."

He doesn't understand how she knows his name.

"Go home," she says. "This place is not for you. Go home," she repeats so quietly that even in the dream he has to strain to hear, "and be a promise to your people."

A tiny intricately carved wooden box appears in her hand. From it she removes a very long and astonishingly bright feather-coat. She throws it over her shoulders and all at once transforms into a Thunderbird of such immense size it could carry a whale in its talons.

Climbing into the sky, the Thunderbird soars so high it blocks out the sun. Its wings make the sounds of terrible thunder, and from its eyes bolts of lightning flash across the heavens. The storm is the most fierce that Dzarilaw has ever seen. He begins to think that he will die here and never wake from his dream.

Drenched and scared, Dzarilaw calls out his surrender. "What do you want?"

"That you remember the day I fed you."

"And the promise?"

"It's in your bones."

For the rest of his life, Dzarilaw had no idea what bargain he had made with the Thunderbird. He became one of the great chiefs of the Pacific Northwest and the People said it was because he had seen the Thunderbird and survived, to which he always answered . . . not yet.

ONE

The sea churned up a trail of foaming water and flapping fish. The only other sounds were the metallic crunch of the engine as it pushed the boat through the cold Pacific waters, and the straining scream of the winch as it reeled in the net, dropping its bounty into the hold.

"Jesus Christ!" the galley mate yelled. "Jesus H. Christ!" he cried again, crossing himself and trembling. He was the first to spot it: a drowned man bound up in the net. He was naked, a deathly blue, and blood trailed from a gash near his belly. Soon everyone saw him and they stopped the winch and he just dangled in the air, caught by an arm and a leg in the netting.

The body swung with the lolling of the ship. No one seemed quite sure what to do. He must be dead, they thought, because he would have to be—this far out to sea and so long in the net—and so there was no rush to do anything until the galley mate crossed himself again and said Holy-Mother-of-God-he-just-breathed, which was impossible of course. They cut him free and laid him down on some old blankets. The cut across his belly wasn't bleeding much anymore but the wound remained ugly, long and ragged.

"Shark," someone said with the calm assurance of many years at sea.

"Hell, that's no shark," another said with equal confidence. "I seen a dozen men shark-bit and that's no shark."

"Dead is dead," the first responded. "Don't much matter what killed him."

And just then a gurgling sound rose out of the blue man's throat and he took a breath.

"He's not dead yet," the galley mate pointed out.

"He's dead alright," Solomon, an older sailor, assured everyone as he joined the group. "I seen dead men do that before."

"That's crazy, Solomon, dead men don't breathe, that's what makes 'em dead."

Once again, the blue man gurgled and his body shook and gasped for air as if he would suck the universe into his lungs if he could, but would settle now for just a little oxygen.

"I'm telling you he's not dead," the galley mate insisted.

"Ssshhhh," Solomon said. "A little respect."

They all grew still and watched as the blue man tried again to fill some small portion of his lungs and fell quiet once more. Very quiet.

"See," Solomon said, "what'd I tell you?"

A raven, apparently as curious as everyone else, landed and perched high up on the trawler's stern gantry. It called out several times—qa qa qa—as though demanding that they attend to the blue man, but its screeching voice made the already nervous men even more anxious.

No one did anything until the cook came up from the galley. He swaggered into the crowd with all the natural authority of the guy in charge of the food and they cleared a path for him. "Sure is a pretty one," the cook, who was not generally given to noticing such things, noticed as he knelt beside the naked blue body. He placed his enormous butchering hands on the stilled blue chest and pressed gently, forcing out some water. The blue man gurgled and the cook pressed on his chest two or three more times, forcing all the water out that would come out. He started on the mouth-to-mouth and kept at it until the dead man gasped and started breathing on his own.

"It's a goddam miracle," Solomon announced somberly, worrying because one should not trifle with miracles—they set the universe off-kilter, make everything possible and render nothing dependable. "Be very, very careful," Solomon cautioned.

—

The wait for the Coast Guard made everyone edgy, especially with the raven on board. It was a bad sign, a raven this far from shore, and when they tried to shoo it away it wouldn't go, not until the helicopter finally came to fetch the drowned man.

Erratic winds buffeted the chopper all the way back to the city, but soon enough the blue man was delivered to the hospital and wheeled through the cacophony of a modern medical emergency. He was dazed, still half-drowned, still hurting, but well aware of the voices speaking words he barely understood or cared to. He listened to the wheels of his gurney as they clattered down the marbled floor to a white-curtained cubicle where a young man began yelling into his face.

"Can you hear me?" the very intense young doctor shouted. "What's your name? Can you hear me?"

The drowned man's name was Jason Ondine and of course he could hear him. Drowning makes you wet, not deaf. He would have answered except that the doctor seemed so frantic, so busy, so preoccupied that it felt like he wasn't really after answers. Besides, Jason's throat was so raw from the salt water that it hurt to try to talk.

Jason Ondine. He repeated the name to himself several times. *Jason Ondine. I am Jason Ondine.* It made him feel good to say it to himself and it became a healing mantra. *My name is Jason Ondine.* He noticed that his body, his entire spirit, seemed comforted by it.

"Where the hell's the gash this guy's supposed to have?" the young doctor, Wayne Elliot, demanded.

Jason was about to explain, but when he opened his eyes, he saw that the doctor wasn't talking to him. He closed his eyes again and remembered how it had felt when he realized that he was caught in the net and could not get free. He remembered looking up at the sun and the few stray clouds beyond the water's surface. He remembered the struggling, the frantic terror—it surged through him once again, there in the hospital—and he remembered how it felt when he finally realized that he would never make it, that he had drowned. A strange, unhurried peace overtook him.

"We're losing him," Elliot warned. "Let's fill him up." A nurse handed Elliot a hypodermic and he plunged it into Jason's chest. Jason bellowed like a mating sea lion. Inside he kept saying his name and soon it relaxed him again and his body went limp. "I think we're going to be okay," the doctor announced, sounding confident. "He'll sleep now and we'll see what we can get out of him in the morning."

"What about the sutures?" the nurse asked.

"You tell me," the doctor challenged. "You see anything to suture?"

No, she saw nothing because there was nothing to see. Other things about the patient made her nervous too. Not medical nervous. There was a spirit sickness here. The nurse, Taryn Stream-Cleaner, was a Haida from a village over on the Island. She'd always been Taryn but the Stream-Cleaner part was a relatively recent addition, a direct translation of her tribal name which no one here in the city could pronounce, not even most of the city Indians. Usually very cool under pressure, it was unlike her to be afraid, but she was trembling. Someone noticed. "You alright?"

"I'm okay," Taryn said, staring at the blue man, but she was not. "The medevac report says a twelve-inch gash running along—"

"A gash like that doesn't heal up in an hour without a trace. I think we can assume the chopper jockeys are just playing with our heads again."

"Well it's not funny." Taryn had no tolerance for sloppy charts, and funny or not, this was sloppy. But in truth, it wasn't the chart that was upsetting her, it was the patient. She couldn't get a fix on it, but she didn't want to get too close to him.

"Okay," Elliot promised, "I'll talk to them."

"It's happened before," Jason said.

All eyes turned to him.

"What happened before," the doctor asked. "Drowning?"

"No, the wound," Jason explained.

"There is no wound," the doctor comforted. "You're going to be alright."

"The shark came at me quick, quicker than I was expecting, and at the last second I twisted away from his jaws. I thought I was okay but his fin caught my belly as he went by."

"There was no wound," Elliot repeated.

"I'd have been dinner for sure because he was turning back for me, but I think the noise from the boat scared him off."

"Fine," the doctor said.

"As long as he's awake . . ." Taryn mumbled, indicating that she had questions to ask of the drowned man. She hoped permission would be denied but the doctor nodded. Sure. Go ahead. "Sir," Taryn said, her pencil poised over her chart, "we need to know your name."

"My name," he said, "my name is Jason Ondine."

Startled, she dropped the pencil. "Ohmygod!"

"Taryn?" one of the other nurses said moving to her.

Taryn backed away from Jason, as scared as she had ever been in her life. She was trembling. *Ohmygod. Ohmygod. It's him. It's him!*

The doctor hurried to her side. "Taryn, are you—"

"It's him. It's Jason Ondine!"

Elliot reached out to touch Taryn but she screamed and ran away. Another nurse ran after her. The doctor went back to look at his patient. "Why is she afraid of you?"

Jason wondered where to start. *Well let's see, a couple hundred years ago when I was just a boy . . . No, maybe metaphor: There is no pack without a wolf, there is no wolf without a pack.*

"Do you know her?" Elliot persisted.

"I'm tired," Jason answered, and closed his eyes. He thought about flying in the sea, about soaring through the water.

TWO

The Chief bellowed with pleasure at the stories they told around the fire, stories they would tell again with even greater relish at his potlatch. These were the days just before they met their first white settlers, so they had no idea what lay before them and told the stories as though the world would go on as it always had. There was no sense of foreboding, no intimation of doom. Stories were still the voice of the universe, the songs by which primal wisdom was carried from one generation to another, from one people to another. These were stories that nourished and instructed them. Stories that protected them.

"Dzarilaw," one of the carvers chuckled as he continued to work on the small box that would become a gift for one of the northern relatives, "tell us the story of the flood."

Dzarilaw smiled. It was one of his favorite stories too. Now, this was not Dzarilaw the mythic animal-hero from the days of creation, but a son many generations descended. He too had been a steadfast warrior, a reliable hunter and fisherman, and a great teller of the old stories. He was loved by all who knew him and held in high regard even by those who had only heard of him. Now that he was old and preparing his potlatch, they would come from all around to honor him.

Night filled the air and drew everyone closer to the fire. The end of August had come quickly and with it the cold. Summer did not come that often to the inside bays along the northern coast. It arrived regularly enough as a season—teeming seas, lush natural gardens, fat mosquitoes feeding on you at their leisure—but it rarely stayed long enough to take the deep chill out of your bones, or prompt anyone to stretch out on the rocks late at night dreaming of relief from the joyous oppression of summer. Instead, fog ruled and it was the nature of the tribe not to notice. Especially the Bear People. The celebrations would proceed unimpeded by the rains and the chill when Dzarilaw, heir of the Bear Prince, gathered all the villages for his potlatch.

"Wolverine," Dzarilaw began, "was the smartest of them all. Smarter even than Bear." He settled into the telling. He could make Wolverine smarter than his own totem because there were no clans to Wolverine. Wolverine's magic was owned by none, and so could be claimed by any. Or denied.

Wolverine is a Trickster, often of a nasty nature, but the story Dzarilaw told about him was one of the more beneficent. It had been told for thousands of years by a people who had never heard of Noah. By a people who had never seen a white settler until they encountered Jason Ondine and his family. By a people who roared with laughter when the Jesuit told them that the one true God had been nailed to a cross.

"Smarter than Bear," Dzarilaw repeated and then paused again because his two slaves had entered through the oval door of the large cedar house carrying the ceremonial blanket that several of the women had completed just in time for the potlatch. The large finely woven blanket was decorated with the detailed figure of a very large grizzly—in honor of Dzarilaw—created with thousands of carefully cut abalone shells that gave the bear an appropriately royal iridescent glow.

The two slaves (Daughter-of-Otter's-Daughter, who was now

growing old, and her son, derisively known as Other-Daughter) held the blanket up for Dzarilaw's approval, which he gave only after all the others had finished admiring the workmanship. A stunning piece of work, it would make a fitting final gift. Dzarilaw would give it to one of the more important visiting chiefs, so the quality mattered. That it was such a fine blanket meant that in the next year or two another village would invite them to a potlatch and return an even finer blanket. The People were all pleased.

Only the two slaves were unhappy. It wasn't that they were treated badly; they weren't. There was the occasional humiliation—like being a grown man known as "Other-Daughter"—and the fact that they had to get used to being chattel, but they were fed and clothed and lived in the wooden houses just like real people. Daughter-of-Otter's-Daughter and her son Other-Daughter were Tlingits from an inland village. They had been captured years ago in a raid led by Dzarilaw one winter when the rivers froze and the seas were empty. It wasn't the slavery that was making them so unhappy, they had long ago been broken to that and ascribed their unhappy fate to retribution for the sins of some ancestors they knew nothing of. But one or the other of them would not live to see the end of this potlatch. Common practice dictated that when a great chief like Dzarilaw organized a potlatch, he would kill one of his slaves to demonstrate his contempt for the notion of property.

"Smarter than Bear," Dzarilaw said for the third time. Everyone liked these stories because they were reminded of the joys of creation and the silliness of the creators. They made everyone somehow feel less foolish about their own behavior. "And a good thing too," Dzarilaw added.

"A very long time ago, in the age of the great floods, when the seas were rising, there came a day when almost the whole world lay under water. Wolverine kept himself dry by hopping from one rock to another, but the rocks were getting farther and farther apart."

Dzarilaw hopped about a little on his haunches, looking very clumsy. Silly. His audience laughed and he knew he had captured some essence of the lumbering wolverine. "Wolverine knew that even these stepping-stones would soon be submerged and the deluge would swamp him and put an end to his life."

Daughter-of-Otter's-Daughter and her son Other-Daughter lingered for the story, lingered to engage Dzarilaw's sympathy. His mercy. He looked over and saw them near the door. Normally they would not be allowed to stay, but Dzarilaw's heart was heavy for them. They had been faithful to their servitude, and while Dzarilaw had nothing bad to say of either one of them, he knew what tradition required of him. He decided to let them stay, and no one seemed to mind.

"So Wolverine called a meeting of all the water animals and asked each of them to help him save the world from drowning. He asked Otter first: Dive down and bring me back some ground. Otter dove deep and searched until his lungs were near to bursting. When he broke the surface he was gasping for air and had to admit that all he could find were weeds and a few fish." Dzarilaw noticed tears streaming down the face of Daughter-of-Otter's-Daughter and he wondered why it was necessary to take a life, even the life of slave, in order to demonstrate one's spiritual purity. He looked away from her. "Wolverine turned to Beaver and—"

One of Dzarilaw's cousins, whose family held the Beaver for its totem, protested that Beaver had done all he could. They laughed at him and so he laughed too.

"It's true," Dzarilaw assured him, "that Beaver dove into the water and did all he could, but still, he too came back gasping for air, and conceded with some taint to his pride that he had been unable to swim deep enough to find any ground. Muskrat," Dzarilaw pleaded, mimicking the high-pitched gravelly voice of Wolverine, "it's up to you."

Cheering hailed this pronouncement, especially among the children, who celebrated with the confidence of people who've heard the story before. "Muskrat wasn't happy that it fell to him, but finally he dove deep into the sea. A long time passed, too long a time, and Wolverine thought Muskrat had drowned. He took it for a sign that from now on, all the world would be covered in water."

The children rattled sticks and pounded on the floor: No. No. No. Dzarilaw let them carry on like that for some time before he finally relented and continued. "When it seemed that all was lost . . . Muskrat surfaced. His mouth was so full of mud that he couldn't talk or even breathe. . . ." The tension in the air was unbearable. Here it was, the moment they were waiting for. "Wolverine put his lips to Muskrat's ass and blew as hard as he could until the ground poured out of Muskrat's mouth, more and more ground, seemingly without end. And more and more."

And with every "more" the children screamed louder with delight, until their mothers came to see what was going on and in mock disapproval led them all away.

"And that ground," Dzarilaw called to the children as they were hauled off, "is the very earth we walk on."

The men laughed. The women pretended not to. The kids made farting sounds through their mouths. Dzarilaw watched Daughter-of-Otter's-Daughter and her son Other-Daughter leave, and though he laughed like the others at his telling of the story, he was too sad to dwell in it.

—

The first time Jason Ondine saw the Pacific Ocean was some two hundred years before the fishermen caught him—blued with dying— in their nets. He was just a boy then, barely twelve, when the pioneers began their trek across the continent. He left the Hochelaga settlement on the St. Lawrence River with his father and mother, an older brother and two younger sisters. They were joined by a Jesuit priest and his altar boy, and half a dozen others. They made a desperate dash through the lower St. Lawrence Valley to avoid getting massacred by a band of marauding Oneidas determined to rid their nation of the plague of the newly ubiquitous Jesuit missionaries, known to them as Black Robes.

Jason Ondine's group met up with other pioneers on the frontier at the western end of Lake Ontario and from there it took two more years of hard travel to reach the West Coast. They started out twenty-three in all, and only seven survived to see the Pacific. They didn't lose a single pioneer through the forests, but once they crossed the Mississippi and met the plains and the ceaseless wearing winds, it began. One of the families—five people—fell to the mosquito fever less than one month out. Others later. Jason's sisters were kidnapped by a frustrated Sioux hunting party all of whom seemed to think potential young wives were reasonable consolation for the lack of fresh kill. The girls were never found.

The mountains were the worst for Jason. So high and cold, so spare of air that he sometimes felt like his chest was trying to explode. His mother died there—of sorrow, his father said—and it left a gaping sadness in Jason. He missed her then and still misses her now.

When the last of the pioneers had almost given up the dream, could not walk another step, they found themselves in the majestic coastal fir forests. They gazed up in awe, genuine biblical awe, as these giant trees reached up to—and probably even touched—the heavens. Consumed by the magic, they were protected from the searing sun by the astonishing canopy, and their feet walked on ground made soft and playful by the generous layers of pine needles accumulated before them.

It took several more days before they finally broke free of the last of the great fir trees and emerged onto a promontory that jutted out high over the Pacific. The undulating waters rolled so far below them that the waves seemed to crash and foam in silence. Two hundred years later Jason still remembered that day with the virgin clarity and blood-surging confusion that froze it in his soul.

It began so innocently. He had found a stone, one that he'd been drawn to by the little flecks of quartz that sparkled in response to the stray rays of sunlight that made their way to the forest floor. Walking on, he kept the stone for the jagged edges that tickled his fingertips. Later in the day, when it had grown ordinary and heavy, he hurled it from the high ledge out toward the ocean. The stone never reached the water. His throw fell short. The stone floated through the air with no apparent purpose until it landed with a sickening thud on the head of a young doe several hundred feet below and killed her.

From that moment on, the future beckoned Jason with a crooked finger.

THREE

In the early 1970s, on the day Lizzie Bennett met Jason Ondine, she was having another one of those intestine-wrenching skirmishes with her mother. In a lifetime crammed with them there had never been a single such encounter that was ever worth having, but the needs of the heart are such that the promise of certain failure never seems to carry with it sufficient warning.

"Never mind," Lizzie snapped, hurting, "just give it back to me." The trembling in her voice was barely audible, sub-sensory to any but a mother.

"What?" Marianne protested. "What did I say?"

This particular skirmish evolved around a thing, as so much of their lives did. This time it was a gift, a frayed fabric not much bigger now than a scarf. A thousand years old, the once vivid pome-granate-red was now a faded hue, vibrant only in the imagination that one was willing to invest. For Lizzie it was the proud remnant of an imperial robe worn by the great-grandson of T'ai-tsu, founder of the Sung dynasty. "Just forget it," Lizzie answered, reaching to retrieve the relic.

"I didn't mean to cause such a fuss," Marianne said, giving the cloth up easily. She had tried to imagine the imperial glamour wrapped up in its frayed threads, but couldn't summon the enthusiasm to overlook the centuries of accumulated decay. Who could know to which places and what purpose this rag had been subject in the intervening lifetimes between the grandeur of the Chinese court and the filthy antiquities dealer in Afghanistan who sold it to Lizzie? Marianne wondered if the seller hadn't been just another impoverished hustler who preyed on Lizzie's daily efforts to redress the inequities of the world.

Lizzie had journeyed through Afghanistan as part of a caravan of sixties bliss that included a classmate from college, a French medical student and his two girlfriends, and a German atheist who had taken a vow of silence just a week or so before he got to Kabul. Lizzie traveled in the good company of new friends and a continuous cloud of smoke from the ready supply of black hash. Her sometimes incoherent but otherwise joyful postcards home had caused some concern at the Bennett dinner table even after she had returned.

It was in the mountains not far from Baghlan that Lizzie found the remnant of the once-proud robe, which she acquired in exchange for a Zippo lighter with a Lucky Strike logo. Anything American was treasured in Afghanistan in those days. Lizzie loved fabrics. The feel of them, the drape, the smells. From very early on they had inspired her, and on this trip she had collected everything from swatches to costumes. Most items were parceled home, but this cloth, this Chinese treasure, she kept with her. Of all the things that she had seen and touched on this journey, nothing spoke to Lizzie of her mother so much as this. She carried the fabric with her the rest of the trip, thinking of how happy Marianne would be to get it, thinking how proud she was about having found the perfect gift. So certain was Lizzie that she even waited until her mother's birthday to present it.

"I really wish you wouldn't take it away from me, Deer Heart," Marianne said, trying to sound enthusiastic.

"I hate when you call me that."

"Deer Heart?"

"You know I hate it."

Marianne had always called her Deer Heart. Those words were, in her mind, the purest link in their relationship. She pronounced it "Dearheart," and certainly the name carried some of that with it, but she meant "Deer Heart." Fawn-eyed. Swift and wary. And when she wrote it—letters, birthday cards, notes—it was always "Deer Heart." The second of her three kids, Lizzie was the only one Marianne had ever felt close to. The first time she looked at Lizzie, cradled in her arms in a hospital bed, she saw enormous frightened brown eyes, huge pools of distant wisdom that seemed to understand too much.

"If you don't want me to call you Deer Heart," Marianne said, trying to settle the issue with false gestures of compliance, "I won't."

If only Lizzie could rip open the cloaks and expose her mother's heart, air out the pain, but she couldn't. It was Marianne's birthday and finally Lizzie gave it up and let her mother call her Deer Heart. If that was all she could have of her mother, she would take it.

"Now," Marianne said, "could I have my present back?"

"Forget it, Mother." Here she was, a full-fledged adult reduced once again to a wounded child in the face of her mother's distance.

"You know, Elizabeth, I think I will never understand you."

Lizzie knew it was so. It simply wasn't in her mother anymore to feel out her daughter's soul, or even her own. Those doors were long since sealed. When Marianne admitted that she didn't understand Lizzie, she meant it with a profound sorrow. Her ability to connect was gone, suffocated by a lifetime of other choices that made reaching out impossible. But Lizzie heard only the rejection, not the plea for absolution. She heard the well-oiled doors slamming shut in her face, not the tears sliding off her mother's heart.

"Deer Heart, maybe you'd feel better if we had some lunch." She meant it more as a prescription than an invitation. Unfortunately, it was salve too often employed, so that it no longer carried with it any comfort and certainly no healing.

—

And so it was, weighed by the gravity of foiled joy, that Lizzie found herself sinking quickly in the sticky quagmire of family. The escape, almost a habit by now, was Calder Cove, a little hidden bay a couple of hours up the coast that she had discovered as a child and still cherished. In all the intervening years she had never seen anybody else there, probably because so few were willing to make the two-mile trek through the woods when they could, after all, get to the beaches to either side of the cove by car.

At Calder Cove Lizzie touched the tides of her life. Here she could settle back into her favorite smoothed-out boulder, curved like a cradle by the millennial slush of patient waves, and play her flute. On this day she began with scales as she watched the sea lions lounging on their own rocks out in the bay. She played until the notes turned to melody and the melody to music and when she tired of the attentions of the sea lions, she closed her eyes and played just for herself.

With her music rising into the air, soothing her, she felt free to wander in her head and wonder about her favorite pestering ironies, like how is it that being smart helps not the slightest to resolve the personal perils of one's own life? And what exactly was smart good for if it wasn't much good for making you happy?

She was enjoying it—the sun, the sounds, the freedom to disengage from Marianne—when suddenly she felt him and stopped playing. She opened her eyes. Far away a man walked toward her across the wet shimmering sand. He was beautiful, and he was naked.

—

Jason Ondine had been lounging on the rocks out in the bay when he heard Lizzie's flute. This was twenty-five years before the fishermen hauled him blue and naked into the boat and saved his life, but it would be this beach and these days that he would be thinking about when they cut him from the net.

Jason loved music and had heard too little of it in his life. Lizzie's gentle serenade was barely audible out there on the water and less discerning ears than Jason's would not have heard it at all. They were tiny notes, lighter than air, and they swept him away. He scanned the shore for the source and the moment he saw her, his heart was lost. In an instant he was transformed. Everything about her excited him: her shimmering brown hair, lanky body, long strong fingers prancing across the flute, and even at this distance her eyes—her big, dark, sad eyes.

Abandoning the rocks, Jason slipped into the surf thinking that what he was doing was crazy, but the anticipation would not be denied and the excitement he felt was too intense to leave room for anything rational. He found himself gliding just below the surface to the shore. With hardly a pause he stood and started toward her, and no one could have been more surprised about it than Jason himself.

His gait was so determined, so easy and fluid, that Lizzie thought she must be hallucinating, and he kept coming. Her heart pounded, beat for step. She thought she should get up and run away, but she didn't. She just watched him, thinking that he radiated danger and menace, but her eyes never wavered. Without any hesitation, he walked directly to her, stopped an arm's length from her shoulder, and stared at her.

"Rrrarr!" he suddenly shouted, a sharp phatic growl meant to startle her, and it did.

She flinched but recovered quickly. "Rrrarr," she growled back, just as suddenly. He flinched. Stepped back. "Why didn't you run away?" he asked, moving closer.

"I have as much right to be here as you do."

"I'm bigger," he answered, still confused by her refusal to be intimidated.

"I can see that," she teased, looking directly at his cock.

It embarrassed him. For the first time since Jason could remember, he was embarrassed by his nakedness. It was an uncomfortable sensation, like shame but more frivolous, and he didn't know how to respond. It set him off guard, but not so much that he tried to cover himself. Not so much that it made him shy. He found himself blustering. "I'm stronger than you, I could just take you."

"I don't think so," she said, dismissing the threat. "This is not exactly the Stone Age."

"The what?"

"The Stone Age?"

He shook his head. He had no idea what she was talking about. It was not exactly an obscure reference, so his reaction puzzled her. She didn't know why, but she had no fear of him. All she felt was an excitement, like she was in the presence of someone whose very existence ratified the nature of her own longing, embodied everything she suspected she'd been missing.

"What are you doing here?" she asked. She meant Holy-God-in-Heaven-how-on-earth-did-you-manage-to-deliver-this-magnificent-human-being-into-my-universe-at-such-an-auspicious-moment, so it was no surprise to her that her simple question, which was intended to carry some authority, came out instead sounding so rounded with pleasure and anticipation.

"I was waiting for you," he answered.

She laughed. She laughed in part because it was funny and it took the pressure off of her, but mostly because that was exactly what she was thinking, and even though it felt foreign and flighty, she knew from the moment she saw him that in some way she had always been waiting for him.

"Or maybe you were waiting for me," he said.

"No," she assured him, feeling exposed, "I often come here." There was a pounding inside her. Wet and thrilling, a primal excitement that inspired confusions and flame. She would have spoken to him in the poetry of mythic adventures: "Here is a golden platter and that beating thing upon it is my heart—take good care of it." But she couldn't say that to him. You can't say that to strangers. Especially men. Not in these days. These were liberated times and there was sisterhood to honor and independence to consider.

He said, "What?" as uncertain as if he had actually heard her.

"I didn't say anything," she said with caution after a moment, while fuming at herself for failing to own her own heart out loud.

Jason reached out and touched her hair. It was dry and silky, not clumped and matted by the sea. His fingers could hardly comprehend the opulent softness they caressed, could not believe the gentleness it inspired in him. These powerful, savage hands that could snap her neck on a whim, wanted nothing more than to caress her softly. More softly. Inside him were fires he was familiar with, desires he had responded to before, but there was something else now, something he had not felt before, and it made him nervous and uncertain. Others he had won with displays of courage or strength, demonstrations of skill, presentations of prizes, or he simply took what he wanted, but it was always simple. This was different. This woman whose hair he barely had the courage to caress was unlike anything he had ever known.

It was too complicated and he knew instinctively that the better thing to do was to walk away, and he would have except that he couldn't bear the thought. He felt like a skittish adolescent, and he did not like himself for it. "You are a very strange woman," he finally said.

"I'm strange?"

He already regretted speaking. He was never very good at it. Not then. Not now. "That's not exactly what I meant."

"*I'm* strange!"

"No. Not strange. I meant . . . something else," Jason tried.

"You come strolling down the beach in your birthday suit and start a conversation with a perfect stranger and you think *I'm* strange?"

"I have no suit."

She didn't see the humor in it. Neither did he.

"I'm sorry," he explained.

"It's not enough."

"I just don't know what to say for you to lie with me."

Now she was scared. Now it was no longer innocent. He wasn't naked any longer, he was just a man with no clothes on. She grabbed her flute and ran.

"Wait!"

She did not. She didn't even look back.

"Wait!" In ways he still couldn't fathom, he felt as if he were slipping away from himself as she ran for the woods. He would have gone after her, but he was afraid to get too far from the water.

FOUR

Taryn Stream-Cleaner took a couple of days off and on the morning she came back to work, the story of Jason Ondine and the vicious incident with the orderly dominated the hospital talk. Petitions were already up in all the locker rooms demanding increased security and better protection for the staff. It was not the first time petitions had circulated in response to some awful incident, nor did anyone expect that the administration would respond any more effectively this time around. Bayshore General was a troubled hospital. It was a government-funded repository for patients with no private health insurance, HMO coverage, or company clinic to protect them. The place was understaffed, badly equipped, and poorly supplied.

Taryn was one of the bright lights. In her early forties and a genuine grown-up, she was a truly outstanding nurse, with an abiding concern for her patients and the gift of a healing touch that she alone was immune to. While Taryn was used to various weirdnesses around the hospital, she was nonetheless taken aback when she heard about Jason and the orderly. She was surprised that it disturbed her so. She'd thought that two days away had dulled her fear of him, but she could feel her pulse quicken in her chest.

"Anyway," her supervising nurse announced, "you're going to have to go up and take some blood."

"Excuse me?" Taryn balked.

"They've got him up in the psycho ward under lock and key—cop at the door, full security, the whole nine yards—and we need the blood. Can't work him up without the blood."

"They've got nurses upstairs." Taryn protested, already thinking, to hell with it, she's not going near him, the job's not worth it. All these years a nurse and she had never, ever, been afraid of a patient before.

"He won't let anyone else do it. He said just you."

Taryn argued with herself all the way up to the fourth floor and decided she wasn't going to let him or anyone else scare her out of doing her job. Besides, the name had to be just a coincidence, there was no way he could be *the* Jason Ondine. And why should she even care? She was Haida, the Ondine legend was Kwakiutl. The Haida and the Kwakiutl were neighbors but hardly brothers, and there was a great channel of sea between the Vancouver Island of her ancestors and the mainland coastal villages of the Ondine story. She attributed her concern to her grandmother, an Island Kwakiutl who had married into the family and brought with her the amazing tales of Jason Ondine. Taryn was a woman of medicine, a modern woman, a worldly woman free of the old superstitions. By the time she got up to the fourth floor, she was perfectly content to blame her grandmother for all this irrational fear.

Jason's room was easy enough to find—it was the one with the uniformed police officer sitting outside browsing through an old J. Crew catalog with the bored mask of a guy pretending to be shopping for sweat socks while in fact searching out compelling young models toned beyond access in even his wildest dreams. He looked up at the sound of Taryn's approaching footsteps. Three old women sat on a bench across the hall from the cop. Crones all. One had long silver hair in handsome braids. The second one, asleep beside her, had short-cropped, equally silvered hair, and the third, probably older than the first two, had long silky black hair. Young woman's hair. They made Taryn nervous, more anxious than she already was, and she was relieved to have to deal with the officer.

Taryn handed him her security pass. He examined it and waved it at the old women. "I told them they had to get a pass," he explained to her, "but they just sit there. Just sit there. Sometimes one of them comes over and looks through the window, but basically, they just sit there." While he fumbled with the door key, Taryn glanced back over her shoulder at the three old—ancient—ladies. The one with the short-cropped hair woke and giggled at her. It made Taryn's hair stand up on the back of her neck.

Stepping into the room, Taryn heard the door lock behind her. She was shaking. Being alone in the room with Jason disturbed her until she saw that both his arms were cuffed to the bed frame.

"Kwakwaka'wakw," Jason said, but he knew by her expression that she was not Kwakiutl and had no idea what he'd said. Then he noticed the slate pendant hanging from her necklace, a small stylized duck sitting on a whale and he knew at once. "Haida," he corrected.

"Yes," she said, not meaning at all to get into a conversation with him.

"All the People carve," he said, "but only Haida carve the black slate." His voice was so soothing and peaceful that it caught her off guard.

"My father gave it to me." Her voice trembled, confused because her anger seemed to be deserting her.

"It's very beautiful," he said and then said nothing else. He seemed perfectly comfortable with the silence, but Taryn wasn't.

"Why did you ask for me?" *Damn.* She hated herself for asking. She just wanted to do her job and get the hell out.

He thought the answer was obvious. "You saved my life."

"Oh, no," she protested immediately. "Oh, no." This was not a burden she was going to take on. "There were a lot of us there and me . . . I . . . I hardly did anything."

"You were the only one there who spoke my name. I hadn't heard anyone speak my name for a very long time. It meant a lot to me, and I just wanted to relieve you."

"Of what?"

"When you save a man's life, you become responsible for him," Jason explained.

Taryn just stared at him.

"That's the way it used to be," he said. "Isn't it the same now?"

Taryn shrugged.

"I'm trying to say that I relieve you of your responsibility. I return your freedom to you. It's the only gift I have to give."

"You know what, all I want from you is a vial of blood."

"It's the least I can do."

Taryn moved close enough to draw the blood and she was terrified. She wasn't afraid he was going to do something to her, she was afraid she'd feel sympathy for him. She was afraid she'd start believing he was really Jason Ondine. Drawing the blood, she couldn't help herself. "Why did you attack the boy?"

"The boy? Is that what they say, that I attacked the boy?"

She was afraid to answer until she pulled the needle from his arm and stepped away. "Yes," she said.

"That's not what happened," he began to explain.

—

After they had brought Jason from the fishing boat to the hospital and patched him up, he slept for two days. When he woke he was thinking about Lizzie Bennett, wondering if there was any way to find her. He'd give his soul to find her, but it had been twenty-five years and if he couldn't find her then, how could he possibly find her now? He was thinking about her, thinking about how often he thought about her, when he suddenly felt a cold chill run through him. It screamed at him: Danger. Run.

It was the middle of the night. Dark. Very dark. A man strode through the door like he owned the ward. He was a big man, a hospital orderly in a worn but otherwise fresh uniform. Jason knew something was wrong because the man had the smell about him of a hunter giving chase to prey.

It seemed like a dream, so inappropriately fluid. Strange thoughts rose from Jason's belly: You will die at the hand of your son! Die at the hand of your son. It was the only part of the curse left undone: Die at the hand of your son.

The man walked past the dying old man, and past the coughing man, and right past Jason to the last bed on the ward. Jason breathed easier, he was not the prey after all. But he was awake now. He had no son and if he did, he would not be one like this.

The patient in the last bed was a boy of seventeen who had been admitted with appendicitis, but the inflammation had gone away and Jason had heard the doctors debating the question of surgery now that it had become elective. He looked younger than seventeen. The orderly sealed the boy's mouth with surgical tape, then flipped him over onto his belly and taped his arms behind his back, all of it executed so quickly that the boy was essentially fully trussed by the time he woke, terrified. He tried to scream through his gag as the man dropped his pants and climbed onto the bed. "Go back to sleep," the orderly told the boy. "Just think of this as a pre-op nightmare. Blame it on the drugs."

The boy kept screaming, but all that came out was muffled complaint, pathetic sounds caught somewhere between his throat and the tape, backing up like sink sewage. "Shut the fuck up," the orderly hissed and pounded him in the kidney. The boy sobbed a great silent shuddering sob. The orderly pulled the curtains closed, creating a cocoon of privacy.

The two old men across the room kept themselves busy dying. They slept harder. The coughing man stopped coughing. They were scared and they all pretended that the closing of the curtain somehow exempted them from acting, excused them from responsibility. It was the ostrich defense.

Abate the rage, Jason thought, but he couldn't. It was already coursing through him, inflaming him. He couldn't stop it. Couldn't even slow it. It's not right, he thought. What was happening here was unfair. Unjust. Not the rape, that was just evil and Jason had long since learned that evil always shows its face. It was the failure to rise up against it that felt so unfair.

The Iroquois had taught Jason to look for justice when he was a little boy, long before he left for the great Pacific shores. They said that the devils come in many forms and cause suffering, and it is the failure to exact just retribution that sets the world off-balance. Neither saintly virtue nor absolute evil is possible in human beings, nor is it welcome. Evil is here to stay, and while it cannot be finally defeated, it must be engaged. It's balance that's required. Moderation. Recognition that every conduct has an effect, that every action exacts a price.

So Jason rose from his bed. His legs were weak from too much sleeping, but his heart was strong with anger. The rubber left his legs, replaced by steady determination in just those few short steps it took to reach the curtain. He pulled the curtain back. The orderly was on the boy, holding him down by the neck. "What the hell," he said, inflamed by the interruption.

Jason reached for the man and grabbed him by his hair. He pulled him from the bed and flung him to the wall.

"You're dead, man," the orderly growled. He charged Jason and when he made contact, he felt like he had run into a redwood tree. It was impossible to imagine that a man could be this solid, especially one fresh from his hospital bed. Shaken, the orderly pulled a scalpel from his pocket and slashed out at Jason. Jason raised his arm to protect himself and took the scalpel in the forearm. The blade opened a gash and went deep into the muscle. It stayed there, attached to Jason like a newly budding aluminum limb growing from his arm. Jason wrapped his arms around the orderly and squeezed. Even with the one arm bleeding, his hold was astonishing.

"I'll kill you," the orderly wheezed, barely able to get the words out.

Unaware of his own strength, Jason tightened his grip until the orderly couldn't breathe and his eyes bulged in helpless rage at

Jason's deadly embrace. Desperate, the orderly jabbed Jason's eye. Jason cried out in pain, then lifted the orderly off his feet and snapped his back. The last thing Jason felt before he blacked out was the stinging *whump* of a security guard's nightstick across the back of his skull.

By the time he woke up, he was in serious handcuffs and deep shit. The story, immediately transformed by institutional conventions, took on a life and shape of its own.

What the police heard when they arrived on the scene was that Jason was raping the boy when the orderly, responding to the commotion, came to the rescue. According to this version, Jason went berserk and tried to kill the orderly. Only the timely arrival of the security guard saved the man's life, but it had left him in a coma. The other patients saw nothing. Admitted nothing. The security guard said that he found Jason naked, that he himself had put the robe on him.

—

Taryn was outraged. This was exactly what she was afraid of, that he would tell her some incredible story and she'd believe him. It made her furious. "Well, then, why didn't the boy tell the police this story! Why didn't *you*? Explain that."

Jason had tried, but no one believed him and no one came to his defense. As for the boy, Jason assumed that he was too traumatized and too scared to contradict the official story, and the other roommates were too wary of what might befall them as patients if they didn't side with the hospital staff. "I need to get out of here," he said.

"What? I don't think you understand. The charges against you are very, very serious. Attempted murder. Rape. You'll be lucky if you don't spend the rest of your life in jail."

"That could be a very long time."

"Exactly," she said, sensing that she wasn't quite getting it.

"No. I need you to help me escape."

Taryn went cold. "No. I'm a nurse. I can't. . . . No."

It would be easy to know if he was telling the truth or not. She moved closer to the bed and looked for the scalpel wound. She checked carefully. Nothing. Not a scratch. She examined the other arm and it too was clean. Not a mark. "You said he cut you!" she said, bristling with indignation.

"Yes."

Taryn didn't know what to think. Was he some monster materialized straight from her grandmother's dreams? Killer or avatar? She hated living in two worlds. She hammered urgently at the door, and when it opened she raced off without making eye contact with either the cop or the crones. She couldn't wait for the elevator and ran down the back staircase, chased by the echo of her own steps. Halfway across the parking lot, she leaned against a lamppost to catch her focus and her breath. What she caught instead was Wayne Elliot out jogging.

"Taryn," he said, full of the robust ebullience of a self-satisfied exerciser, "are you alright?" The running always buoyed him. He was up to three miles and was hoping to boost it to five pretty soon. He never told anyone, but in the back of his mind was the notion that he could work himself up to a marathon. Maybe not this year, but someday, maybe. "Taryn?"

"Oh, hi," she said with a smile meant to affirm that he was still her favorite doctor.

"Are you okay?"

"I'm fine," she assured him, meaning that she thought she was losing either her mind or her soul, neither one of which could she do without.

"Can I help?" he said, hearing the pain, not the words. He'd always been a good friend and seemed to have a knack for showing up when she needed someone to talk to.

"I guess I'm confused about this whole Jason Ondine thing." Taryn had spent her life escaping from the restraints and stigma of the past. She became a nurse, a pragmatic woman of the sciences, more to mark her emergence from the world of superstition than anything else. She wasn't ashamed of being Haida; in fact, she loved the culture. The stories warmed her, but she understood them to be just that—an old magic with no place in the new world. So how then was she to account for this Jason Ondine and the terrible spiritual aching that possessed her when she was near him?

"You mean the business with the orderly?" Elliot checked.

Not quite what she meant, but the orderly was certainly an easier issue to talk about so she agreed to it. "He says he was defending the boy."

"I've heard that."

"He says the guy attacked him," Taryn continued

"I wasn't on, but Karas says there was a scalpel buried in his arm."

"He stitched him up?"

"Actually, no. He said it was weird. He said he checked it real carefully and it didn't need stitches."

"Oh, Christ," she said.

"What?"

"There's not a mark on him. Nothing."

Elliot hadn't stopped thinking about Jason since the first night. The report that Jason had a gaping wound when he was hauled aboard the fishing boat and that it had healed by the time they got him to the hospital was intriguing. Now this. Elliot didn't know what was going on, but if it were true, there was something in Jason that held untold promise. He was a modern miracle waiting to be reported. Elliot could already feel the possibilities swelling in his mind. "You seem to know something about him."

"Not really," Taryn said. "Just some old wives' tales."

"Listen," he said, excited, "can I buy you a coffee?" He was racing way ahead of himself, shaping his research. Controlled cuts. Clean ones. Some deep, some vital. He was already rehearsing his approach: "Jason, hi. Listen, I'd like to try a little experiment."

FIVE

Like most of the communities along the Pacific Coast, Dzarilaw's Village was built above the shoreline, every house and every lodge facing the sea. They were magnificent buildings of planked cedar supported by enormous poles and fluted crossbeams. The towering entrance posts were carved with mythical birds and bears, wolves and whales, all of which almost always sat atop a gaping mouth carved large to swallow visitors in welcome. The village was usually known as Eulakon, but in these days of the great potlatch everyone was calling it Dzarilaw's Village again, not for him, but for his great-great-great-great-grandfather the Bear. There were many soaring totem poles, some as tall as eighty or ninety feet, and every single one of them carried at least one image of the original Great Bear.

The sun was already setting on the third week of Dzarilaw's potlatch and he was still giving gifts away, such was his honor. The People had already begun to say that this was the potlatch festival of a great chief, and Dzarilaw was humbled to hear it.

People came from far away to help Dzarilaw shed his possessions. They came and accepted their gifts and stayed to dance and drink and tell stories and argue about whose version was right. It was important to argue about how the world began or who saved it when it needed saving. Was it Wolverine with the mud he sent others to fetch from under the sea, or was it the trickster Raven and the giant serpent? It was important to argue and even more important to accept on faith that everybody's version was correct.

Sometimes the questions assumed a level of veneration worthy of a Talmudic engagement or Papal conference, as was the case after Dzarilaw told his version of Wolverine and the mud. Everyone agreed that Wolverine had indeed saved the world from drowning, but there was intense competition over who had failed first, Otter or Beaver, and what that might mean to the way men conduct their lives and fight their wars. Dzarilaw insisted that his version was correct because he had heard it from his father, who had learned it from his father and so on, all the way back to the original bear of bears, the Bear Prince Dzarilaw himself.

It had to be Otter who failed first, common sense decreed, because Otter was the sleekest and the fastest and Wolverine would most certainly have sent him first because there was no time to waste, and the lesson was that the obvious battle plan was not necessarily the best, and any warrior worth his responsibilities should take care to order the world correctly before engaging in combat, hunting, marriage, or any other dangerous undertaking. Others argued that Beaver was actually sent first, because he was the smartest, the only one of them all who could build such fantastic houses and the only one who would know what kind of mud to bring back.

"But he failed," Dzarilaw reminded them.

"Yes, but he failed first!" Proving that wisdom is often not even worth its weight in mud.

The big question on everyone's mind, however, had to do with the rumor that was circulating, now openly, that a group of Pale People were on their way to the potlatch. They would be the first Europeans ever to set foot in the village, and there was considerable excitement about it. Dzarilaw took it as a very great honor that they would come all this way to pay their respects. He was most anxious to see them because he had heard, as long ago as his grandfather's time, that they had blue eyes. He was grateful that in his own life he would get to see if this was true or if, as his father had explained, only demons had blue eyes.

Everybody was having a good time except for Daughter-of-Otter's-Daughter—chained to a log to await her fate—and her son, Other-Daughter, who spent most of his time beside her, feeding her festival food and trying to comfort her.

—

On the fourth day of the pioneers' trek, Jason's group arrived, eight strong, having picked up a Tsimshian shaman who had been to the forts on the plains and spoke enough European to translate for them. By the time they arrived, the village knew all about Jason. The story of his killing of the doe had traveled by footpath and canoe with magical embellishment, and while the others were welcomed, Jason was greeted with awe and suspicion. The People didn't know if the story of the doe presaged the arrival of a great hunter or an evil child. In either case, he was not embraced.

He had dark brown eyes, which disappointed Dzarilaw and made it impossible to brand him a demon and dispense with him. It would take more thought. The general consensus was that the boy should be dispatched, but the People were reluctant to challenge the gods without a little more evidence that killing him was the right thing to do.

The Tsimshian didn't translate everything, but Jason didn't need to hear the words to understand that he was not regarded well. When the Tsimshian kept stealing glances at Daughter-of-Otter's-Daughter chained to the log, he wondered if he too was in grave danger. Daughter-of-Otter's-Daughter did not look away from Jason, and he saw in her eyes a despair that marked for him the beginning of a loneliness so deep that no mortal life could ever comprehend it. It was a loneliness he knew at once he would never shake, except for one brief, shining moment so far into the future that he could not yet even imagine it.

That night Daughter-of-Otter's-Daughter was brought to Dzarilaw before the fire. She would be one of Dzarilaw's two final gestures in this potlatch. The last one would be offered tomorrow when he would present the blanket with the bear on it. Daughter-of-Otter's-Daughter was trembling. Other-Daughter was weeping and he was taken away to spare the guests his unbecoming behavior.

"It is a young man's deceit, the gathering of property," Dzarilaw announced to all who had gathered to see the sacrifice, "and tonight I cast off the last of it."

There were murmurs of approval, a sure sign that at least those present were satisfied with their gifts. "You were a great warrior," someone shouted out of the darkness, "and now you are a great chief." Dzarilaw acknowledged the high praise with a glance. Inside, it made him glow but it would not do to smile. Smiling might be taken to mean that he was susceptible to flattery, a certain invitation to the great Spirits to bring him to ruin.

At first Jason and the others didn't quite grasp what was happening, but as it began to take inexorable shape, they were horrified. The Jesuit stepped forward, speaking in French, invoking the mercies of Christ. The Tsimshian tried to translate but Jesus was a spirit none of them knew or cared about, and the Tsimshian was quickly silenced and with him the priest.

Dzarilaw approached Daughter-of-Otter's-Daughter and looked directly into her eyes, something he would never do under normal circumstances, even to a slave. He didn't know what to say to her, how to explain that this was not personal and that there was no choice. No escape for either of them. He wanted to tell her that she had been a boon to his household and that they would all remember her well. He wanted to tell her that he would use his best knife and that she would feel no pain. "I have prayed," he finally said, whispering to her, "that the Shadows catch your soul and return it to your people."

"What will become of my son?" she pleaded.

The fate of Other-Daughter had weighed heavily on him, and now he saw that he could lift the burden from his shoulders by doing something lofty for Other-Daughter. But what? At first he thought he would give him to clan relatives who had come from very far north and had no slaves of their own, but Dzarilaw worried that having no slaves, they might not treat him well and decided against taking that chance. There were friends who had come from the east, near the Great Mountains, but they were not blood family, and relatives were sure to be insulted if he made such a gift outside of the clan. He was troubled.

"Without me," Daughter-of-Otter's-Daughter asked again, "what will become of him?"

"He will have his freedom," Dzarilaw promised her, "and my protection to find his way home."

"I am content," she answered, tears welling in her eyes. She was crying, happy for the first time since she'd been brought here those many years ago. Dzarilaw put an arm around her and drew her to him. She rested her head against his chest and listened to the beating of his heart. With his powerful arm, he held her pressed tight so she could not make a sound. He drove his knife between her shoulder blades until it pierced her heart and he could feel it explode. He held her pressed to his chest until she was dead, and then he let her slide to the ground that her good blood could seek out the comfort of the earth.

—

The next day, in the heat of a high clear sun, Jason was summoned to appear before Dzarilaw. No one could know that Dzarilaw was in the process of deciding whether the boy should live or not. In fact, he was well-disposed to Jason, perhaps because it was early in the day and he was still feeling the effects of the barks and herbs he'd been smoking last night. There might have been no question at all, except for the blundering efforts of Jason's father and the Jesuit to appease.

"We are honored by your journey and the difficulties you have braved to be with us for this great festival," Dzarilaw greeted them.

"He welcomes you," the Tsimshian translated.

"It is we who are honored to be welcomed among you at this special time," the Jesuit answered.

"They accept your gracious protection," the Tsimshian interpreted. And so it went, the translations so squeezed and twisted by the Tsimshian that no one was quite sure exactly what was going on. Jason's father and the Jesuit could tell that their Tsimshian was nervous, but not why.

As a sincere gesture of goodwill, Jason's father opened his carrysack and from it presented Dzarilaw with a ruby brooch he had owned all his life, a memory of his own mother.

Dzarilaw was speechless.

The Tsimshian was astonished. Afraid. Those standing close enough to see what was happening were shocked.

The Jesuit meanwhile retrieved an ornate silver cross from his purse as his offering. The Tsimshian stopped him. The Tsimshian was sweating. It wasn't just the boy who was going to die, they were all going to die, him included. "Great Bear Prince," he said to Dzarilaw, "they mean no wrong." Several of Dzarilaw's warriors moved in closer. Jason's father and the Jesuit knew they'd crossed some invisible lines, they just didn't know what they were.

"You can't bring gifts to a potlatch!" the Tsimshian hissed at them. "You're going to get us all killed."

The whole point of a potlatch was divestiture. Separation from property. A great chief gives up everything material so that he can focus the rest of his life on matters spiritual. He gives everything to the tribes, and for the rest of his days the tribes will give him everything—anything—he needs. There could be no greater insult—no more pointed desecration—than to bring Dzarilaw a gift.

"Kill them," Dzarilaw said calmly to his warriors.

"No!" the Tsimshian shaman screamed. "It's not their fault."

Dzarilaw glared at him.

"They're just stupid," the Tsimshian explained.

Dzarilaw's glare softened.

"These Pales, they can't help themselves . . . They're just stupid."

Dzarilaw laughed. He told his warriors what the Tsimshian had said and they laughed too, more because Dzarilaw was laughing than because it was funny. "Stupid," Dzarilaw said to the Tsimshian.

"Very stupid," the Tsimshian encouraged. "You can see it in their eyes."

So Dzarilaw decided to keep the ruby and the cross because they were as useless as anything he'd ever seen and were without value, and he laughed again and the crisis passed, at least on the surface. Inside, though, Dzarilaw was incensed. These ugly strangers had tarnished his potlatch, and although he had acted magnanimously and forgave them in front of everyone, he couldn't be sure that the gods were not offended. So when he turned his attention to Jason, he was surprised to see the boy staring at the trees. They spoke to each other through the Tsimshian.

"What are you watching?" Dzarilaw wanted to know. "What are you watching that is so powerful to you that it takes your attention away from me?"

"The old woman sitting in the tree."

Dzarilaw turned to see. On a middle branch sat a raven. Others also turned to see. Some of them gasped audibly. "You see a woman?"

"Very old."

"I see only a raven."

"Very old, but she has very young hair, long and black and shiny," Jason continued. "Very beautiful hair."

They were suspicious of him before. Now they were afraid of him. Several of the women covered their young children's eyes and took them away. This blanched-skin boy was too dangerous to be looked upon casually. And clearly, if he had Raven's protection, he was too powerful to be dispatched. Probably.

Dzarilaw was not convinced. He handed Jason a bright red berry and indicated that the boy should offer it to the old woman. Jason held out the berry and while the old woman never moved from the tree, a second raven swooped down out of the sky and snatched it from his hand. Dzarilaw was impressed. It made no sense to him that a spirit should come to his village in the shape of a pallid boy, but he knew better than to question this spirit in its ways.

He walked over to Jason and put his arms on the boy's shoulder. It was a mark of his friendship, but more important, he was testing himself, testing to see if he had the courage to touch a spirit, testing to see if in fact he had chosen the right time for his potlatch, if he was indeed ready to pursue spiritual life. The boy's shoulder felt like any boy's shoulder, but Dzarilaw's courage in having touched the spirit did not go unnoticed. The old woman in the tree scowled at Jason and jumped down from the branch. She hopped around a little and then she flew away.

SIX

Under normal circumstances, Dr. Wayne Elliot was a reasonably ethical man. One of the good guys. He knew that experimenting on his patients violated both his medical oaths and his own personal standards, but extraordinary opportunities require extraordinary measures. The coffee with Taryn Stream-Cleaner had lasted for a couple of hours. Although he learned very little about Jason, he nonetheless left inspired. At the very least, Elliot took it for a sign that he was on the verge of something important, finally.

He was a good doctor but he was supposed to have been a great one. Everyone assumed it of him, and he toyed with the idea that Jason was his last great chance to rescue himself from fading expectations. He had been third in his class in med school but was considered by most to be the pick of the litter. Professors included. There was just something special about him. Maybe it was that he was a genuine natural healer. The books and the classes didn't bring him the power but they did unleash it.

Wayne Elliot was what they meant when they said that medicine was an art. He had an instinct. He could somehow distinguish, for example, between berylliosis and sarcoidosis without the sophisticated immunologic techniques every other physician required, and the science inevitably proved him right. He could isolate cardiac disorders with a stethoscope that others could barely find with an EKG. He seemed to know, with unerring precision, which bacteria he was fighting long before the cultures ever came back.

The point is, Elliot had a gift. He was a doctor of infinite possibilities who had opted for a lucrative practice instead of an interesting one, and the dreams went away and the promise soon faded. He became, fairly quickly, just a good doctor. A doctor with a well-run office, exorbitant fees, and two *pro bono* days a week at Bayshore to assuage the guilt and combat the growing emptiness. There was simply a limit to how often you could stick your finger up somebody's ass and still feel good about what you did for a living, and he had reached the limit. He'd give it all up now for a return to the promise, but it was as gone as last year's daisies.

He was full of regret and desperate to find the spark for his life, so it was no surprise that Jason Ondine set fire to his soul. He felt badly for Jason but he pressed on, compelled by what he knew to be the demands of a higher order. What he was about to do was for all humankind. His was, he kept assuring himself, a noble quest, not a selfish one. Jason had a miracle in him and Dr. Wayne Elliot was the man to unlock it, the porter to carry it to the world.

—

For reasons he could not possibly fathom, Elliot found the three old ladies on the bench near Jason's room somehow disturbing. One of them smiled and he looked away. The police officer let him in and closed the door behind him. Elliot loathed what he was planning to do, but he was determined to go through with it. He took cover in his best bedside manner. "Hello, how you feeling?"

"Like a trussed mountain goat," Jason answered.

"The restraints? You don't like the handcuffs?" It was a stupid question, not worthy of an answer. "Well, you haven't exactly proven to be a model patient."

Jason kept his impulse to defend himself in check. As the lone voice descrying his innocence, he knew it had to sound like the plaintive wail of every criminal on the wrong side of an accusation and he decided to spare himself and the doctor.

"Do you remember me? I'm Wayne Elliot," the doctor explained. "I took care of you the night you were brought in?"

Jason remembered everything, and it was not always a blessing. That night he had come to the boat in the first place for the music. Human contact was rare for him these days and such random encounters with music held a special lure. In this case it was some Slavic chorale blaring in the rather tight quarters of the ship's galley. It was difficult but inspiring music, and its insistent tones beat against the hull and out into the water, where they carried some distance. Jason was several miles away when he caught the first strains.

The boat was lolling, quiet except for the occasional creak, and Jason lost himself in the music, diving through the water down under the boat and slicing back, rolling with the eager wail of the chorus and its ardent invitations. So lost was he in the music that he failed to notice the approaching shark until it was too late. Jason twisted away, but the shark still cut his belly and would have had him for sure on the next pass except that the winch started up and the noise frightened it off.

Jason was half-dead—more—when they hauled him up in the net. He remembered not breathing and listening to the men pronounce his death. He remembered the awful pain of the suffocation and the fear. He remembered flying to the hospital, and he remembered Elliot sticking that giant needle into his chest. Of course Jason remembered, but starting down that road would surely lead him to a tirade against Elliot's complicity in his current humiliation. Best just to suffer it with grace and remember it for later. "Yes, I remember," Jason agreed, "and I have forgiven you."

It spooked Elliot and infuriated him. He hadn't done anything, what right did this man have to forgive? *Fuck him,* Elliot thought, and it made it easier to do what he had to. He took Jason's pulse from one of his handcuffed wrists without even really noticing that he was doing it. He was in many ways a creature of habit, and

taking a pulse had become absolutely automatic. He'd often calcu-
late the rate and enter it in the log without any conscious recollection of having done so. From his bag he brought out two scalpels
and a jagged-edged hunting knife. "Jason," he said, "I'd like to try
a little experiment."

Jason screamed at the scalpel's first cut. It was sudden, and in his
eagerness Elliot had cut much deeper than he'd intended.

The cop rushed into the room. "You okay, Doc?"

"Fine. I'm fine"

"He's cutting me up!" Jason yelled.

"He won't let me give him his shot," Elliot explained.

"I don't need a shot!"

"You a doctor now?" the cop joked, mocking Jason.

"Just something to quiet him down," Elliot explained. "Don't
want him getting into any more trouble."

"His screaming is agitating the old ladies. If you need me, I'm
happy to help."

Elliot accepted the offer, and with Jason cuffed to the bed it
wasn't much of a job to pin him for the shot. It was quick and, for
everyone but Jason, painless.

"Don't leave him alone with me," Jason said, already beginning to
slur slightly. "He's trying to kill me."

"Like the orderly tried to kill you. I heard it all before," the cop
answered. "You need me, Doc, I'm right outside."

Elliot waited for the officer to close the door before he checked
Jason's arm, and he was astonished. The cut was already beginning
to heal. "My God," he said, as his mind raced to comprehend
what was going on. Forget the Fountain of Youth, this was the
Godhead he was seeing. This was the blessing of Eden before the
Fall. This was . . . his.

"Jason, you understand that it's not my intention to hurt you,
don't you? I mean, that's the last thing I want."

Another cut sliced deep into Jason's shoulder. He felt the cold
steel touch his skin and cut through. It was suddenly hot, searing
into the muscle like a molten metal made of his own blood. Elliot

made a total of fourteen cuts, some shallow, most deep, all painful. He made eight with the scalpels, six with the knife. And as he watched, he saw the wounds heal before his eyes. He was witness to miracles, and as soon as he discovered the secret, it would be science. *Goddam Nobel Prize science,* he thought for just a moment before he dismissed the notion angrily, chastising himself. He was a doctor, for God's sake, and this wasn't about winning prizes or stroking his own ego.

On the other hand, he couldn't stop wondering how far it actually went: If he pulled off a nail, would the nail grow back? If he cut off a finger, would it regenerate? And if a finger grew back, would an arm? And most important, the experiment that he knew he could not avoid: Did Jason's powers allow him to defy death? If a fatal wound were inflicted, would he survive?

SEVEN

For two years after Dzarilaw's great potlatch, Jason enjoyed the protection and affection of the Chief but he was mostly shunned by the rest of the village. The other bloodless whiteskins were embraced. Loved. Celebrated for their insights and good humor, for their strange ways and awkward gait, for the stories they brought of faraway places. But Jason was held at a distance.

At the end of the first year, Jason's father decided to return to Hochelaga to recruit more pioneers. After much soul-searching, he decided that crossing the continent twice more was just too much for the boy, and Jason was to be left behind to wait for his father's return. No explanation or reasoning made the boy feel any better. So, when winter broke and the gateway opened for the journey, his father said good-bye and climbed into one of the three big canoes that launched the trip. "I'll be back as soon as I can."

"Don't go!" Jason pleaded.

"I have to, Son."

The betrayal felt lethal. "Don't go!" Jason screamed after the departing boats, terrified. He ran into the river. "Wait," he screamed. "Wait!" The canoes slipped into the current and moved off swiftly.

Jason charged into the water, up to his waist, but he couldn't swim and could go no farther.

"Wait! Wait!" He stood unsteadily in the choppy flow of the water, still screaming long after the canoes were out of sight. Dzarilaw stood outside his lodge and watched the boy. He wondered whose fears were greater, the father's or the son's.

In a village—a world—in which social ties ruled both the core and the periphery of daily life, Jason lived alone. Abandoned. He would never forgive his father, he would never get the chance to.

Jason was nominally in the Jesuit's care but that carried no weight with the tribe. Even Dzarilaw's advocacy and persuasion didn't help, and Jason soon found his life ruled by the damning weight of loneliness. The story of his rock killing the doe had branded him, and the incident with the raven sealed his reputation. He could turn out to be a legendary hunter or a wondrous warrior, he could even turn out to be a great spirit, he could become almost anything, but he could never be one of them.

"Why, Grandfather, why not?" Jason demanded of Dzarilaw, speaking the language flawlessly. He had learned it in just a few months, another magical turn that engendered more mistrust.

"They're afraid of you."

"I didn't do anything."

"You saw Raven without his mask," Dzarilaw explained.

"I saw an old woman."

"And we saw only a bird."

"And if I had seen only a bird, would I have lived past that night?" Dzarilaw smiled. "Yes, I think so."

Jason lowered his head, ashamed of the feelings that overwhelmed him. The old man wiped a tear from the boy's face. "It is not a sign of weakness," he assured him, "to suffer pain."

The comfort Jason got from Dzarilaw didn't help much, but it was all he had and he would hang onto it with the tenacity of a homing salmon. The village had made Jason into an icon, conferring upon him a fate heavier to bear than the slaughter he had escaped. They shaped attitudes and notions around him that made him seem not quite real to them, and not quite whole to himself. To a people whose very survival was utterly dependent on their harmony with the natural world, Jason's killing of the doe indicated an apparent disdain for the creatures of the forests and the seas that was utterly incomprehensible. It provoked considerable distress among the People and an almost palpable desire for revenge.

If they would not love him, Jason could at least make them fear him, and he saw to that with rare dedication until finally he was embraced in the breach. When a hunt went badly, Jason could be blamed. When a sickness overtook someone, it was believed to have happened because they had looked Jason directly in the eyes. If a season shifted out of phase with the moon, it was Jason's doing. Jason had become the back end of creation. While he was ignored with ritual precision, he was as integrated and essential to the tribe as some of its most venerable elders.

When Dzarilaw died, exactly thirty-two turns of the moon after his potlatch—a date that he himself had picked years before—life in the village grew considerably more difficult for Jason. With his family gathered around him, Dzarilaw asked for Jason to be brought to him. "Hold my hand," he told the boy, "so your spirit can guide mine through the shadows." Dzarilaw was prepared to take the journey, although it seemed more comforting to believe that once he closed his eyes, his eyes were closed.

Jason held his hand and neither of them said much for the rest of the day. The old man hoped that by calling the boy to his side, his protection might outlast his life. He hoped that the People would see his fondness for Jason and in his absence take the boy into their hearts.

It didn't happen.

With the last spark of his life, old Dzarilaw turned to Jason and said only, "Don't be afraid." Then he closed his eyes and never took another breath.

Outside the house, dancers danced and drummers pounded out their sorrow in ancient rhythms, and they were comforted. "Ay yi yi Dzarilaw," they chanted, meaning: *We-mourn-in-great-sorrow-for-you-*

Dzarilaw. In fact, *ay yi yi* was no words at all, just sounds of pain rising up from the heart, and everyone knew them to be sounds of grief and sadness.

"Ay yi yi Dzarilaw," they sang. "Ay yi yi kwakwaka'wakw." Kwakwaka'wakw was the name they called themselves and all the tribes that spoke their language.

They mourned for him and they mourned for themselves. A very great chief had left them. "Ay yi yi Dzarilaw," they sang. "Ay yi yi kwakwaka'wakw." They sang and wept for two days before they buried him.

After that, Jason went from fearsome spirit to fallen angel. Cast out. Without protection. Still powerful of course but somehow less awesome. More despised. More token than totem. When Dzarilaw was alive, Jason could be blamed for a wide variety of ills but never punished for them. Now he was served up to appease troubles, distract misfortune, or otherwise beguile the moods of the gods. If it rained when it should not, Jason was set out on display until it stopped. If a hunt promised to be difficult, he was often dragged along as bait for the unsettled spirits, a distraction for their trickiness. A warning against their interference.

It was for this honor in the breach that Jason was taken on the gray whale hunt for protection.

"No, no! I don't want to go." The great whales were making their journey north and wouldn't pass this way again for several months, and then in deep waters, too far out for the canoes. There was no time for coddling Jason's fears. Besides, terror hurts the stomach, not the boat. "Don't! Let me go! I'm not going!" He pleaded to be left behind. He was afraid of the sea and the idea of challenging it in one of their massive canoes was more than he could handle.

As a younger boy, back in Hochelaga, Jason had felt comfortable in the canoes. He paddled well for a child, with considerable promise that he'd become a reliable riverman as he grew up and his arms and shoulders began to fill out. But those birch-bark canoes were relatively light. They sat high on the water and were extremely maneuverable. It was hard to get into trouble unless you ran into very bad rapids or turned over in the currents.

The birch-bark canoes were made to be handled, but these canoes were ocean-going monsters. They were forty or fifty feet long, shaped from the giant trees of the coastal forests, and required many men, grown men working in concert, to control them. They were heavy, they sat low in the water just begging to get flooded. Worst of all, Jason feared, any boy in fact not yet grown enough to man an oar would be fairly expendable if they ran into storm seas or other trouble out on the water.

Jason's petitions fell on deaf ears, however, as did the warnings of several of the women that he was bad spirits and would ruin the hunt. "He is more useful here at the village searching for mushrooms with us women."

The men laughed. A chief's wife who had dreamed bad dreams of Jason challenged their arrogance. "There is not a self-respecting whale in all the sea that will feel anything but disdain for you if Jason goes along. Not a single one who'd be willing to give up his spirit to feed the likes of these." She said "these" with a sweep of her hand so charged with scorn it must have taken years to perfect.

The men laughed and took Jason anyway. There were twenty-two men in his dugout canoe, twenty-six in the other, and only Jason was scared. He was scared when they attacked the waves, and more scared when they got out beyond the waves and lost sight of the land entirely. For the others it was a celebration, a threshold crossed. "The boats and the shore are no longer joined."

Jason so feared the open ocean that he began to mock it, hoping the waters would object and chase them back to shore. He mocked the great whales themselves, shouting that their meat spoiled quickly and their blubber was rancid, but the sea stayed calm. He turned to taunting the very spirits of the sea and it was for this, the legend goes, that a squall formed out of nothing in an instant and a great swell overtook them and swamped their boats and hurled them into a giant angry whirlpool.

Jason froze in the panic that consumed him. It was midday but the howling, thundering squall so darkened their world that not a single man could hear the grisly cries or see the desperate struggles of the others. These extraordinary teams of sea hunters, bound to each other in the clockwork precision born of generations of rehearsal, were all dying separately, each in his own solitary terrors in a roiling sea of finality. Men shouted for help. Screamed out to their protector spirits to help them, but it was futile. They were all swirled round and round at dizzying speeds in the vortex of the whirlpool, slapped to the sides of this terrible funnel of water, barely able to breathe.

"I can't swim! I can't swim!" Jason screamed, in English, so even if anyone could hear him over the cacophony of disaster, certainly no one could understand him. In fact, language didn't matter. Everyone knew that Jason was responsible and anyone who managed to catch even a glimpse of him summoned all the courage and strength they could to get away, assuming it was just the boy and not them the sea was after. Jason, his lungs exploding, his mind blinded by panic, choked on the sea water that flooded him.

—

The very best men of a very proud village had been wiped out in the period of a wave, sucked down in the trough that swallowed them up as certainly as the killer whirlpools of Keagyihl Depguesk. This surprised everyone because it was commonly understood that the monster spirit of whirlpools had promised Hanging Hair that he would stop doing things like that. Hanging Hair was a beautiful spirit who dwelt among the trees. Deep in the dark forests it often seemed that her long black hair had captured pieces of the sun for its own keeping. Apart from Jason, few had ever really seen her, though many thought they had, especially when the winds blew so that the branches swayed over the water and sunlight glinted through the leaves as though she herself were walking by.

In the earliest of days, dismayed that so many brave young men had lost their lives to the capricious whirlpool, Hanging Hair had called a great feast to arrange that Keagyihl Depguesk should be disappointed of his prey. She invited all the great monster powers of nature and each one demonstrated their own particular power—some falling as cliffs, some freezing as ice, some burning like forests—but all of them entered peacefully into the Festival House which was deep under the sea.

Each was given their own place on the bench around the wall, and they were joined by Hanging Hair's older sister Sedna, Mother of the Sea. Sedna often roamed the sea in the shape of Orca, the killer whale, but in honor of this festival she came as a woman, with long, long hair like her sister, but it was silver-white and done in braids.

The sisters brought each guest the very rare and tasty kidney fat of mountain goats, but by magic each piece became a large ball of the most perfect fat and they all ate until they were full. With everybody feeling good, Hanging Hair told them that it was time for them all to have more consideration for human beings. She said that people who made offerings to the whirlpool must not be cheated and destroyed, and therefore the powers of Keagyihl Depguesk must be greatly reduced. After much discussion it was agreed. There are still serious controversies around tribal fires about exactly how this was accomplished, but everyone knew that it was agreed. Which is why the men of Jason's village were so surprised to be taken by a whirlpool.

—

Jason fell free of the swirling and sank, wafting like a leaf through the deepening darkness of the ocean. His lungs were bursting, his legs and arms flailed weakly against the heavy water, his eyes wide with horror. The pain peaked and he began to feel somewhat lightheaded. He saw an enormous whale approach. An orca. Killer whale. Swimming closer. It looked like a woman with flowing silver-gray hair. It looked like a whale. It looked like a woman. It bumped him, nudged him. Everything was so cold except when the whale put her hand on his face and it felt soft and warm. She nudged him again and again, moving him slowly toward the surface, which Jason could see was much too far away. He blacked out. "He closed his eyes," the stories tell, meaning that he had died.

Whether Jason had actually died or not always remained in contention but what was never in question was that he woke on the mainland shore, cold, soaked, and exhausted, with both Hanging Hair and Sedna, Mother of the Sea, arguing about it. "He should have been allowed to die," Hanging Hair insisted, sadly, because she had always liked this one and he was so young. "It's not our place to interfere."

"We interfere all the time, besides, it's not for his sake I did this," Sedna had to explain. "It's because Keagyihl Depguesk continues to abuse his power. I took this one from him as a warning."

"You'll have to throw him back," Hanging Hair persisted.

"I can't."

"Why not?"

Sedna was embarrassed and hesitated to say, but Hanging Hair would find out sooner or later and so she simply told the truth. "I breathed spirit into him."

Hanging Hair was shocked by the confession. She held her tongue because it was on fire with rage and it would do no good to flick that at Sedna. And so she waited, and Sedna waited. For two days the sisters waited while Jason lay entranced on the sand, until Hanging Hair regained her composure. "Is he the one, then?"

"I don't know."

"He saw me once in the village," Hanging Hair confessed.

"You allowed him to?" Sedna was surprised.

"No, he did it with his own eyes." Hanging Hair had been impressed when it happened, and now Sedna was too. "Are you afraid?"

Yes, she was, and they were both confused and couldn't decide what to do. There was a third sister, Adee, and they sent for her. Like Sedna, she had silver-white hair, but hers was cropped short and feathered like an eagle. She was very very old and no one had ever said of her that when she was young, she was beautiful. Hanging Hair and Sedna told her everything, and after she had considered it all, she told them what she thought they had to do. "Cut him open and tear out his soul."

"We tried," Sedna explained. "We sliced him open from his throat to his cock—"

"But his soul wouldn't come loose," Hanging Hair complained. "It just slipped right through our fingers. It was impossible to take hold of it."

"And then he healed right back. Not even a scar," Sedna offered.

Adee sighed, as hugely disappointed in her sisters as usual. "Then the only way for him to die is at the hands of his son."

"I don't understand people like you," Sedna attacked Adee. "You are so rigid."

"I don't make the rules."

"Rigid," Sedna hissed.

"He's a boy," Hanging Hair explained. "He has no son."

"If he's ever allowed to grow into a man," Adee explained with arrogant patience, "he will one day be strong enough to destroy us all."

"If we can't kill him," Sedna demanded, "then just what are we supposed—"

"He has to be kept in the sea," Adee announced, as though stating the obvious.

"And then I'm responsible for him forever!" Sedna complained. Hanging Hair and Adee both glared at her. Sedna hated having to be responsible for everything she did, but her sisters were clearly not going to back off, and she finally accepted. "Then what should I make of him?" she asked.

"An orca," Adee suggested, thrilled with the thought of a spirit-powered killer whale challenging Sedna in her own seas.

"A sea lion," Hanging Hair announced, trying to keep the peace and get this settled, "seems about right."

"And he would remain a sea lion . . . forever?" Sedna wanted to know. Needed to know. It was always a little unpredictable dealing with human beings.

"Yes," Adee assured her, and after a moment added, "probably."

EIGHT

Jason woke in the middle of the night. While the cuts had in fact all healed, the pain lingered. That would take a lot longer. He knew Elliot was coming back and it was not hard to imagine what the good doctor had in store for him. "Let me out of here," Jason bellowed, further confirming for everyone that he was irrational and dangerous.

At one point a nurse came in to offer some comfort. She was a good Christian, there for any patient who needed her. Hate the sin, not the sinner. If this one assaulted the boy and destroyed an orderly, God must have a reason. The patient is still in need of comfort.

Jason tried to explain about Elliot, but when she asked to see the cuts, he had none to show her. No scabs, no scars, and pain—as ever—was invisible to all but the bearer. "You have some visitors outside," she said, "but they don't have a pass."

"A pass?"

"They can't get in without one," she explained, displaying her own pass.

"The old ladies," he said. "I don't want them in here." The nurse was perplexed, but nodded as if it made sense. "They like to see me suffer," he explained.

"They don't look like—"

"No, no. It's been going on for years."

"You've only been here a few days," the nurse reminded him.

"Believe me, they can make an afternoon seem like a lifetime."

"I have aunts like that myself."

"Aunts . . . yes, " Jason mused. "Aunts"

"Aunts," the nurse echoed, wondering if she was missing something and certain that he wasn't going to explain. "Maybe I can get you some Valium or something, Hon," she said, soothing.

"He's going to kill me." Like Elliot, Jason had no idea how far his own recuperative powers extended. Mortality loomed for him as it did for everyone, and captured, bound like this, unable to protect or defend himself, Jason was frightened. "He's been cutting me. I think he wants my liver."

"Aw, no, Hon. He's a doctor, he's just trying to help."

It was pointless. Once they decide you're crazy, everything you say sounds crazy. He kept thinking that he had to get back to the sea, that he'd be safe there, but wishing wasn't going to make it so.

"You're scared, Hon. I don't blame you. I'm happy to sit here and hold your hand if that'll help."

Jason didn't need his hand held but he didn't object. It was comforting and there was no point making yet another enemy in this place. "Will you stay and hold my hand when the doctor comes?" It wasn't fear that prompted the question but calculation, manipulation, and it felt powerful, thinking like a man.

"Sure, Hon," she promised. "If it's okay with the doctor."

Jason smiled. An ancient response to futility.

"That's much better," she told him. "You have a lovely smile."

She was still holding his hand when Elliot arrived and, after a brief exchange of professional pleasantries, was asked to leave.

"He'd like me to stay," she said, and then whispered, "I think he's a little scared."

Elliot fixed his best do-what-the-doctor-says look on her and it was sufficient.

"I'll be back later," she told Jason and hurried off.

—

It was two o'clock in the morning when Elliot had decided to come to the hospital. Excited and too uneasy to sleep, he believed that if he could find and isolate the magic that was in Jason, it would be like touching the face of God. He'd come too close to let it go, but with the threat of Jason's arraignment looming, he feared that the courts were going to snatch the prize from him. Once Jason was officially charged, he'd be moved to a prison hospital and Elliot's grand opportunity would be lost. Forever.

Determined to take his research to the limit, he knew that morning might be too late. It had to be now. He parked a couple of blocks from the hospital and walked the rest of the way. To avoid being noticed, he climbed to the fourth floor on the rear service stairs that hardly anybody ever used. He saw the old ladies but didn't think they noticed him. Already apprehensive about being there, discovering the nurse in the room didn't help. He wondered if sending her away had made her suspicious. He paced. He had a lot on his mind. He had things to say to Jason but he didn't know where to begin.

"You know this is wrong," Jason warned him.

"I'm not happy about it. You think I like this!"

"Yes. You're making the choice. Yes."

"Well, you're wrong. I'm doing it because it has to be done, but inside it's tearing me apart," Elliot explained. There it was. Conscience. Bold and aggressive. The problem with conscience is that it is more often employed to justify evil than to defy it. It was the thing that made one feel human even while performing despicable acts. It was what would permit Elliot to kill Jason in the name of science or humankind or truth or justice. Or greed. Or the simple pervasive desire to suck some love out of a universe expanding without any care or conscience whatsoever.

"Trust me," Elliot assured him, "you're better off in my care than in some heartless prison hospital where they'll carve you up every which way to Sunday trying to see what makes you tick."

"And what you're doing is different?"

Elliot was upset. Offended. Conscience questioned always is. He turned away. "Have it your way," he barked, meaning don't muck with your keeper when your keeper has all the keys. He took a deep breath and opened his bag. Even while reaching for his scalpel, he could barely believe that he was actually prepared to sacrifice Jason's life for the sake of this inquiry.

—

Outside the room the cop sat in his chair dreaming of a desk job. The three old women sat on their bench across the hall. Eventually, Hanging Hair got up and walked over to him.

"It's like I told you, Grandma," he said as she approached, "I can't let you in without a pass from the court. That's the rules."

She didn't like him. Not at all. She didn't mind the pass business, everybody has rules. Even the Spirits in the days of creation had rules they had to abide by. Nothing was arbitrary, and when it was it had to be corrected. That's why they were here, after all. There was an immediate impulse to correct the impudent officer, both to entertain herself and to teach him to respect his elders. She could vaporize him, turn him into a fleeting wisp of steam. Or into a squirrel, a particularly chattering, annoying squirrel. Twisting his head off and making him sit on it had some appeal, especially when she thought of having him watch while ants carried away his limbs.

None of this developed beyond the stage of pleasant thoughts, however, because it would cause such a fuss and her sisters would be pissed off. "Rules are rules," she replied to the officer who had not the slightest inkling how close he was to oblivion.

"That's right," he said, in a tone of voice that made her think, *What the hell, he'd be better off as a scurrying mouse,* and she was just about to do it when he added, "If it's too hard for you to get to court, I can drive you over when I'm off duty."

He'd saved his own ass by the narrowest of margins. A little respect was all it took. Hanging Hair relented and said, "No, that's alright." Then she reached over and touched his shoulder. His body froze. He was virtually dead except that his heart kept beating. Later she would release him, and he would not know that anything at all had happened. He would remember nothing, would have experienced nothing. He wouldn't even remember the conversation. It was an act of mercy.

—

Taryn Stream-Cleaner was also having a hard time sleeping that night. She made herself some hot cocoa, thinking that might help, although it never did because she made it with water instead of milk. She had a CD on and was listening to "La fleur que tu m'avais jetée" from Bizet's *Carmen*. It wasn't the music that calmed her so much as the memories of her second husband that it brought to mind. He had introduced her to opera, which she treasured because it took her as far away from the reservation villages as it was possible to get.

Opera was passionate and persuasive and it made her feel more cultured and uncommon than she was used to—almost Italian, because he was Italian. He was an educated, sophisticated, sensitive man who stole her car and all her jewelry when he left with that woman from Georgia, but Taryn considered it a fair trade for the music. These seemed like better roots than the ones she was born with.

Sitting on her bed, drinking the cocoa, she was thinking about him—about making love with him while soaring on the wings of extravagant arias played loud—when she was suddenly interrupted by the very much less than melodious squawking of what looked in the dark like a big black crow hovering outside her window. When she went to look, it was gone. She knew it had to be her imagination because crows can't hover.

The next thing she knew, Taryn was walking down the hospital hallway, feeling a little dazed, as if she were in a trance. She took the keys and the nightstick from the frozen cop and let herself into Jason's room.

Elliot was just about to begin his proto-fatal surgery and was startled by the intrusion.

"What the hell are you doing here!" he snarled.

"I'm not," Taryn answered, "I'm just having a dream." She raised the nightstick and struck him hard. She stepped away as he folded senseless to the floor.

Jason was grateful. "I see you've changed your mind."

"No," Taryn replied, "A bird came to my window."

Hearing that, it wasn't hard for Jason to know just whose dream this really was. "A raven?"

"Yes."

"With long black hair?"

"Yes! Like a woman, yes. How did you know?" she asked, unlocking the cuffs.

"She wants my spirit."

Taryn dismissed it as dream talk. Unintelligible by its very nature. She finished releasing the restraints and handed Jason the bag of clothes she was carrying, which she had no recollection of assembling. Later, back at home, Taryn woke suddenly in her easy chair in the living room. The music was still playing and Jason was standing at the window looking out.

"Ohmygod!" She couldn't believe this. "It was supposed to be a dream!"

"Sometimes dreams are more real than you think," he explained.

It was strange but she did feel curiously well except for the part about aiding and abetting. "Will I go to jail too?"

"For helping me escape?"

"For hitting a doctor!"

"I have a feeling he won't remember any of it."

In fact, at that moment Elliot was in the hospital cafeteria nursing a terrible lump on the side of his head. He had no idea how it got there.

NINE

Dinner at the Bennetts was always a formal event, even when the family dined alone, and it was always at precisely the same time. By the clock it was seven. By the vodka it was when Marianne took the last sip of her cocktail, and if you had your eye on Robert Bennett—which the family always did—it was twenty-two minutes after he got home and had his gin and began to think about having another. This was Lizzie's third dinner home since the day at the cove, and she was no less distracted than she had been for the previous two. She seemed present. She smiled and nodded, but she was very far away.

"Deer Heart, aren't you hungry?" Marianne urged her, because Lizzie was staring at the candles.

"Yes," Lizzie smiled, "thank you." She reached for her napkin and held it in her lap without removing the sterling ring or unrolling it.

Her father was talking about something—tennis, Lizzie assumed—but her own thoughts were dominated, owned by the naked man on the beach. She couldn't stop thinking about him, and didn't want to. She kept seeing those magical eyes, imagining that through them the world looked whole, imagining in them repositories of every questing promise.

"Deer Heart, your father's talking to you."

But Lizzie was . . . distracted. She was still holding the rolled-up napkin, caressing it absently. Stroking it, in fact. Up and down. Not even noticing.

"Lizzie!"

"What cock?" Lizzie blurted out.

"Excuse me?" Bennett noticed.

"Cock-of-the-walk," Marianne announced, laughing like it was some old joke between her and her daughter. It brought Lizzie back to the table and she smiled too and realized that he wasn't talking about tennis but had been asking about her grad school applications. Marianne was always jumping in to protect Lizzie in situations like this, whether Lizzie needed it or not. It was because of the sophomore thing. "The difficulty," as Bennett referred to it. Since then, any real connection between Lizzie and her father was mere show. She used to be his favorite, and he hers, but that was over now. It would never be like that again, because she wouldn't ever trust him again and he wouldn't ever let her see that it mattered.

Bennett's antipathy toward his sons had been apparent from the beginning. As far as he was concerned, they were a disaster, which left Lizzie as the only possible beacon of his dynastic responsibilities. With Lizzie his hopes for the Bennett future had soared. Here at last, he thought, were the genes in full flower, but his dreams were dashed that sophomore year and now she too was a disappointment to him. It was not a burden Lizzie wore well.

Progeny of enormous privilege, they were all, without exception, frightened off by it. The money made them crazy. They simply had too much of it and it preempted their lives, constricted them in impossible ways. The money held them together like the grip of death, and drove them apart the same way.

William, first son and oldest child, was currently in a gender-questionable ashram in the eastern Caribbean. He was by now a genuine monk by calling (a master of the denial of selfhood) but by temperament and training the captain of the guru's yacht and the movement's single greatest-ever fund-raiser. Bennett, having experienced the Second World War, knew he was supposed to respect the principles of religious tolerance, so he never vented his disappointment in William with epithets like Towelhead or Buddha-suck or Karma King. However, he had missed the gender wars and thought nothing of referring to his son as "the faggot." Owen, the youngest child, should have been the joy of the pride but was instead a nineteen-year-old drunk at Princeton. It would never change for him and, recognizing that, Bennett froze Owen's trust funds. "To protect him," he said. In fact, it was to keep control of his proxy. Lizzie had all the necessary tools to follow in her father's footsteps but turned her back on it. In light of what he referred to as "this betrayal by Lizzie," he gave up on all of his children and regretted ever having them.

Family lore had it that the rupture came in Lizzie's sophomore year, but the seeds were sown in Mexico when she was eight. They were walking through the village and were besieged by beggars. It was her first exposure to poverty. Men and women, children, tugging at her skirt, pleading for something. Anything. The hotel guide shooed them away and Marianne told her to pay it no mind. "It's alright, Deer Heart, just don't look at them."

The next day William and the parents went out scuba diving and left Lizzie and Owen with the nanny. When the nanny fell asleep with Owen out at the pool, Lizzie went to the hotel gift shop and filled up the largest shopping bag she could carry with treasure. She knew adults smoked cigarettes and kids liked candy, so that's how she filled the bag. "Gifts," she told the clerk with a smile that assured everyone her parents knew what she was doing and convinced the clerk to let her sign for it. She knew there would be too much to explain at the front entrance, so she went around back and left through a service door.

Alone in the village, absolutely unafraid, she gave away her gifts. They were all gone in minutes, and when she got back to the hotel, she lay down on her bed and cried. She knew she hadn't done enough.

When Bennett found out about it, he was furious. The nanny was fired. The clerk was fired, and the manager's career with the hotel chain had suddenly reached its ceiling. "God knows what could have happened to her out there. Eight years old!" But what had really frightened him was the fear that he had caught a glimpse of the real Lizzie. He didn't mean he had seen a concerned and compassionate human being, he meant that what she had done was crazy, and that brought to mind his schizophrenic sister, Clarice, dead by her own hand some ten years by then. That's what scared him.

Lizzie, however, had learned that good intentions were never enough, and it started her on a road of failed designs. She had ambitions and dreams, but from then on they all began with the promise of failure somewhere at the core.

It was the connection in his mind between Clarice and Lizzie that was really the engine behind sophomore year. Armed with the sixties paranoia that a single joint could drive some people irretrievably round the bend, Bennett couldn't stand it. Lizzie might, after all, still be his last best hope. He hired detectives to keep an eye on her, and when a report came back that they had seen her smoking something in a hookah at a college party, he lost it. She was yanked from school and sent to rehab. If nothing else, Bennett was a man of prompt actions and knew that if intervention was to be effective, it had to be quick and decisive. No delays for him. No soul-searching. No conversations with his daughter to try to figure out if he was out of line. "I have sired nothing but heartache," he complained to Marianne. It was true that Lizzie smoked a little dope now and then, not much more or less than anyone else who was paying attention, but she didn't deserve this. And it didn't last very long, the rehab part. "She simply left," they reported to Bennett one day, and he was very upset.

It was fairly easy to get out. She had picked a lock, bribed the night watchman, and was gone. She took with her a genuine pot-head—at rehab on a court order—and off they went in his crumbling psychedelic VW bus to tour the country. After about six months, completely fed up with the unrelenting scent of grass and the constant shattering rattle of the van, Lizzie surrendered and went back to school. She did extremely well. Straight A's in everything—except the business courses, which she found herself to be exceptionally good at but which she intentionally screwed up as a thank-you note to her father. She began volunteering at a corporate-watchdog think tank that specialized in environmental class-action suits. Rat-shit collectors, Bennett had called them. In fact, he was so deeply upset, she couldn't have been happier.

The rehab question was never discussed between them, but Bennett never forgot it, or forgave it. Ever since, anytime Lizzie did or said something that didn't quite meet with his approval, he attributed it to the drugs. Flashbacks, he'd think. Or she was "on" them again. Or they had permanently disabled her. No documents were signed, no gauntlets thrown, but neither Lizzie nor her father—both shattered by the experience—would ever forget or ever forge a truce.

"Deer Heart, are you going to answer your father or not?" Marianne pressed.

"Oh, the applications?" she said, gathering herself as she straightened out her napkin. "No, I haven't sent in any of the applications yet."

"Time's a-wasting," Bennett reminded her. "You did say you'd attend to it when you got back from Nepal."

"Afghanistan," Marianne corrected.

For him it was a simple matter. Decide what you want to do and do it. Graduate school, business, charity work, whatever it was going to be, get on with it. "You must know by now what you want to do?"

"Yes, I think I do," she said in a tone that implied it was something he'd approve of. "Yes," she said, thinking only about the cove and Jason, and feeling, finally, like she'd won a round.

Lizzie was a child of destiny, although the shape it would take was beyond anything she might have imagined.

—

For two hundred years Jason lived as a creature of the sea. He came ashore only to lounge on the rocks and warm himself in the sun or frolic with his harem. But on that day of blue skies and soft winds when he first heard Lizzie's lonely flute, everything changed. The music summoned him from the sea and he saw her face. A longing so profound and consuming welled up in him that it scrambled everything two hundred years of experience had taught him.

He remembered the Jesuit telling old Bible stories in the village. About the solemn strains of David's harp soothing the troubled evil spirits of old King Saul's tormented mind. Or Elisha calling on the minstrels to play when the people were without water for three days in the wilderness, and then the water came. In each instance, the Jesuit had pointed out, the music played to a higher power. This time it was Lizzie's majesty that touched the gods and set him free. She had made Jason a man again.

Following the siren of her flute, Jason shed the sea lion skin he had worn for so long and walked—*walked*—across the sand. He felt his legs carry him, upright and swift, something they had not done all these years. To feel his arms swinging at his sides was monumentally thrilling.

When he spoke to her and words issued from his mouth instead of the bellows and barks he'd grown accustomed to, it fired him with a familiarity and comfort he had not known since he was a young child.

He had come home—to her—and knew at once that it was love that brought him here. He hadn't ever experienced it in the sea, but it was not hard to recognize. He'd known passions in the sea, lust and bonds and tenderness. Caring and concern. Delight, but not this. With all of their powers as creatures of the sea, with all the primal force of their lives, none of them had ever felt this. Love, but not like this. Love that confirmed, but not love that transformed.

He waited a second day and then a third day on the beach in that isolated cove, but there was no sign of her. He had felt the connection, scented the interest, and yet she hadn't come back. He ran twenty miles into town that night and back again, just to find clothes in case that was what was keeping her away.

He chanted to the Spirits.

He prayed to the Jesus though he couldn't remember much about him. He prayed to the Jesus because it felt powerful in him, but he was embarrassed because Christ had seemed like such a puny god in Dzarilaw's eyes.

For Dzarilaw, a god who made himself a man was no big deal, that happened all the time. But a god-man who behaved like an ordinary man—it just made no sense. That he allowed himself to be crucified like some vanquished warrior, there was no honor in it. Not for a god. Not for someone who could make miracles. He chose to die, the Jesuit had tried to explain, for our sins.

"Then what do we die for?" Dzarilaw wanted to know. "If he died for us, it didn't work then, is that it?"

"No. You don't understand."

"No, I don't. I definitely don't."

"He died to pay for our sins," the Jesuit repeated.

"Pay who?"

"God, the Father."

"You said he was his own son."

"Well . . . yes."

"Then he died to pay himself!" Dzarilaw had roared with laughter. It was the stupidest thing he'd ever heard.

"You just have to open your heart," the Jesuit had screamed. It was the only time Jason heard the Jesuit scream, except for the day some years later when they cut his heart out with a knife carved from a whalebone.

"Gods or not," Dzarilaw answered calmly, "fathers taking their sons' lives to prove a point is not something I want to open my heart to."

Still, there was something about the Jesus that made Jason feel he should be included in his prayers. Maybe it was just in case. If he was the one spirit with the influence to bring Lizzie back to the beach, it would be stupid not to include him along with Tornarsuk or Qagwaai or Rhpisunt or any of the others. There certainly was no harm in it.

TEN

Of all the gods and spirits, Jason never knew to whom he owed his gratitude, but on the fourth day, after he had fasted and prayed to every magic he could imagine, Lizzie returned. It was of course Hanging Hair to whom he owed this moment, and to keep from spooking him she remained well hidden, just another raven in the trees. But she was a very happy raven. "Finally," she cawed in a voice only her sisters could hear. "Finally it begins." He was sleeping and the flute woke him. She was playing something she later told him was called "Reveille," and when he opened his eyes she was sitting cross-legged beside him on the sand. "Rise and shine," she cheered. "You can't sleep forever."

"Yes you can. Lazy Boy could do it. Night Hunter did it too, but he was dead."

"Excuse me?"

"He was dead."

"What have you been smoking?" Lizzie asked.

"Nothing. I used to smoke a little bark but I didn't like it much."

If she weren't in love with him, she would have thought simply that he was just too weird and left it at that. But she was and everything he said made her happy. All his words came to her in the most glowing light, and what she didn't understand she attributed to her own shortcomings. It wasn't just that she loved him, it was that she was already part of him. That he was already part of her. That it was no accident they had found each other. This much was clear. If they were going to spend much time together, they were going to have to do better at making English a common bond. So far it was getting in the way.

"You make me laugh," Lizzie told him.

"I'm sorry. I didn't mean to."

"No. That's a good thing. I like to laugh."

"I thought you would." He wanted to take her in his arms and lose himself in loving her, but he knew he couldn't, not without the truth. It would be unfair—unjust—to take her without telling her who he really was. What he really was. But he couldn't. She wanted a man and he was not that. He didn't know exactly what he was. A spirit? A sea monster? A dream? Maybe whatever he was was more than a man, but it was also less than a man and he was ashamed. He felt inferior, unworthy. Afraid to admit himself to her.

The easiest thing would be to take her and then tell her. It seemed to make good sense to his swelling cock, but the rest of him objected. "There is something you need to know," he finally said to her.

"Maybe it's better that I don't."

"I am not what you think."

"Oh?" She really didn't want to hear it. It felt good being near him, and now real life was going to intrude. Now she would hear caveats and warnings. Complications. Messiness was about to intrude in the guise of truth and honor and would surely screw up everything. She'd been there before and ran all the possibilities through in an instant. He was married. Or too recently divorced. Involved with someone who was coming back Friday. Not ready to make any kind of commitment. Syphilis. Lice. The clap. Chronic impotence. Vows of celibacy or promises to conquer the world before he settled down. He's going to jail or coming out of it. He's a cop and not worth getting involved with because he's going to get killed on the job sometime soon. He's studying for the priesthood.

She could have gone on for a long time, but he foiled her by speaking before she had a chance to stop him. "I'm really not a man," he told her.

I knew it, she screamed inside her head, patting herself on the back with one hand and crushing her heart with the other. "Could have fooled me," she answered, trying to keep it light and pretend the universe wasn't crashing down around her.

"Most of the time I'm a sea lion," he confessed.

"Thank God," she cried out, laughing.

"You're not upset?"

"No. I'm relieved."

"Maybe you need time to let it sink in."

"No. I'm a little dazed, I think, but compared to some of the stuff I thought you might say this is . . . a piece of cake."

"Cake?" He had bared his soul, exposed his fears, risked her love, and she compares it to cake!

"Fruitcake."

He was appalled. "It's a land-based joke," she told him by way of explanation.

"You don't believe me."

"No, I do. The crazy thing is I do, I just don't know what to do with the information." And it was true, she did believe him. It was bizarre. It was insane and no doubt mythic, but she trusted it was true. She leaned over to him and he put his arms around her. Arms around her. He had hungered for this for two hundred years. Arms, holding this woman who filled him with her fit. Close and warm. A moan built up in her belly and escaped in a sigh. He had never before experienced anything so erotically sensual, so carnally romantic.

"I think I've been looking for you all of my life," Jason told her.

"I wish you had found me sooner." She was overwhelmed by his gentleness, startled by his strength.

He was startled by his appetite. "I never meant to make you wait."

Her clothes fell away like a morning dew. She took him throbbing in her hands. Hands! He had never felt a woman's hands on him before, caressing him like this. She took him into her and they made love on the beach. This was beyond their hungriest invention, neither of them had ever imagined that appetite could be so overwhelming.

"Your hands," he whispered in mounting surrender as her fingers worked his legs and back. Singing lilting pleasure to each other, only the sea shared the bounty of their craving. Only the sea heard the shuddering music of their moans.

"Oh God."

"No," he answered, determined to keep things honest. "I'm just some kind of spirit."

She laughed. He didn't understand why, but he laughed back, sharing her joy until the lust once more subsumed the pleasure and they returned their attentions to absorbing each other.

"Yes."

She screamed and the gulls screamed back.

"Yes."

He bellowed in the agonies of his delight, and two seals quit the rocks for the safety of the sea.

—

For three-and-a-half months they were inseparable. They took to the world in one endless celebration. She showed him cities and he reveled in the cacophony of sensory overload. He could barely believe her when she said that no, this wasn't some kind of special gathering, these people lived here all the time. She introduced him to concerts large ("Just like a rolling stone . . .") and small ("Freedom's just another word . . .) and ubiquitous ("All you need is love . . ."). He was so overwhelmed by the soaring simplicity of the quest for peace and love that he asked her if this meant the Messiah had returned and she said no, it was still a dream.

He took her up into the high mountains and they lay naked in an alpine brook still babbling with fresh winter runoff, and they fell asleep under the caressing blanket of its skimming sparkle. ("And she fed him tea and oranges that came all the way from China . . .")

The hard part is that there is no respite from bliss. Caught up in it, every moment inspires and exhausts. Every mountain is The Mountain, every cloud The Cloud. Every blade of grass a signal for the perfect universe, and every freshly harvested blackberry is a personal gift from the gods. Or God.

Day by day he felt more human, more like a man. Day by day he was recovering himself, restoring himself. Day by day the sea receded from his soul, becoming more of a karmic memory than a primal imperative. He was beginning to remember what it felt like to know the excruciating triumphs reserved exclusively for creatures afflicted with the blessing of mortality. Their comfort and connection remained simple and perfect, beyond anything either of them could have imagined. It was a blindingly bright time, and all too brief.

—

Lizzie's mother was frantic when her Deer Heart ran off with this unknown companion, but it wasn't until Lizzie called home one day and told her mother that her lover was a mythical creature from the sea—a silkie, a transformed sea lion, a totemic legend—that Marianne Bennett got scared. It was not unlike Lizzie to say or do crazy things, but this crazy thing was clearly somewhat more serious.

"It's one thing to soar on gliders," Marianne responded on the phone, "or traverse the continent in that ratty VW van, but it is quite another to consort with fish."

"For God's sake, Mother, that was just a metaphor," Lizzie replied at once. "I was just teasing. Joking." She realized she had gone too far, said too much.

"You know what, Deer Heart, I think you should come home for a little while."

"Mother, I'm fine. I promise."

"Of course you are, Lizzie," Marianne said, but she was nowhere close to believing it. In fact, she was scared, scared in the way she now understood Bennett had always been. It wasn't so much the fish thing, she hadn't quite decided about that, it was that Lizzie sounded so damn happy. Just incredibly happy, like Clarice before she took all those pills and drove her car into the lake. Officially, it was ruled an accident, but the good-bye note from her that came in the mail two days later made it clear that this accident was of her own design. The only appropriate response now was to trust that Lizzie was in fact in serious trouble, and if she'd learned anything from Bennett, it was to act quickly and decisively. She didn't hesitate to use the family's wealth and influence to effect a rescue.

Jason and Lizzie were staying at a dinky California clapboard motel with no redeeming features other than its view of the sea and the short walk to the beach. That morning, Jason woke early. Lizzie did not. He tried to rouse her to go for a walk but she just pulled the covers tighter, so he kissed her on the forehead and hiked up into the woods on his own to feed his hunger for the feel and smells that had eluded him for so many years. It was all still so fresh to him. The soft crush of pine needles under his feet, the warm heavy air, the sudden bolting of a startled deer or a frantic thrush.

One day he saw a coyote and tried to talk to it but, to no avail. It was just a coyote, not Coyote. And he began to realize the ravens he kept seeing were just ravens, not Hanging Hair. He took it all to mean that day by day, he was freeing himself.

Lizzie stayed in bed. Dreaming, as she often did, of him, while outside the motel the forces of their misfortune gathered. Marianne was out there, sitting in a plain beige rented sedan just up the road. Little bouts of tears kept erupting, and she was never sure if it was because she was doing a good thing or a terrible thing. The man driving the car—from the detective agency she had hired—said she was a very brave woman, that made her feel better.

Outside the motel, two more private detectives and two uniformed off-duty California Highway Patrol officers prepared to launch. Everybody drew their guns. One of the CHP guys, burliest of them all, put a boot to the door and knocked it off its hinges.

Lizzie screamed.

They rushed her and pinned her to the bed. One scanned the

room and another checked the bathroom for signs of Jason. He wasn't there and they were relieved. Boyfriends were often a problem in these kinds of situations. They get protective. Crazy sometimes, and people get hurt and the private dicks hate it when it's them.

They wrapped Lizzie in her blankets and hauled her out to the waiting off-duty patrol car. "It's okay, Ma'am," the smaller of the two patrolmen assured Lizzie, "It's all perfectly legal."

Pinned inside the blanket, all Lizzie could do was scream and bite. She got deep teeth into the forearm of one of them, and after that they were all a little more circumspect about how they handled her.

Up in the forest Jason heard the screams. Not just because his hearing was sharper than most people's, but because he was paying such rapt and close attention to the sound of the woods that Lizzie's cries came as an invasion. He knew at once it was Lizzie, and he turned and ran. The trail was too circuitous, snaking back and forth, so he left it, skittering down embankments, blazing through brush, trampling new paths as he forged his way in as direct a line as he could manage, until he emerged from the woods onto the highway a goat-spit from the motel.

It was too late. He was drenched in sweat, gasping for air. "Lizzie!" he screamed. "Lizzie!" The door to their room was open. Lizzie was gone. Everyone was gone.

He ran to the manager and was once again too late. The man had been well paid.

"Nope. Didn't see nothing. She left without saying anything to me."

"She wouldn't just leave."

"She did. Hitchhiking, I think."

"I heard her scream," Jason insisted.

"Nope. Been no screaming round here."

Jason still hadn't adjusted to the notion of being in cars, and he certainly wasn't getting into one without Lizzie, so the only thing to do was walk. He started north. Sometimes along the road but mostly on the beaches and pathways closer to the water. Four hundred and some miles. With every step he felt himself slipping away.

By the time he was halfway back to the beach where he had first found her, he could already feel his heart returning to the sea. It wasn't many more miles before he felt his soul going out after it. By the time he got back to Calder Cove, he was but a heartbeat removed from the curse that had claimed him for so many years, and he was losing the struggle. He was lost if he didn't find her.

He walked the sand of the cove for days. Not eating. Not sleeping. Calling for her. Finally, filled with despair, unable without her to hang onto himself, he gave up. He plunged into the waves and returned to the ocean.

For two more years he never left the bay. He swam the waters, patrolling day and night, scanning the shore for signs of her. Listening for her music. She never appeared.

He became famous along that section of the coast. It excited people to see him. Look! Look! There he is. That's the most magnificent sea lion I've ever seen.

He's beautiful.

He's majestic.

Listen. Listen he's singing!

For two years he patrolled, calling for her. For two years he mourned. Then, late one afternoon, his heart broken, he dove deep and headed for the open seas.

ELEVEN

Malcolm Brae was listening to Nanci Griffith on FM. He loved
Nanci Griffith and considered himself lucky because you usually
didn't get to hear her much on the radio. He had every CD she put
out, but this was an official car and there was no player. He wasn't
even allowed to install his own.

"It's a squad car, Brae," the captain yelled at him.

"I was just asking."

"You wanna listen to CDs, go home."

"No, I don't wanna listen, I was just asking."

"Jesus Christ," the captain announced to the rest of the detectives.
"He thinks I'm sending him to a damn rock concert."

"Hey, Cap, cut the kid a little slack." Thing was, they all liked
Malcolm, and hell, it wasn't his fault he was the new kid on the block.

"Hey, if I cut him some slack," Captain Adachi shot back, "there
won't be any left for you when you need it." Tom Adachi liked
Malcolm, wouldn't razz him if he didn't. On the job Adachi was a
real hard-ass and he was only polite to cops he didn't like. That's
how you knew you were on his shit list. "Go on, Kid, get outta here.
Go catch us a crook."

"Just one?" Malcolm challenged as he headed for the door. Adachi flung a donut at him. Malcolm caught it and took a bite without breaking stride. The guys cheered. Even Adachi smiled. There was consensus about very few things around here, but the catch confirmed for everybody that they were right to have lobbied so hard to snag Malcolm for this division—he was going to be a real asset to the softball team. His reputation as a ballplayer had preceded him and the catch felt like verification.

Malcolm was rangy and strong, and so fresh-faced it was hard to believe he was a plainclothes cop. Off-duty traffic maybe, but a gold shield? Two days a detective and it made him feel like he was on top of the world. It would wear off in a while, but in the meantime it felt great.

It had always been a problem for Malcolm—things wearing off. It was like nothing ever took hold deep enough. He always felt like he was sliding away, like his roots never dug into the ground. When he was a kid, it scared him. Later it just made him sad, gave him those eyes.

Who knows by what special grace Malcolm ended up on this side of the law. It could just as easily—perhaps more easily—have gone the other way. Malcolm Sr. had spent twenty-one years on the force and dreamed that his son would follow in his footsteps, that one day they would serve together. Malcolm dreamed it too, more for his father's sake than anything else, but he was always in so much trouble growing up that becoming a police officer felt out of reach.

As it turned out, Malcolm joined the force a couple of months after his parents were killed. They never got to see him in the uniform, and Malcolm never won the satisfaction of his father's approval.

Adachi had become a sort of mentor and had in fact championed Malcolm's rise through the ranks. They had bonded when Malcolm was still a fresh uniform and reunited Adachi with chopsticks. Adachi had given them up as a kid because they were just too issei for him, too old country.

The Japanese heritage ran deep in Adachi's blood but not in his brain. He was proud of where he came from but knew little of the details. Imprisoned as an infant with his parents in Tule Lake internment camp during World War II, he had that in him. But once the war ended, Adachi became just another American kid who thought baseball (not sumo) was at the center of the world. He'd made one trip in his life back to the old country and returned astonished at how neat and tidy everything was. It made him a little uncomfortable, but he loved the way things were packaged, and now he had his own little *tsutsumu* collection, more than thirty examples of these traditional Japanese wrappings. Adachi never cared much for sushi, sashimi, or fish of almost any kind, but after Malcolm restored him to chopsticks, he loved, *loved*, ordering Chinese and Thai take-out.

—

Now, barely six years out of the police academy, Malcolm was a detective, heading off on his first serious case in the company of what he considered a very good sign: Nanci Griffith on the radio. He pulled up to the main entrance of the hospital and reviewed the file while he waited for the song to end. It was the Jason Ondine case. When it was still basically a routine rape (the seventeen-year-old Cottie Prusch) and assault (the comatose orderly), they had handled it at the precinct. They liked the publicity and it was good for morale. Now that Jason had escaped, and the case was threatening to become political, the media was stoking the coals and the case was kicked up to Division. *Kicked up to me,* Malcolm chuckled. Hell of an idea, something getting kicked up to him. He knew of course that the fact that they had sent him out alone was a strong indication that the brass expected the matter to implode, and they didn't want any senior players sprayed with the fallout. Let the rookie take it.

Adachi had a phrase for these kinds of cases: County Crazy. Years of wasting scarce time and tighter money had taught him that hospitals often breed craziness and it rarely amounts to anything. It was a high-stress environment that prompted lots of complaints and no follow-through. In the bright light of bureaucracy, nobody had the stomach for justice.

Malcolm figured he'd see Dr. Elliot first. Jason had escaped from his care, so it seemed a reasonable place to begin the investigation. Elliot had already given fairly complete statements to Precinct, so it was really just a way in. He wasn't expecting anything that wasn't already in the file. The door to the little lab was open, so Malcolm knocked and walked in.

"Roll up your sleeve," Elliot said without looking.

"I'm not a patient," Malcolm explained.

Elliot had a big bruise on the side of his head and despite the obvious discomfort seemed quite focused on his research. Still without turning his attention away from the microscope, Elliot pointed at the sign on the door: "Prepare all ye who enter here, to shed a vial of plasma."

Because his research was . . . unofficial, the only way for him to get benchmark samples to compare to Jason's blood was, as he put it, to "depend on the kindness of strangers." Staff joked about it, and Elliot never applied any real pressure, but he got enough volunteers to create a reasonable sample base.

Malcolm gave it up out of curiosity. They talked and it was easy. Malcolm sounded like a lawman and Elliot like a distracted physician, except that he seemed too anxious to have Jason back in the hospital. Other than that, Elliot ran straight down the party line. Everything he said was so close to his original statement—too close— that Malcolm knew not to trust him. He knew Elliot was withholding something, but he didn't know enough about the case yet to know if it was anything that mattered. "You know, Doc, if I was you, I wouldn't want this guy back in one of my beds. I'd want him locked up somewhere a little more secure."

Elliot issued some platitudes about being a doctor and Jason needing medical care. He obviously wasn't going to give away anything, at least not today, and Malcolm thought he'd better get out of there before he had to part with yet more bodily fluids. Malcolm had hoped that Elliot was just a warm-up and that things would improve from there. He went around asking lots of questions but no one had anything to add to their original statements and Malcolm ended up feeling that despite the bulging file he had started with, he really had nothing.

In order, he talked to: the cop who'd been on duty and who still remained bewildered about what had happened; Taryn Stream-Cleaner, who acted like she could barely remember a patient named Jason Ondine, but sweated over her eyebrows when she talked about him; the security guard who had clobbered Jason on the night of the rape; the gift shop volunteer who had told the original investigating officers that she thought she saw Jason leave with one of the nurses. So Malcolm was pretty damn frustrated by the time he finally went upstairs to talk to the boy and he was nervous about it. In uniform he'd talked to several rape victims, and he'd been a good cop to talk to, but they'd all been women. This was new to him and it felt shitty to be uncomfortable about it.

"Prusch?" Malcolm asked the teenager in the bed. "Cottie Prusch?"

"I don't remember anything," the boy answered.

"You don't remember your name?"

"I don't remember anything about what you want to ask me about."

"Okay," Malcolm said, "you don't want to talk about it, I understand."

"I don't have anything to say."

"You know," Malcolm said, trying to make the boy feel a little more comfortable, "there's nothing to be embarrassed about. You got nothing to feel—"

"Fuck you!" Cottie answered, embarrassed.

Malcolm had a knack for seeing past the surface, for seeing more of people than what they wanted to project, and it was clear to him that this boy's embarrassment had nothing to do with sexual humiliation. It had to do with what he was trying to hide. Malcolm put his pad and pen away. He turned to the patients in the other beds and they looked away, so he knew before asking that they weren't going to remember anything either. When he did ask, they said they'd been sleeping. Hadn't seen a thing. "I don't know how you people can breathe with all the bullshit in here," he announced as he walked to the door.

"You can't talk to us like that," the guy with the cough piped in.

"It's a technical phrase," Malcolm explained. "I got a bad guy to catch and refusing to help makes you all a bunch of assholes. You don't deserve any respect. Not from me."

"I'm going to report this," the cougher threatened.

"Call 911," Malcolm encouraged. "Tell 'em you been insulted, see how fast they get here." He left, pleased with his performance, hoping it would prick a conscience or two. Cap was right, he thought: County Crazy. Adachi would have been pissed about it, but Malcolm was more generous. They're just scared, he figured. Somebody'll come around.

—

Taryn could not believe it when she discovered Jason Ondine in her apartment. She had absolutely no recollection of how this had come to pass, and even Jason's three attempts to describe what happened elicited no memories.

"I hit Dr. Elliot?"

"With the nightstick, yes."

"Knocked him out?"

Jason nodded.

"OhmyGod."

"I don't think he'll remember any more about it than you do."

His assurance did nothing to assuage her anxiety. "I want you out of here. I want you to leave." To begin with, she expected the law to break down her door any minute and haul them both off to jail. Then there was Elliot and the question of whether she had sufficient seniority to keep her job after clobbering a doctor. What bothered her most, however, was that this man—this white man who had not spoken a single word to her on the subject—was making her feel more like a Haida than she had since her grandmother died, and she didn't like that. She had worked her entire grown-up life to shed the stigma of her origins and to assimilate, to be like everyone else, to feel like everyone else. She didn't need this man around shaking the foundations of the world with which she was, finally, comfortable.

"Please. You have to go," Taryn begged.

"You said you would help me find Lizzie."

"I said I would try."

"Okay." That was enough for Jason.

Gathered at the dining room table, Taryn plugged in her laptop, waited for the software to settle, and signed in. Jason was thrilled. He had no idea what the little box was for, but he loved the pictures flashing by and the little beeps and noises that it made, and when she finally connected to the server and the laptop said, "Hello, Taryn Stream-Cleaner," he burst out laughing.

Never mind that Taryn wanted him the hell out of her life, there was another part of her that was all a-twitter. It was, she had to admit—to herself, not to him—very romantic. Never mind that Jason was a stranger, the strangest stranger she ever met. He was searching for a lost love, on her laptop! Well, it was wonderful. It transformed her notions of her computer from a fancy calculator to something hot and passionate.

The little laptop whirred and beeped and Jason loved it. Having missed the electronics revolution altogether, he had no computer phobia, no notion of hard drive crashes and data losses. He just thrilled to the rhythms, not unlike the ceremonial drums he had learned to understand as a child. But this was different than the old days and he was grateful. Searching for people back then was all-consuming. He remembered the frantic, futile search for his sisters when he and his family were crossing the plains, how they could travel for days without even finding anyone to ask. Now you hit a few buttons to get a list of everyone from the Escondido chili market to the Bath Iron Works in Maine.

Her fingers were flying. His mind spinning. AOL finally got him to the National White Pages. She selected the Pacific Region. "Elizabeth Bennett," she said as she typed it in.

A few seconds. His heart leaped as the response came back, right there on the screen. He read it aloud: "Elizabeth Bennett—Aptos, California." They were both ready to celebrate when a second name joined the screen: Elizabeth Bennett—Moorpark, California.

"Two of them," Taryn announced, trying to assure Jason by her tone of voice that a simple phone call would resolve the question.

Elizabeth Bennett, the computer continued, Yucaipa, California.

Elizabeth Bennett—Seattle, Washington.

Elizabeth Bennett—Las Vegas, Nevada.

Elizabeth Bennett—Scottsdale, Arizona. Elizabeth Bennett—Shoshone, Idaho. Elizabeth Bennett—Sandy, Utah. Elizabeth Bennett. Elizabeth Bennett. Elizabeth Bennett.

It was a wild ride for Jason, up one side of the information revolution and down the other in a handful of seconds. From possibility and prospect to overwhelmed and defeated in the flash of an active-matrix screen. He had hit the wall. Jason Ondine, this is computer-shock. Computer-shock . . . Jason Ondine.

"Goddammit," Taryn fumed, "half the country is named Elizabeth Bennett." She stormed away from the table and paced before hitting upon what she hoped might resolve this impasse. "I can print out the list, and you can take it with you and . . . you can . . . you'll have . . ." Staring at her, it was clear he wasn't going anywhere. "What did you think, I'd get on the Net and bingo you'd have an answer? Look, five minutes ago we had nothing," she scolded. "Now we have a list. We start making the calls, one by one, until we find Lizzie."

She made the first call to demonstrate how easy it was. She picked an Elizabeth at random and dialed. "Hello, is Elizabeth in?"

"Who is this?"

"You don't know me but—"

Click. Dial tone.

Taryn's confidence was unshakable. She dialed a new Elizabeth. "Hello," she said, quite cheerfully, considering, "I'm looking for Elizabeth Bennett?"

"She's dead. Hit by a truck."

"Oh . . . I'm sorry." That was a possibility they hadn't considered. "I'm very sorry."

"Hell, she was a hundred and seven. She was gonna die any minute anyway," the voice responded.

Undaunted, she turned to Jason as cheerfully as she could. "You see? There's nothing to it. We'll be through the list in a day." She handed the phone to Jason and he made his first call. Literally his first-ever telephone call. Another miracle, but he was afraid to let it excite him the way the computer had. One modern miracle crash per day was enough.

"Hello," he said to the woman who answered. "Is this Lizzie?"

He listened, then turned to Taryn. "What is a telemarketing call? She doesn't accept them."

Taryn took the phone. Too late. Elizabeth was already gone.

The next Elizabeth had a Polish accent. Sorry to bother you.

Then came teenage Elizabeth: "Bobby is that you? If it's you just say it's you. You're such a baby."

Jason was in hell and it didn't much matter because he was numb. Lizzie? No. Lizzie? No. Lizzie no. Lizzie. No Lizzie. No. There had to be another way.

TWELVE

Marianne Bennett had grown bitter and frail over the years. Now, looking back, she was filled with regret and remorse over the way she had interfered in Lizzie's life. Hardly a day went by that she didn't punish herself in one way or another. Sometimes she'd go sit up in Lizzie's room and cry. "Deer Heart, Dear Heart, I'm so sorry."

It had all worked out so badly, nothing like what she had planned.

"I thought I was doing the right thing," she said to a little framed photo of Lizzie dressed as an elf on her eleventh birthday. The idea was an old one. She'd spirit Lizzie off to Florence or Paris for a few months and when they got back the girl would be cured of her misguided romantic adventure and get on with her life. Find someone appropriate, settle down, and raise little board members. Instead, it all got so complicated and spiraled into hell.

"Mother, why are you doing this to me?" Lizzie pleaded.

"Because we love you, Deer Heart. It's for your own good."

"He'll come for me, you know."

"I don't think so, Sweetheart. His kind have a way of fading away."

"His kind!"

"You know what I mean. He's just not our kind."

"Like Father? Is that what you want for me? A man who couldn't find your bed with a searchlight?"

Marianne slapped her.

Lizzie locked herself in her room.

They hired a "nurse" to look over her during this "transitional phase," which they knew would be difficult for everyone. The nurse (a retired Bulgarian weight lifter) seemed nice enough, although, embarrassed by her very thick accent, she hardly ever spoke. She was there to keep Lizzie from running away or hurting herself. Also, to some extent, to keep Lizzie from hurting anyone else, although no one in the family ever really believed she'd do anything like that.

It was Robert Bennett himself who put the noose around Lizzie's neck. "The woman is—"

"The woman!" Marianne barked back. "She's your daughter. She's your child."

"This child is a legally responsible adult, has been for some time, and controls fourteen percent of our holding company."

"I don't need a lesson in family economics."

"Marianne, she is non compos mentis. Who knows what she's capable of doing? I will not have the family's economic welfare jeopardized by a crazy person."

"Crazy is not . . . maybe she just needs a little time away."

"She's in love with a fish!"

"She never said fish."

"Sea lion, what's the difference."

"The difference is it's just a metaphor." It was one thing for Marianne to think Lizzie was losing it, quite another if Bennett latched onto it. Marianne had limits, he had none. "She just means he has some primal connection to the sea, to the source of life as we know it."

"That's crazy enough for me," Bennett snapped

"What are you going to do?"

"Whatever I have to do to protect the family."

It was chilling. Marianne had seen this kind of resolve in him before, like a jackal on the way to a kill.

Perhaps she said it to distract him, to dissuade him, to bring him back to questions of blood. In more honest moments in later years she'd admit to herself that she said it to hurt him. Crush him. She couldn't have kept it a secret forever anyway, but the timing, the timing was deliberate. "You'd find out eventually," she began, "so I might as well tell you now."

"Tell me what?"

"Lizzie's pregnant."

"Hardly an insurmountable problem," he answered without hesitation.

"You are one cold bastard," she said, removing her napkin from her lap. She deposited it dramatically on the table as she got up and left without another word. Though he deserved much more, it was the only time she could remember ever swearing at him.

—

It was a long time ago. It shouldn't have been so vivid in Marianne's mind but it was. Memory was unfair. It distressed her that the happy times didn't stand out in such relief, that their shared moments of rejoicing never amounted to enough to be indelible.

There was a knock on the door. "Telephone, Missus," the cook, Carmen, announced.

"I'll be right there."

"Will you need some help getting down the stairs, Missus?" Carmen offered through the closed door.

"No, Carmen, thank you. I'll take it in my bedroom."

Marianne returned the little framed eleven-year-old to the night table. "You'd be what now, Deer Heart? Forty-nine? Fifty?"

She knew exactly, but asking questions made it seem more like a conversation. "I miss you something terrible." She blew Lizzie a kiss and answered the phone. "Hello?"

On the other end of the line Jason was stunned. Even in a single word she sounded so much like Lizzie that it threw him. His voice stuck in his throat and he had to tell himself to relax before he could speak. Even with Taryn Stream-Cleaner's insistent pursuit, the search on the Internet for Elizabeth Bennett, Liz Bennett, E. Bennett, L. Bennett, and so on was getting them nowhere until Jason apologized for his lack of faith in her magical little machine and wondered why they just didn't call Lizzie's parents.

"Hello, Mrs. Bennett?" he managed to say, "I'm trying to find Lizzie."

He thought he could hear, even over the phone, that her heart was racing.

She took a breath, it was sharp and frightened. She didn't know how, but she knew instantly that it was Jason. She'd never spoken to him before, so it wasn't as if she could recognize his voice, but a chill sliced through her, so sharp and charged it took a moment before she gasped and shuddered.

"Mrs. Bennett?"

"No," she shouted at him, full of panic, and then hung up. She ran to the top of the stairs, moving faster than she had in years. "Robert!" she cried out, hoarse with fear. "Robert! It's him!"

Bennett would not at first believe her, but when she finally convinced him, his concern turned to Lizzie and he notified the police.

THIRTEEN

Jason was on his way to Lizzie and riding the train reminded him of early lessons in courage. It was not so much the heat as the rhythm of the wheels that brought it to mind. *Clackity-clackity. Clackity-clackity.* The sound reminded him of an old greeting, a command really, that he hadn't heard for a couple of hundred years: Kwax'eedus-kwax'eedus. *Clickity-clack.*

"Kwax'eedus," the Chief kept saying to the strange young boy Dzarilaw had brought to visit. "Sit down," he repeated, pointing at a spot so close to the fire that Jason thought if he weren't careful, he could become the roasted dinner. The Chief was called Yalis, after the village where he was born. But he was called this name only since he left the Island to live on the mainland. He was a jealous man, angry that he was not revered like Dzarilaw, angry that he alone thought he was the better hunter, braver warrior, wiser chief.

Dzarilaw had hoped to bring Jason here with him for the Cranberry Feast, but other obligations made it impossible. It would have compromised everybody's honor, hosts and guests alike, if Dzarilaw had also missed the great Grease Festival, so they had come. The festival, by habit and tradition, was a drunken debauch that always left one feeling that there may in fact be such a thing as too much of nature's bounty.

The flames licked out at Jason in such constant affection that he was certain all that kept his skin from blistering was the sweat pouring down his brow. Under any sensible conditions, he would have moved, but here he could not. Dzarilaw had carefully explained the rules, that it was the custom for the Chief to torment his guests. His songs and actions were designed to ridicule his rival—or his rival's surrogate—who was supposedly unable to match the host's exuberant generosity and sheer wastefulness. Fish oils were regularly poured directly onto the fire, and the resulting flames leapt in dramatic display, threatening all who sat too close. Any form of protest was simply unacceptable, a mark of inferiority, and critical dishonor.

"Dzarilaw," the boy whispered.

"Yes," the old man whispered back, touching Jason's hand, "I am as comfortable as you."

For Dzarilaw's honor Jason would sooner have his flesh seared from his bones than move, but he was losing the war of his will. He turned the pain inside, as the old chief had taught him. He went deep down inside searching for additional courage, and just when he thought that he could find no more, he stared deep into the fire and saw there something no one else could see. He saw Raven. He saw Raven laughing, mocking the fire, and it made him smile. When Yalis saw Jason smile, he knew that he would have to pour enough oil on the fire to burn his house down before the boy would move, which he thought to do but then decided better of it.

"Now on to my feast!" Yalis announced, preserving both his own house and this young boy, whose heart apparently danced with flames.

Clackity-clack. Clack clack. Jason could feel the train slowing down. His eyes were closed and he could feel the flames again, and Dzarilaw's hand on his.

—

White Meadows is less than an hour from the city, but it feels very far away. Rural and separate, somehow protected from urban invasion. It's invisible to most of the world but famous among those who can afford it. This was about as far from a snake pit as one could imagine. *Idyllic* was the word they most liked to tender in describing the place. Idyllic atmosphere. Idyllic setting. Idyllic attitude. Idyllic footpaths and idyllic decor.

Idyllic electric fences around the perimeter. Idyllic lithium schedules. Idyllic no-nonsense security people. Hard to get in uninvited. Impossible to get out. Idyllic electroshock in the early days. Less now because these days ECT is considered less than . . . idyllic.

It was the perfect place for those who could afford to dump family they didn't want to have around. Mothers and fathers and sisters and brothers. Blood that was simply too difficult to care for at home. Sometimes just blood that was less than convenient. With Bennett's influence in the community, it took very little leaning to get Lizzie committed. It was, Bennett explained to the psychiatrists involved, for her own protection. He wasn't going to have another suicide in the family. "I couldn't forgive myself if I let what happened to Clarice happen to my daughter."

For most of the first couple of years, Lizzie spent enormous energy trying to effect either release or escape, neither of which turned out to be possible. This was not a college rehab program, this was the real thing. Important families invested a lot of money here to have their loved ones "protected," and one doesn't just escape that kind of sanctuary. To keep her sanity, Lizzie turned her energy to charitable work. The family approved of her intentions, so her trust executors were instructed to allow any reasonable goodwill checks she wrote to go through. They hated the groups she chose to support, but true to their word, they did not interfere.

Under the pseudonyms "Anonymous" and "A Friend," Lizzie sent money to environmental groups, political candidates, watchdog organizations, struggling schools, community clinics, historical preservation societies, literacy groups, scholarship funds, and so on. As time went on and she got to do more reading and studying, her checks were often accompanied by astonishingly clear letters of policy analysis or organizational notions. She would then often see her words quoted, usually unattributed, in organizational newsletters, newspapers, and political speeches. Had she lived on the outside, she might have been celebrated. On the inside, however, she just did her work and remained anonymous. It wasn't freedom but it carried with it a certain satisfaction. If her life was being wasted, she saw to it that her mind and her money weren't.

For her personal well-being, Lizzie turned to her fascination with textiles and costumes. She took it to a level of involvement that amused her because she understood with singular clarity that her consuming interest in fabrics was just a silly substitute for the real passion of her life—the deep and immutable conviction that Jason was coming for her. Deep and immutable at least in the early years.

—

Books, magazines, articles, phone calls. She learned of master weavers and designers, magicians whose ancient methods yielded reams of exquisite fabrics—capes, rugs, shawls, tapestries—and who were now often remembered by a single coat or the remnants of a bolt from their workshops. She discovered whole villages that turned out masterworks of ingenuity like the salmon-skin coats from the Ainu of Hokkaido or the alpaca weaves of Patagonia.

Her room at White Meadows became a dizzying museum in riotous counterpane until one day she realized that it was too much. Drowning in a cauldron of colors and patterns, she was no longer able to see any one thing well. She began giving select pieces away to staff members and patients for special occasions: birthdays, anniversaries, Tuesdays. The rest she stowed in a special storage room that White Meadows kindly provided, and she'd bring up one piece at a time to feature in her now splendidly simple room.

—

"C'mon, Hon, we got to go in. Be a good girl," the young nurse said to Lizzie, who was almost thirty years her senior. There was extra security around her these days, ever since Jason had called the house. Bennett had contacted White Meadows with his concern that Jason might show up there. White Meadows understood these things and considered themselves notified.

"Be a good girl, Lizzie," the young nurse repeated.

"I'm not a girl, you little jerk," Lizzie snapped back. Twenty-five years Lizzie Bennett had been here and they hadn't managed to break her. Her heart, yes, that was broken before she arrived, but her spirit was strong and could still rise in righteous indignation against the daily affronts.

For twenty-five years Lizzie had been a—the word they used was "guest"—here. She had endured shock, lithium, Prozac, talking cures, T-groups, ceramic rehab, dietary antidotes, experimental medications, and every other therapy, panacea, prescription, and distraction the place had to offer. There was no chance of a cure because there was no chance that Lizzie would ever deny Jason.

"It's bad enough you're pregnant, Elizabeth," her father had said to her for the last time that day, the day they decided to send her away, "but to insist that this was done to you by some mythical silkie freshly emerged from the sea is unbearable."

"Nothing was 'done to me.' I'm not some hapless dupe that—"

"You sure look like one to me."

"Thank you."

"I want to know who this person is, where he comes from, what he does. He has obligations here, Elizabeth. Responsibilities."

Resigned, she began the litany again. "He comes from Hochelaga. When he was just a boy he—"

"Hochelaga is now Montreal. It has been for a couple of hundred years. Will you please stop playing at crazy and tell me the truth?"

"He comes from Hochelaga. When he was just a boy—"

For the pregnancy, she was demeaned. For the madness of steadfastly refusing to deny the existence of her magical lover, she was treated, relentlessly. For the first ten years or so, she waited for Jason. Expected him. Prayed that he would come, and believing it buoyed her spirits and strengthened her resolve. Every day she anticipated his arrival, and every day she forgave him because she knew that if he didn't get there it was because he couldn't. She trusted him and knew above all else that he would never betray her.

After ten years or so had passed, she began to notice her image in the mirror. How much she had changed, how old she was getting. She was no longer the beautiful young woman he had found on the beach. She was growing older faster than was necessary, more quickly than intended. Now instead of anticipating his arrival, she began to fear it, and then to dread it. She could survive anything but the look of surprise and disappointment that would cloud his face when he walked in and saw her. Not that she could blame him. It wasn't her fault. Time ravages. It wasn't his fault.

She began to pray that he would never find her. That he would always see her for what she had been, and never see her like this. She would, she began to know, spend the rest of her days alone, and took what comfort she could in the knowledge that she was making the best of it. Whenever she wavered or began to fall, it wasn't to rescue by Jason that she turned for courage, but to the memory of the tragedy of their son. It had made her fearless. When she lost Jason, it confirmed her worst suspicions about a capricious universe and made her more fearful. When she lost her son, there was nothing left to be afraid of.

—

From the small rural train station—nothing more than a small platform onto which a moving train could drop a mailbag—Jason took a taxi to White Meadows. He went directly to the reception desk where the woman seemed somehow to be expecting him. Betty Hesperson. Her bearing was contained, well ordered, but underneath she seemed high-strung and disappointed.

"I would like to see Elizabeth Bennett," he replied to her solicitation.

She was friendly and forthright and quite firm. "These are not visiting hours."

"I don't know hours very well," Jason told her, "but I've come a long way." He could hear her pulse pounding. They were sounds he was attuned to, sounds he hunted by in the sea. They announced her fear and alerted him to be wary.

"I'm sure something can be done," she answered. Her heart was racing, pulse pounding. They had been warned about him. "I'll be right back," she assured him and walked off to an office down the hall to call the police. She was told to do anything she had to to keep Jason there, so when she came back to the lobby, she said, "I'll have an attendant show you to her room. You just have a seat and he'll be right with you."

Jason declined the offer. He preferred to pace. He was nervous. It just didn't feel right, but the excitement he felt knowing how close he was to Lizzie overwhelmed everything else. Caution was no longer on the menu.

It had been relatively easy to find Lizzie once he got on track and called the right Bennett house.

"I don't think they're going to exactly welcome you with open arms," Taryn reminded him. The only part of the story he'd told her was that the family had stolen her from him.

"You can't catch fish without getting wet," Jason answered.

"What?"

"Where I come from," Jason began.

"Where do you come from?" Taryn jumped in, sensing an opening she'd been anxious to discover and afraid to explore from the beginning.

"Up the coast," he told her, protecting himself and closing the subject. "We used to dance."

"I love dancing," Taryn announced, wondering why she was getting so sucked in when all she wanted was for Jason Ondine to be out of her life.

"Usually the dancers wore the masks. My favorite was one of monster birds." It was a heavy mask, very hard to wear. It was of a giant bird, from whose head grew two mythical birds, Kotsuis and Hokhokw. They were the centerpiece of a winter ceremony and the dancers controlled their great snapping beaks with strings.

"Did you wear it?" Taryn was fascinated. Her grandmother had once told her about wearing one of the masks.

"No," he laughed, "I was just a boy." It was to him a comforting explanation. He didn't have to explain that he was an outcast. Just a boy was fine. At this distance, love plays tricks. In fact, mostly it was his youth, not his pain, that he remembered.

There were masks of great chiefs with proud wooden helmets and masks of lurking ogres who devoured children. Masks of ancestors and Raven and Bear. Masks to frighten and to enlighten, to protect and to intimidate. Masks for worship. Masks for funerals. Masks just for fun. Masks even for Wolverine, which Jason was about to describe when Taryn jumped in again. "I don't think I much like wolverines," she announced.

Jason touched her hand. He liked her but modern people were very strange. They seemed to know so much and understand so little. "It is not for you to like or not like the great Spirits," he explained. "All you have to do is respect them and learn from their triumphs and their mistakes." Taryn apologized. She said she felt terrible but her family were all Christians now, and this was the harder part to admit. They didn't know the dances anymore.

"I'm not a priest," Jason explained. "I didn't say you had to apologize, only that if you wanted to, there were ways to do it. Truth is, a lot of people don't like Wolverine. He can be pretty nasty."

"Thank you," she said, taking it for absolution, "but I still don't understand what the masks have to do with anything."

Jason wondered if it was his imagination or if people really used to be much smarter. "It means," he clarified, "that we can often choose what we want to seem to be." He explained to Taryn that he would go to the home of Lizzie's parents in disguise. Wearing a mask, so to speak. She told him he had better be very careful, the police would be looking for him. He was touched by her concern.

He went dressed as a delivery man bringing fresh crayfish to the Bennett estate. While the family was indeed on alert about Jason Ondine, they never suspected the delivery man. They were screening for a man in his fifties, maybe sixties, and Jason was young and strong and obviously could not have been more than a child twenty-five years ago.

He was sent around to the kitchen and Carmen invited him in. He recognized her voice from his phone call. She did not recognize his. Carmen left him for a few minutes, long enough for Jason to look up Lizzie in Carmen's Rolodex. He called the number right from the kitchen. On the other end someone answered, "White Meadows."

Jason asked for the address and it was given to him. It was all so easy, in fact, that Jason had to believe the three Sisters of Creation were helping things along. Hanging Hair at least.

"Mr. Ondine?" the attendant, Stanley Stevens, called. "We can go over there now."

Jason followed Stevens from the Administration Building across the quad to one of the satellite patient buildings. Jason did not like it here. It reminded him of the other hospital, but it also had a weirdness all its own. There was pain everywhere. Deep angst and fear and confusion. He could feel it.

Stevens led him to the second floor and along to the end of the hall. His breath quickened. Lizzie was near. He could feel her. He didn't know exactly what it was, but he was even more sensitive to her presence now than he had been twenty-five years ago. He felt a kind of excitement he had never quite experienced before. It was full of anticipation, but equally charged with melancholy.

They got to her door and Stevens turned back to Jason. "You should wait out here. I'll go in and . . . you know, prepare her."

Part of that was true, Stevens was concerned about Lizzie. The other part was that he had been instructed to stall because the police were on their way. He went into the room and closed the door. Jason stayed in the hall, trying to find a calm center. He could not.

"No!" Lizzie screamed. "No! I can't see him."

"You have to see him," Stevens told her.

"I'm begging you. Don't let this happen."

"It's not up to me, Lizzie."

"Stanley, please. Please. Don't let him see me like this." She caught a glimpse of her reflection in the window. "Oh God, no."

Stevens had seen her scared, before but nothing like this. This was sheer animal panic. Her eyes darted every which way looking for an exit. There was none. It was part of what her family paid for. For the first time since he'd known her, he was glad there were bars on her windows. "It will be alright," he assured her, not understanding at all what this was about. "I'll be right outside the door if you need me."

As Stevens walked back to the door to get Jason, Lizzie was in agony. How would she explain what had become of her? How would she explain what had become of their son?

Jason stepped into the room and Stevens closed the door behind him. Lizzie froze. Seeing him took her breath away. He was as stunning as the first time she had seen him at the cove. He had, in fact, changed not at all. Aged not at all. It made it all so much worse. She turned away in shame.

"Lizzie," he said, mistaking the gesture, "it's me."

She couldn't bring herself to turn back and let him see her.

"You're angry," he said. "I don't blame you. I'm sorry, I didn't mean to take so long to find you."

There was a catch in her breath. Tears streamed down her cheeks.

"Forgive me," he said, so quiet and full it was unbearable. "Please."

She turned to him, drawn by demands much stronger than her fear and her need to hide.

He was overwhelmed by the sight of her.

"My God, Lizzie," he said. "You're even more beautiful than I remember." He went to her and took her in his arms, and she let go of the years and the doubt and the pain, and she wept and trembled and kept touching his face.

—

Outside in the hall, Stanley Stevens slipped the bolt and barricaded them in the room.

FOURTEEN

The Jesuit had grown old in the years since Dzarilaw died. He made very few converts, but he was allowed to live among the People and was considered by most to be almost one of them.

Every few years he would make the long trek back to one of the growing string of western forts for trade, the company of Christians, and for confession where possible. On his first trip he brought back hymn books and cord, fishhooks, tin pots, nails, and other assorted supplies, most of which went unused by the People, including the iron blades that seemed so much less useful than the whalebone knives they'd been carving since time started, back in the Spirit days that they tell of in the stories.

On this last trip he brought back the blankets. They were meant as a gesture of generosity and support, a treasure from one world to another, and he never ever considered the possibility of smallpox. He came down the river with several canoes, and the People lined the banks of the settlement to greet him. Even though they were not always fond of this crazy white priest, they were always overjoyed when someone returned from a journey. Anyone. Any journey.

Reunions were about much more than old acquaintances renewed, friendships rekindled, or familiar bonds fortified. They were about the ebb and flow of life, a confirmation that the way they saw the world was the way the world was. Sun rises, sun sets. Winter settles, then recedes. People go, people come. So while the Jesuit didn't carry the weight of an avatar, he was still a gift-bearing indication that the ancestors remained mindful.

Over the years the Jesuit had also come to believe that life was played out in full view of those who had come before, and he thought so mostly because of the seal hunting. He had tried to teach them that Mankind had been given dominion over the animals of the earth, but such a notion was a denial of everything the People knew to be true. It demeaned their hunting, abrogated their prayers, and insulted their ancestors.

"If the animals were not equal to human beings," Skaai explained, "if they were not as sentient, if they were not as possessed of spirit and soul as we are, then our lives wouldn't work, the People would not thrive, our prayers would not be heard."

"Jesus teaches us," the Jesuit began to reply, but Skaai stopped him.

"Has the Jesus ever hunted seal?"

Everyone knew the answer, so it wasn't necessary for the Jesuit to say it out loud.

"A man who has never hunted seal cannot know very much about the cycles of life, can he?"

"He sends me to learn," the Jesuit ventured, a desperate attempt to salvage some honor for God. Everything here is about the seals. When the Jesuit had first arrived, with little Jason and the others in tow, he thought, as he had been taught by his priests, that Man simply harvested what he wanted. But he learned from the People that that was not how it was.

"In the first place, there is no hunter good enough to catch a seal who doesn't want to be caught," Skaai explained.

Skaai, a little man with old broken limbs and only one eye, had earned his way as the greatest poet and storyteller in the entire tribe.

Fractured and hobbled since childhood, unable to hunt, Skaai was still the most loved man in the village.

It was Skaai who made Jason a legend. It had come to him in a dream, when he was already old, shortly after all the men in the two large dugout canoes had drowned at sea. In Skaai's dream he saw that while all the others had perished, Jason was saved and banished forever to the lonely burden of a permanent life in the sea. It was a vision that set Skaai apart from all the other poets.

Fabled for his patience, Skaai was sorely tried in every serious conversation he tried to have with the Jesuit.

"God gives us the seals, as he does all things," the Jesuit proclaimed.

Skaai was frustrated by the Jesuit's obstinacy but persisted by reminding himself that the Black Robe was simply a little feeble-minded and required extra patience. "The seals come willingly to be hunted," Skaai explained again. "It is like a dance, and all we can do is keep the way open for the seal to approach. The task of the good hunter is simply to keep the way clear—don't foul the waters, keep the blowholes open in the ice, return the spirit to the river, and so on—and the seal will then honor the hunter by offering up his meat."

The most important symbol in the dance was the seal's bladder. After all, the meat was taken, the bladder was inflated and returned to the sea, where it would be restored so it could return the following year to meet with the hunter.

"They need Jesus," the Jesuit complained.

"They need only each other," Skaai assured him, thinking he should pity the priest because the man was a pagan, "and the dance. We are nothing if we do not restore the seal."

—

Jason was the first to see the Jesuit's returning band come down the river. Jason was on the rocks where the river begins to widen to the sea. He liked it there because he could survey the sea and keep an eye on the village at the same time.

The big canoes excited him because he thought that maybe this time his father would be on one of them, maybe this time his father had returned, but he had not. It had been thirty years since Jason was first consigned to the sea and he still hadn't given up on his father, still hadn't managed to let go of his connection to the village, still hadn't accepted his fate and taken fully to the water.

He kept thinking that somehow the People would recognize him, somehow they would transform him, take him back. Over the years he saw old familiars die, he watched the village grow and shrink with the fortunes of the hunt. He began to develop perspective.

What surprised him most in the beginning was how much more powerful he was as a sea lion. Even from his rocks out at the mouth of the river, he could see the village with absolute clarity. The smiles, the tears, the subtlest shift of mood were all evident to him. He picked up the scents and smells of the village as though he were right there, in its midst. And in matters of reflex and strength and courage, he had all that in measure way beyond what any man could know. But it was not enough. The People didn't know him, and when they saw him, they didn't admire him, they just wanted to eat him. Return his bladder to the sea.

"There! There!" one of the young guides in the second canoe behind the Jesuit yelled. "On the rocks!"

"It's me!" Jason cried out as he had a thousand times before. And as it had been a thousand times before, the only sounds that came were the challenging bellows of a magnificent sea lion bull. A great prize for any hunter.

They got as close as they could, and Jason continued to bellow excitedly—hoping against hope because he already knew better—in a desperate effort to make contact. When they got close enough, they launched their spears. None caught him with any but a glancing blow, but it hurt his feelings and made him angry. He dove into the river and came up hollering in thunderous bellows under one of the canoes, breaking it in two and dumping its cargo of half the mission's blankets into the deep river channel where they would never be found.

The guide who paddled this canoe was hurtled through the air and continued to flail wildly when he hit the water screaming. He was calling for help in a language Jason couldn't understand. He was shouting that he couldn't swim. He was swallowing water and choking on it. Jason studied the fear in the man's eyes and it surprised him because he had forgotten how terrified men were of drowning. He'd forgotten how terrified he had been.

"There he is! There he is!" the Jesuit shouted as if to organize the rescue, but the other canoes, fearing another attack by the raging sea lion, did not turn back for the guide. He was a Cree from very far away and it made no sense that one of the People should risk his own life for a stranger, even one who had traveled all these miles with them. They paddled hard to get away from the rampaging sea lion as Jason continued to thrash at the water with the ferocious power of his immensely muscled body, intentionally chasing off the boats.

The Cree kept calling out to gods that Jason had never heard of. He swam to the Cree and stared directly into his eyes. The man shrieked.

"Don't be afraid," Jason said, "I too am a man." But to Jason's dismay, his words sounded to the horrified Cree only like the bellowing of the sea monster he appeared to be. The Cree fainted.

Jason swam under the man and lifted him onto his broad bull back and swam him to the shore. Jason crawled across the sand and rocks to a dry place where he left the Cree cold and terrified and convinced that he was dreaming. Then, from behind every tree, every rock, every shadow, the People appeared in full strength and Jason thought, yes, yes at last they had recognized him. Yes, they had come to welcome him.

And then he saw the spears and knives and clubs, and he understood that they had come to slay him, and they charged as one.

The sheer muscled bulk that made him such a power in the sea was a handicap here as he struggled to move his massive body back to the water. They moved across the beach much faster than he could possibly manage, and all he had on his side was thick skin and sheer determination. He felt the blades pierce his body. Over and over. He looked back and saw the Cree urging the hunters on, and he saw the Jesuit kneel and pray.

That night in the village there was much to celebrate, and the more they danced the more they argued. Some said the Cree had been saved by none other than Jason Ondine. "It must be Ondine," several insisted. "Who else cares about drowning men?"

Others said that was impossible, Ondine was evil and if it had been Ondine, he would have ripped the Cree in half and swallowed him in two bites. "Swallowed him whole, bladder and all, if it was really Ondine."

Now this was only thirty years since the drownings and there were still those in the village who had actually known Jason as a boy, who had touched him or talked with him. Those few were endowed with a certain authority that was, as a matter of tribal courtesy, rarely challenged. "I once touched his face," one of these women said, and in fact it was true. She had nursed him through a fever. She hadn't wanted to, but Dzarilaw ordered it, and she was certainly more afraid of Dzarilaw than of any adolescent spirit. "They said there was evil in him . . . I don't know."

"I held his arms once," one of the hunters announced. "He wanted to swim and his arms made him feel clumsy, so he took them off and I held them until he came back."

"You are a drunken fool," Skaai reprimanded. "Of course it was Ondine. Who else could have survived such an attack?"

They argued through half the night and the Jesuit handed out some of the blankets. They were warm and welcome, and by morning, half the village was asleep around the embers of the fire, wrapped happily in their new blankets.

—

Throughout the night, Jason stayed close to his rock and nursed his wounds. It was the first time he discovered how quickly his body healed, and how much longer it took for his soul.

FIFTEEN

It was almost an hour before Malcolm got the message. He was off-duty so they never ran him on the radio. Okay. But, goddammit, he had a pager. Private issue. Paid for with his own damn money just for a situation like this. He was at the softball game. The Wednesday game. On Sundays he'd play for the precinct. Sundays was a fancier game. Tougher competition and a better workout. It was on Sundays he had made his reputation in the department, long before he became a detective. But it was the Wednesday game that got him there in the first place. It was the success of the Wednesday game that got him thinking about becoming a cop at all.

All his life Malcolm had felt this pit, like a hard little black hole somewhere in his belly. There was always an ache to it. Never a physical pain, just some sort of distant yearning. Sometimes he thought of it as the repository of his tears. It felt like that, like a far-away sadness all wrapped up in this frighteningly little black hole. Even when he was little, his parents used to say, there was something lost about him. Something they never saw in other kids' eyes. They said it felt like he was born tormented, as if there were a fire consuming him from the inside, keeping him empty. When he was a boy, he said it was like being hungry all the time, but not for food.

"It's like I got this leak inside me," he once told a friend back in junior high.

"What do you mean, you gotta piss?"

"No, Paulie, I don't gotta piss." Malcolm burst out laughing and threw an arm around his friend. "I love you, Paulie," he said, scaring the hell out of him.

Paulie took Malcolm's arm from his shoulder. "C'mon, Mal, there's people watching. You can't go talking like that."

It was the accident that did him in. He couldn't have been more than fifteen or sixteen. He was doing what he always did, bouncing between heaven and hell. One minute soaring with the angels— sometimes with chemical boosters, sometimes without—the next wallowing in hell. It was often hard from the outside to tell which was which.

"I swear to God," he lied.

Drove the car off a tree and into a laundromat.

"I swear to God, this kid ran right in front of me."

And it was a stolen car. "I swear to God . . . I didn't know. This guy lent it to me."

The judge sentenced him to community service, in deference to Malcolm Sr.'s unblemished record in uniform and his promise to keep a sharp eye on the boy. It was a generous sentence, considering all the damage.

"I swear to God . . . for a damn car, it's not fair," Malcolm complained outside the judge's hearing range. And then he got lucky. Softball. It was a soul-saver, an elaborate colloquy with his own emptiness.

It came to him in a flash. Some people get E=mc2. Origin of the Species. Love thy neighbor. Get married and have kids. The gray horse in the seventh at Aqueduct. There are all kinds of flashes to be flashed. Malcolm got softball. Actually, he'd always had baseball, always had the reflexes. What came to him in the flash was the idea of sharing it, of bringing it to people for whom stuff didn't come so easily.

He collected equipment, starting with a sizeable donation of used gloves and bats from Snyder's Sporting Goods—Paulie's father—and ragged bases from the high school. For the very first game he rounded up fifteen other guys—all of them homeless, living in doorways and underpasses and shelters—and they had a great time.

They played eight a side and you had to pitch to yourself—the hitting team supplied the pitcher. It was the best game of baseball Malcolm or anyone else on the field had ever played in their lives. Grown men bayed with unshackled delight when they got a hit or made a snazzy defensive move. These were men who had not experienced a moment of joy for as long as they dared think back, and softball restored it to them.

The game was meaningless, as ephemeral a triumph as the gods had ever devised, but the moments were pure, and restorative, and healing. The moments were mountains climbed by men who on some days couldn't climb a sidewalk curb. Malcolm Brae had made them men again.

Before long the game was attracting thirty or forty guys (never more than half a dozen women among them) and they had to play two games a night and the whole thing took on a life of its own. Several of the regulars set aside one day a week in which they dedicated their panhandling exclusively to the game. (Excuse me, sir, could you spare a buck for a rosin bag?) They bought themselves T-shirts and caps from a seconds shop that gave them a special deal and eventually they were collecting enough to turn softball night into a barbecue where they'd feed not only the players but anyone else who showed up hungry.

For a little while, that knot of emptiness in Malcolm's belly lightened up. A year later, when he reported back to the court on the state of his community service, the judge handed him a brochure about the Police Academy (which he'd been given by Malcolm Sr.) and told Malcolm that the next time he showed up he'd better be wearing a uniform. Then he shook Malcolm's hand and told him that his homeless softball game was a wonderful gift to the community.

Malcolm kept the brochure but it wasn't until after his parents were killed that he ever looked at it.

—

It was the middle of the first game of the night. Malcolm had just driven in a run with a deep sacrifice fly to left field and was feeling good until he heard his beeper. He returned the call to discover that it had taken the station almost an hour to notify him that Jason Ondine was at White Meadows.

"Jesus Christ! What the hell's the matter with you?" he yelled at the civilian phone handler who worked, alone and embittered, in the station basement.

"First of all," the woman answered, "I'm not your mother, I don't gotta go looking for you to deliver personal messages."

"It's not personal!"

"Second of all," she continued, ignoring his defenses, "you keep raising your voice at me and you may never ever get another page outta this station."

The thing about people with real power, Malcolm remembered, is that they're not afraid to use it, so he knew to be afraid of her. "Yeah, well lemme tell you," he barked, "I got no right talking to you in this tone of voice."

"What?"

"You heard me!" Malcolm stressed.

"Detective Brae?"

"No harm done a decent bottle of wine couldn't fix," Malcolm informed her.

"What?"

"Alright, I'll send you a bottle of red, but that's it. Let that be a lesson to you." He pocketed his cell phone thinking that if he'd just learn to make his mouth a little slower than his temper, he wouldn't be out a bottle of wine. "Asshole," he said, addressing himself.

"You talking to me!" the shortstop bellowed, throwing down his glove and stomping off the field in Malcolm's direction. "You fucking talking to me!"

"Who you think I'm talking to!" Malcolm shot back. This was baseball and no time to abandon jock posture. On the other hand, he was thinking, *I'm about to instigate a bench-clearing brawl between a bunch of lunatic vagrants and that's just dumb*, so he backed off. "Sorry, man," Malcolm announced, waving off the encounter. "My fault."

That stopped everybody in their tracks. There was a collective gut-wrenching wave of disgust. There are a lot of things one can say in a confrontation like this (Oh yeah! Says who! Fuck me?! Fuck you! C'mon big shot, try me! Take your best shot asshole cause you ain't getting a second chance.) And so on. And usually they are pretty much the right things to say to defuse the situation. Everybody gets to do a little semenistic venting and the game goes on.

But Sorry-my-fault is not in the lexicon of encounter. It's something you say to your own teammates. You drop a fly ball—sorry, my fault. You try to steal and the guy behind you gets picked off—sorry, my fault. But never, never are you allowed to say it when somebody's coming to throw a punch. It just confuses everybody and can turn a purely game-based brawl into something personal. Now everybody was staring at him.

"I gotta go," he said and they realized that's what he'd meant in the first place, not sorry-my-fault but I-gotta-go, and it was a big relief because in fact all the guys really respected him and wanted it to stay that way. He drove off and the game went on without him. He looked back in the side mirror thinking this was a hell of a price to pay for having stolen a car when he was just a kid. Not even the one he'd wanted. He had taken the Honda only because he couldn't get the Grand Prix parked beside it started.

—

Half of the White Meadows staff was out on the lawns and paths of the main quad, gathering as they always did in little groups—to avoid alarming the patients—when something exciting might be going on. Last month it was a suicide. A man who had been checking himself in and out for several years with bouts of depression hanged himself from the church steeple. Now they gathered because word was out that a madman had taken one of the lifers hostage and was holding her in her room. Patients also collected on the lawn and shuffled nervously, regretting that one of their own had been culled and grateful it hadn't been them. They were there for the impending blood, there to confirm it wasn't coming from them.

Betty Hesperson greeted Malcolm at the front door of the Administration Building and handed him a mug of coffee. "It's a long drive. I thought you might like this."

"It's not that far with the siren on."

"You don't want the coffee?"

"No. No, I do." He warmed his hands on the mug. He was poised and confident, but not so practiced that Betty couldn't read his anxiety.

"He's in the West Meadow Building," she volunteered. "On the second floor in a secure room with bars on the windows and a barricaded door."

Malcolm nodded, as though he expected no less. "Does he know you called—?"

"No, I don't think so. I was very discreet."

Malcolm had already spotted the gatherings so he knew she couldn't have been all that discreet, but he gave her points for thinking about it. "Ma'am, if you could show me the way?"

She was very happy to. It gave her considerable status. She knew it wouldn't last long, but it felt good. She'd probably get three or four days out of it, a week if she was really careful about parceling out the details of her conversation with the handsome young detective.

They walked across the lawn, the bounce in her step matched by his own. This was going to be his first official detective-level bust. There is an excitement to firsts that is hard to match. Not exactly a match for the anticipation of his first woman—girl, really, they were thirteen— but there was certainly a magic about it. The almost exuberant anxiety, the fumbling fear, the carnal sense of impending danger. In the case of the girl, failure and humiliation loomed, here it was only death.

They walked up the hallway and could hear the music from a long way off. Stevens had been joined by two other attendants—he'd called for backup, just to be on the safe side—and by now they had all heard the story of Jason and the orderly back in the city and were all thinking how they'd like to get their hands on him, for two minutes. That's all they wanted, two minutes alone with him. Malcolm asked for a rundown and it didn't take long. There wasn't much to run down.

"What happened when he tried the door?"

"I told him it was policy to keep it locked during all visits."

"Stanley," Betty began to admonish, "the policy is just the opposite. The doors should be . . ." She trailed off as her thoughts caught up with her mouth and closed it.

"What did he say?" Malcolm wanted to know.

"Nothing. He didn't say nothing. I mean, he said like, okay or something like that and then they turned on the radio and started dancing."

"And that was . . .?"

"Maybe an hour. Maybe a little less."

"And you think they're still dancing? Jesus," Malcolm admonished.

"The radio's still playing," Stevens pointed out in his own defense. "What the hell else do you think they're . . . Oh, Jesus, you got to be kidding. At her age!"

Malcolm knocked on the door.

They ignored him. They didn't even bother to turn the music down.

"Mr. Ondine?" He waited. "Mr. Ondine, this is Detective Malcolm Brae. . . . I'd like to talk to you if you got a minute."

"Jesus," Stevens repeated to Betty, "at her age?"

"Mr. Ondine, all I need to know right now is that Ms. Bennett is alright."

"Oh God," Betty blurted out, recognizing for the very first time that Lizzie Bennett could be in serious danger. "Oh God, he wouldn't hurt her, would he?"

"He hurts that sweet lady," Stevens announced, "and I'll tear his heart out with my bare hands."

"That's my job, Sport, and I think you better back off."

"I'm here to—"

"Back off! All of you. Do it. Now!"

They did, even before he reached into his jacket and pulled out his gun. He spit the clip, checked it, and set it back. "Mr. Ondine, I don't hear a good word from Ms. Bennett in the next five seconds, I'm coming in and I'm coming in pissed off."

He said it, so he was committed to it. He'd never killed anyone before. He always knew that someday he might have to, he just never expected it to come this soon. He was what Captain Adachi called a review virgin, a term spoken with some resignation if not outright contempt. A review virgin was an officer who'd never shot anybody and so had never had to face a review. For Adachi it meant a cop who hadn't yet really been tested, and so couldn't yet really be trusted. "I don't want no virgin watching my back," was his most preferred use of the term.

The irony of the music coming through the door was not lost on Malcolm. Nanci Griffith, singing that it was just another morning: "And it's a miracle that comes around every day of the year."

He released the safety on his pistol. "Ms. Bennett? Can you hear me?"

Nothing. He slipped the bolt on the door. "Ms. Bennett?"

He who hesitates is just screwing around. He put his boot to the door and shattered the frame as he kicked it open. He rushed in behind the cover of the clatter. He knew that about sudden noises, that they gave you an advantage of a second or two, usually more than enough to save your ass in situations like this even though, he reminded himself as he was in full flight, it was something he'd learned at the movies, not on the street.

Exploding through the door, thinking movies, he knew he had to say something. Something. The lines ran through his head as if he could hear all the movies at once: "Drop it, Scumbag!" and "Freeze motherfucker!" and "Police! Nobody move!" There were endless standard tough-cop choices, but what he found himself yelling when he came through the door was "Shit!" because he was too late.

There was no one there. The window was wide open and the steel bars were broken and bent away. Ondine was gone and he'd taken Lizzie with him.

It was a big room, maybe not worth the bucks they were paying for it, but it was a nice room. Simple. Lizzie had made it very simple. A few pictures, some seashells, a painting of a sea storm on one wall, a white filing cabinet, a gorgeous quilt on the bed, and flowers. Three small flowers in an elegant little crystal vase. And the radio. It sounded tinnier up close.

Malcolm was mesmerized by the room. Almost spooked by it.

"Everything alright?" Betty interrupted, sticking her head in the door.

"Uh . . . fine." Malcolm put his gun away and switched to his cell phone. He got through to Adachi immediately. "Got a situation here, Captain."

"What the hell is it, Brae, you let him get away?"

"Uh . . . he took a hostage. The Bennett woman."

"Jesus, Brae, how'd you let that happen? The guy's a killer, he'll clock her out soon as he figures he's clear. Christ!"

The evening news took it on like a soap opera. It had all the elements: an innocent crazy lady taken hostage by a psychopathic killer. It was as wrong as it gets, but it fit neatly into three minutes and set the tone for the duration. Armed and dangerous. Do not approach. Shoot to kill.

Malcolm sat in the chair beside Lizzie's bed. He reached over and touched the pillow. It felt full of tragedy and it sent a chill coursing through him.

SIXTEEN

Love laughs in many ways. Sometimes explosive and full of fire, sometimes just a simple sigh. Or a scream. Sometimes love liberates, and sometimes the law is on your ass every way you turn. For Jason and Lizzie it was all of this all at once.

"It's because I'm rich," she told him. "If I was a welfare lunatic, nobody'd even be looking for us."

They crouched low in the woods, well hidden by the abundant growth, and studied the roadblock a hundred yards up ahead. Lizzie laughed.

"Sshhh" he told her, touching his finger to her lips.

"I can't help it."

"They may look funny," Jason whispered, peering toward the deputies, "but they're dangerous."

"It's not them, it's you."

He was puzzled, and somehow pleased. He touched her lips again and smiled.

"It used to be," she explained, "that I saw you only in my dreams, and it always made me sad. Now I see you and you're really here and I can't help it . . . it makes me laugh."

And he laughed. She put her fingers to his lips to stop him and they were both laughing and saying stop we're going to get ourselves killed and this is crazy and shhh shhhh and they couldn't stop because love laughs in many ways and joy is its greatest treasure.

Her heart spilled over and tears poured down her cheeks. He kissed her face over and over and over, and it almost felt as if the agonies of the past twenty-five years had been worth this moment.

They couldn't stop laughing, and one of the deputies at the roadblock turned to another and said, "What the hell is that?"

"Cats, maybe," another answered.

"That's no damn cat," the first one said and the others had to agree. Three of them drew their guns, powered up their flashlights, and started into the woods.

—

Jason had known almost as soon as he arrived at White Meadows that the police were coming for him. While he had somehow retained the strength and the acutely developed senses from his life in the sea, he still hadn't quite adjusted to the fact that they were unusual powers for an ordinary man. Unusual powers even for an extraordinary man.

While Betty Hesperson was calling the police from the office, she thought she was far enough away from Jason to be talking in private. She had even closed the door and whispered during the entire call, but Jason heard every word. Her description of him, was, he thought, all things considered, fairly flattering. It didn't take much to know that the smart thing to do was to leave immediately, but he hadn't come this close to Lizzie just to jump ship.

Sometimes, when he lived in the sea and the hunting was difficult and he was hungry and there was nothing to do but wait for dinner, for a school of fish perhaps to swim into view, he could feel the anxiety building in him. It wasn't that the waiting took a long time, it was that it became everything and so it was all of time. It was forever, which is how it felt waiting to be taken to

Lizzie. It was all there was—waiting. From now until the very end of time, or until something happens, whichever comes first.

When finally Stevens ushered him into the room and he saw Lizzie, his heart was transformed. For the first time since he had last seen her, it felt like the heart of a man, and it filled him with humility and with pride. And he was overwhelmed.

"Forgive me," he said.

In two hundred years of living in the sea he had never felt the need to apologize for anything. In the sea he had been an integral part of the ebb and flow of natural rhythms and impulses. He was, simply, a part of the puzzle.

But here he was a human being, and with that came a sense of choice, of responsibility. Here will had a role. Here he was accountable for not having seen her for all these years. "Forgive me. Please."

She turned to him and the moment he met her eyes he knew it was done. She allowed him the burden of his responsibility. And she made him human.

"My God, Lizzie," he responded, bursting with love, "you are even more beautiful than I remember."

He held her and she wept. Love laughs in many ways.

She turned on the radio and they danced, hardly moving, clinging to their own rebirth and after a while he said to her that the police were coming for him and they had to leave.

"Stanley bolted the door," she reminded him.

"We'll go through the window."

He still had no idea how strong he was, but he opened the window and tested two of the bars. Steel. He remembered how much the People had hated metal. Some attributed the end of their world to the arrival of iron. They said the animals lost their soul when they were killed with metal blades. They said metal was why game was becoming so scarce. It was why they had to chase the game now, why they could no longer simply clear the way and invite them to the hunt.

Jason tugged on the bars with a real anger for the steel and they bent in his hands, and snapped.

"What was that?" Stevens called from outside the door. "Miss Lizzie, you alright?"

"I'm fine, Stanley," she called back. "It's just the chair."

Lizzie tied some sheets and blankets together. "This is very clever," Jason announced after testing the knots.

"You see it in the movies all the time."

"I'd like to see a movie," he told her as he lowered their rope out the window. He turned and walked back to her. He held her shoulders. "I pledge to you," he announced with heartfelt solemnity, "that I will never let anything ever hurt you again."

She pulled away, angry. "You can't say things like that. I'm a grown-up, Jason. I know better. You make pledges like that and life will make you a liar."

"I would risk anything for you."

"And me you, but I can't save you from hurt and pain."

"And I can't save you?" he asked.

"All you can do is try to be there when I need you."

"I will never leave your side. I swear it."

"And I release you from that pledge."

"I don't understand, Lizzie. Aren't you coming with me?"

The question stunned her. Until now, now that reality loomed, filled with urgency, it had never been a question. Her mind was reeling. She wasn't ready to say it, but how could she go without telling him that she'd borne his son, and lost him. "Jason, there's something you have to know."

"Lizzie, all I need to know now is if you're coming with me or not."

"Of course I am," she said. She'd tell him soon, she thought, feeling like a deceiver.

—

The three cops split up in the woods and followed different trails toward where they thought they had heard laughter. The lead cop found himself on a trail that wound slowly to the low rise where Jason and Lizzie were in fact hiding.

They stopped laughing and watched the fractured flashlight beam sparkle through leaves as it made its way closer and closer. Lizzie got quiet. Very quiet. Jason got silent. He pointed to the back slope of the mound, but when they turned, there was another flashlight coming their way. They were trapped.

The lead deputy was closing, and the closer he got the more nervous he felt. He'd been a cop a long time and faced danger regularly, but this was the first time he ever felt the hairs stand up on the back of his neck. It was the first time he felt spooked. "Kim?" he called out, more to calm himself than to collect information, "got anything?"

Kimetashka called back from the far side of the small rise. "Nothing here," he answered, also feeling unusually unnerved and glad to hear a voice. "Coming your way, Graj."

Lizzie was edgy, ready to bolt. Jason touched her hand and it calmed them both.

Graj, the lead officer, was less than ten feet from them. He hadn't seen or heard them yet and he was scared.

Jason could hear the man's heart beating, a frightened heart, and it steeled him for an attack. He'd let Graj get a foot or two closer.

Suddenly, with a terrifying shriek, a raven dove from an overhead branch and screamed by, inches from Graj's face. The deputy screamed. He fired two shots. Wild. Into the bush.

"Graj!" Kimetashka hollered. "Graj!"

"Where the hell are you!" Graj called back in a panic, sounding farther away than he meant to be.

Jason and Lizzie remained hidden as the raven circled and cackled. "Graj!"

Three or four more birds flew by cackling. Laughing.

"Jesus Christ," Graj muttered to himself, waiting for his heart to start again. "Jesus H. Christ."

"Graj!" Kimetashka called again, running.

"I'm okay. False alarm, I'm okay."

Kimetashka got there just in time to see Graj put his gun away. "You okay?"

"It wasn't cats," Graj told him, "it was birds or something."

The third deputy joined them momentarily and they all walked back through the woods together, full of recovered bravado by the time they reached the roadblock and reported.

"Some fucking crows," Graj explained to the others.

SEVENTEEN

The plague of the smallpox came down upon them like dreams from demon skies. There was no place to run to, no one who could hide. The Jesuit priest and the other White Ones had enough immunity to protect them, and they escaped the deadly scourge. Only the People died. More than half the village by the time it was done.

It came upon them so suddenly it was impossible to see it as anything but a curse. A week or so after the incident with the sea lion and the Cree, the sickness broke out in lodge after lodge. All at once. Terrible chills that quickly turned to ferocious fever. Vexing rashes that filled the hands and feet and spread to the trunk when there was no more room on the arms and legs. Ugly sores swollen with puss and then filled with blood, and bleeding that would not stop.

"The Lord is my shepherd, I shall not want." The Jesuit, who had not the slightest idea that his blankets had brought this scourge, walked among the People, reciting psalms. He saw in all of this not only tragedy, but opportunity. A chance to capture souls for God. A golden gateway for bringing new converts to Jesus.

The future and the past died first. Little babies and great-grandmothers. Aging warriors and hunters weakened by old wounds never quite properly healed. A visiting Klamath who had actually been feeling poorly when he arrived. The very best totem carver in the area, a relatively young man who was known for his weak lungs because he coughed a lot, probably, they said of him, because of all the dried bark and wood chips he constantly smoked in his stone pipe. The smoking made him crazy, they said, and agreed that it was probably necessary to be a little crazy to carve such fine poles.

The People prayed. They prayed to spirits and to ancestors. They prayed to their totems and their neighbors' totems. Even those who never prayed, who really didn't care much for the spirit world or didn't believe the Spirits intervened anymore, prayed.

They prayed to the Bear Mother and to Tlenamaw, the Monster Dragon. To Qagwaai, the killer of dragons. To Killer Whale and Grandmother White Mouse. To the trees and the rocks and the night sky and the day.

And almost everyone prayed to Hanging Hair, whom they called Gyhldeptis, and she wept for them because she couldn't save them or comfort them. All the trees of the forest bent their branches in sorrow and the People kept dying. She made herself into Raven and perched in a great tree to the east of the village and cursed her impotence, which she blamed on her sister for having breathed spirit into Jason, upsetting the delicate balance of natural powers.

Some of the People blamed Jason too. Those who thought the sea lion was Jason thought the smallpox was his revenge for their attack on him.

"Crazy!" Skaai railed at them. "Crazy talk!"

"You always defend him," they said. It was true. Ever since Skaai's dream about Jason being rescued from the whirlpool, he had seen Jason as a hero. A rescuer.

"Tell that to the men he drowned."

"You can't blame him for that. He drowned with them," Skaai replied.

"Then what was he doing in your dream?"

"He came to say we should not fear him."

"It was a false dream."

"Dzarilaw loved him," Skaai answered. "Was that a false dream too?"

"Ask the men who drowned." It had come full circle.

"He will return," Skaai declared.

"Not if he is drowned."

"He'll be here when the People need him."

The Jesuit could not resist. "Jesus is here now," he announced.

Everybody looked around. Any salvation would do.

"No," the Jesuit explained, "you can't see him with your eyes. It takes your heart. You have to open up your heart."

And just as quickly as the door had opened, it snapped shut. He'd lost them once again and knew it. He stumbled over his words, rushing to win them back, but it was impossible. "Jesus died for us!" he shouted, "so we could live with him forever in the Kingdom of God."

"It is too far away," one of the old women shouted back at him. She had dying children. She had no time for this.

"Open your hearts! Open your hearts!" the Jesuit called.

Even while Skaai was dying of the smallpox, he clung ferociously to his belief that Jason Ondine was a spirit created to comfort the People in their time of greatest need. These times were the worst that Skaai had ever seen, so it was not beyond reason for him to suspect that now would be a good day for Jason to arrive. In fact, when his fevers ran especially high, he believed that when Jason had swum in with the Cree on his back that day, he was coming to announce himself and save the People from this plague. That they chased him off with spears and knives simply sealed their fate.

"Superstitious bug food!" Skaai hollered through the fever at his people. "Look what you have done to us."

It was their lack of faith that most disturbed him. How would they ever receive miracles if they couldn't see them! He took it upon himself to teach them better about Jason Ondine.

Once each day, for the last three days of his life, Skaai told stories. He told creation stories (how the world came to be) and allegory stories (how the world came to be what it is now), and he told stories intended to clarify the legend of Jason Ondine. His favorite story was the epic of the Boy-who-went-to-live-with-the-seals, and on the first night he told it in a traditional way, observing to begin with that the ways of the ancestors compelled a young person to go with the seals out to the sea.

"This is the story of a young boy who went out with the seals and lived with them under the sea. He was the only child of a great hunter who worried that after he was dead, the boy would have a very difficult time, for he had no brothers and no sisters to hunt with him. So the hunter went in search of a shaman who could tell him what to do. To make certain he was choosing the right shaman, the father prepared a test. He hid one of his most valuable whale-bone knives and approached the shaman, asking if he could help him find it.

"He went first to the most esteemed shaman in the village and, as was the custom, gave him a reward and asked him if he could help him find his missing knife. The shaman chanted and sang and danced, but he could not find the knife.

"And so it went, shaman after shaman failed to find the missing knife. Finally, the hunter went to the poorest shaman in the village, for he was the only one left.

"As he approached, the shaman said, 'Whatever you want from me can wait, but you should hurry back to the edge of the village and pick up the knife you forgot there before you lose it.'

"So the hunter knew he had found a shaman of real power and explained his problem. 'I need a shaman who has enough magic to help my son become a prosperous hunter.' They discussed it for several hours and the shaman devised a plan. That night, when the rest of the village was asleep, the hunter would bring his son to the shaman's house. There was a hole in the back wall just big enough for a boy's head. The boy was to put his head through the hole, then the shaman would secure him there with a rope. 'As soon as he is secure,' the shaman warned the hunter, 'you must strike him with your knife and sever his neck.'

"The hunter was shocked. 'That is what you must do. If you are too distressed, if you fail to strike, it is you who will destroy any chance he may have of becoming a great hunter.'

"That night he brought his one and only son and drew his head through the hole in the wall. The shaman signaled for him to strike.

"The father lifted his knife . . . and he could not. He could not kill his son.

"The shaman was furious at the hunter for ruining his son's life. The father bowed his head. He had a feeling of immense remorse and tremendous regret. The father pleaded seven nights with the shaman.

"Eventually, the shaman said to him, 'If you can avoid mourning and grieving over him, we can let the seal bladders take him away. That's one thing I can do for him.'

"So they agreed, and when winter came and the month for the lifting of the bladders was upon them, the shaman said special prayers and sent the boy on his way with the bladders which contained the life-force of the seals.

"The boy became one of them. He swam in the sea and caught fish in his mouth. He soon discovered that the people on the ocean floor, who were constantly moving and covered with sores, were the spotted seals. And the small men with big eyes were hair seals. He actually saw them as human beings.

"The men who sat around near the walls and never ventured far were bearded seals and they hardly ever hunted, but their companions brought them food. The giants, the largest of the seals who swam by from time to time, ignoring the rest, were sea lions. The boy thought they could be gods.

"The boy lived with them for a very long time. He learned to think like the seals, to see like the seals. He learned everything he needed to know to be a great hunter. Even among the seals he was greatly admired."

"After many years," Skaai told his audience, "the boy came home."

—

On the second night before he died, Skaai changed the story. Almost everyone came to hear because they knew he was going to change the story and that made the night a very solemn and important event.

A storyteller never changed a story just for the sake of it; a story arbitrarily altered loses all its power. If Skaai was determined to change this story, on the eve of his death, it would be considered, by one and all, to be an event of extreme importance. Like being present for the creation itself.

The story line remained basically the same. The hunter went to see the many shamans and so on. The differences were these: The boy was given a name, Jason Ondine, and his father was not of the People but was a white-faced man, a hunter from very far away who had come to live with the People. Skaai had known him. "I knew him."

—

On his last night Skaai said the boy was sent to live with the seals, but the seal bladders were too small to hold him and he burst forth from his, deep under the seas, and went to swim with the gods—the great sea lions—and became one of them.

"He will come back," Skaai told them. "He will return for the sake of the People."

—

In the days after Skaai died, the People were furious and scared. They had prayed and chanted and danced. They had told stories. They had cried and they had mourned, and yet the dying continued. Raven no longer perched in the high branches at the edge of the village, so the People said that even Hanging Hair had abandoned them.

They were desperate and decided that there was no longer any choice but to follow the path of the Jesuit and make the ultimate sacrifice. They went to search him out and found him praying in his lodge. They took him, struggling, by his arms and his legs and brought him down to the river.

Jason was lying on the rocks in the mouth of the river when he heard the shouting. He lifted himself up and saw them carry the screaming Jesuit to the river's edge.

"Open your heart," they chanted. "Open your heart."

They held him on the ground and a shaman danced in circles around him.

The Jesuit screamed at them. "You don't know what you are doing!" In his language and in theirs.

They answered back, chanting in tones of reverie that blanketed his terror, and they heard only silence from his moving lips. The shaman held a whalebone knife aloft as he danced. It was an offering. It was the very best whalebone knife in all the village. It had until now only been used to butcher the very first seal of the season, for as many hunts back as anyone could remember. They assumed his Jesus would be pleased. The Jesuit screamed and fought, and when he had no more strength left, he cried out for God. He stopped screaming and he prayed, losing himself in the names he recited.

The shaman knelt beside the Jesuit and told him that he hoped his Jesus was a compassionate spirit and would save him from the pain. He thanked the Jesuit for his sacrifice and promised that they would send his bladder out to sea. Then he plunged the whalebone knife into the priest's chest and the Jesuit screamed out in agony, a wail that pierced even the chanting of the People

The shaman cut out the Jesuit's heart and set it on fire. They let his blood run into the river. It was an offering they hoped would satisfy the plague.

Within days, the dying stopped. Those who were still sick, recovered. It was over. They held a large feast in gratitude, to honor the Jesuit and the power of his sacrifice.

Jason left. It was the last time he saw the village. It was the last time the People saw a sea lion resting on the rocks in the mouth of the river.

EIGHTEEN

They made it past the roadblock that first night and kept going, exhausting themselves in the effort to get as far away from White Meadows as they could before morning. They covered three or four miles on dark and sometimes treacherous trails until Lizzie just couldn't walk anymore and Jason carried her. Another eight miles. Over rocky terrain, through open fields, and often along creek beds to mask the route. Several times he backtracked just to test the scent, and when he couldn't pick it up, he knew there wasn't a dog in the world that could find it.

They stopped that night at a small sheltered clearing high up near the crest of the range, just short of the spine. The ground was soft under a layer of moss, and Jason collected fans of cedar for a cover. He held Lizzie in his arms and they slept hard for almost three hours.

When the dawning sun warmed and woke them, they made love. It felt like they had never made love before. It felt like they had never stopped. Memory and desire flooded them in great rushing torrents of pleasure. He lay inside her on the soft mossy ground. They absorbed each other, humming lilting elations, hardly ever moving at all for several hours until she whispered yes and they erupted, bursting with twenty-five years of anticipation and howling to the risen sun.

Her skin was at once new to him, yet every inch was familiar. He could feel her pleasures in it, and her agonies. Her flesh was not just the cover, not just the container, but a mirror of all she had collected in her soul through these years, and he could feel it even when he couldn't understand it.

His fingers were so sensitive to her, it was as if he could feel her life unfolding in his touch. It was so powerful, so intimate and over-whelming, it made him angry that he had gone all these years without hands.

They walked and they ran and they made love again and again, leaning on trees and lying in creeks. In open meadows under the moon. On day-warmed boulders in secluded knolls. They went after each other with a hunger born of all those missing years. And even so, she couldn't bring herself to tell him, couldn't open up her words to him so that he could really see into her heart, could really see what it was that tore her apart and built her spine.

They made love until her masks were all used up and she was left transparent and trembling, and still she couldn't say it.

They were trying to catch up and weren't even getting close.

—

They kept to the deepest woods and the least-traveled mountain trails, soft paths left by generations of fox and deer, wild dog and occasional hikers. Every so often he'd pick up the smell of old coyote piss or last year's bear dung, and although he hoped they were Spirit droppings, they turned out to be only what they seemed to be—old shit from wandering coyotes and well-fed bears. It was slow-going but safer than the roads, at least for the moment. Food was plen-tiful—berries, roots, mushrooms, edible grasses, small game—and as long as the weather held, it was fairly comfortable. He couldn't believe how much harder it was to catch birds on land than it had been in the sea where they just floated around waiting to be picked off from below. They never tasted very good, but sometimes just answering to your belly mattered more. It was the feathers mostly. He hated the feathers in his mouth.

One night they camped against the cliffs on a richly pebbled riverbank. The stones were so rounded and smoothed by the river that they felt almost soft underfoot. It was a place of such soothing serenity that Jason just couldn't understand why Lizzie looked so sad. "It's nothing," she said. "It's okay."

It wasn't okay but she was entitled to her privacy, her silence. Among sea lions there were lots of feelings, lots of ideas, lots of thoughts to share, but no words. No specific words, and without them there seemed to be no need for privacy.

With human beings it seemed to be words that caused most of the difficulty. The words were very precise and always inaccurate. The words bred anger and shame along with intimacy and bliss, and the words were what created the need for privacy. It was always the words that were too much to bear.

Jason went into the river to fish, thinking that thinking was also too much to bear. Bear. Bear. Bare bear. He'd always admired them. Always been jealous. All those years owning the ocean and he was envious of bears because he would watch them in the river grabbing fish with their great claws, and he had none. No matter that he was a far better fisher than they ever were, that they had arms to fish with aroused his resentment.

Now it was over. He stood knee-deep in the river swatting fish out of the water with his hands. It was so easy. He could pluck fish from the river with the ease of Lizzie picking berries from a bush. It was incredible. It made him laugh. It made him happy.

They built a fire—with matches, another miracle—and ate until they were full and made love on a driftwood timber until Lizzie came and burst into tears.

"You still look sad. . . . Is it still nothing?" he asked, stroking her cheek, wondering if she'd had enough of privacy, enough of wandering around alone in her own head giving more consideration to random thoughts than they often deserved. Thinking,

Jason had come to believe, was a human technology far more out of control than these new electronic gadgets everyone seemed so concerned about.

From the moment Lizzie found out she was pregnant, the only thing she wanted more than the baby was to tell Jason, and she never got to. She had tried it and rehearsed it so many ways that she herself was never sure which version would pop into her mind: *I'm pregnant. We're pregnant. I'm having a baby. A girl. A boy. We're having a baby. We're going to have a baby. I bore you a son. Our son was born today. Just as the day was dawning. Our son. Our son.*

"Oh God, Jason, he's dead. He's dead!" she blurted out.

"No, no. It's alright." He held her close. "Nobody's dead," he assured her, thinking she meant him.

"It's Nathaniel."

The name meant nothing to him. He continued to hold her, to stroke her. "Nathaniel?"

"He is our son, Jason." Jason felt a rush of pride, but she choked it off. "And he's dead."

They had no son. Jason didn't know if he felt cheated or numb; all he wanted to do was quell her pain. It felt peculiar not to feel anything for a son, even one he never knew he had. He had never seen him or held or comforted him. He had never known that a son was even possible.

"He was three days old," Lizzie said, sobbing. Of all the pain that she had ever known, none bore so deep or weighed so profoundly. No loss had ever come close to this, not even losing Jason. It was the worst moment of her life and she relived it every single day. The pain had not diminished in twenty-five years. Not in the smallest measure.

They had moved her from White Meadows to a maternity hospital in the city for the delivery. Her father was determined that she receive the very best care possible, and it went well. Less than ten hours of labor. No stitches. No fear. She suckled him almost immediately and dreamed that Jason would somehow know and come to them.

"He's a beautiful baby, Deer Heart," Marianne gushed, trying on her new role as grandmother.

"He needs his father," said Lizzie.

"Deer Heart, are we going to go through this again?"

"You promised you would look for him."

"I did."

"I don't believe you."

"Well, then it doesn't matter whether I did or didn't, does it?"

For two days Lizzie mothered Nathaniel. For two days he flourished. He gazed up at her face when he nursed. He slept easily on her chest. He gurgled when she stroked him.

On the morning of the third day, Lizzie's father came into her room with the terrible news. He sat on the edge of the bed and took her hand. "Lizzie, I'm sorry. I'm so very sorry. This is the worst news I've ever had to deliver."

"What? What are you talking about?"

"Nathaniel died this morning."

"No! Nooo!"

"In his sleep."

"Nooo!" She bolted from her bed, racing, screaming. "Nathaniel!"

Bennett grabbed her before she reached the door. To comfort her. To protect her. She pushed him away.

"Nathaniel!" She ran down the hall calling for him. "Nathaniel! Nathaniel!"

When she got to the nursery, he was already gone, taken away two hours ago. They were sorry, the two nurses told her.

The funeral was held the next afternoon. Very quiet. Very private. Very solemn. Few people came, not even all of the immediate family. They gathered in the Bennett family parcel of the cemetery, a section of burial estate secured several generations earlier. Lizzie could barely stand, broken by grief and sedatives. She trembled as she watched the tiny maple coffin lowered into its grave. The funereal words recited by the minister were no more than a distant droning in her ears.

Someone handed her a gleaming spade and she dropped the first shovelful of earth into the open pit. It felt as if her life stopped when she heard the mud and stones land on the maple box.

"They returned me to White Meadows," she told Jason by way of rounding out the story. "I went back once to see the tombstone. It was too much. I never went again. I talk to him instead in my heart."

Jason was shaken, more for her ordeal than the loss of the son. The son remained an abstract notion to him, not nearly as real as the many sons he sired in the sea. She went to her little bag and brought back an old photograph. Of Nathaniel. Swaddled and held in her arms, though the picture shows nothing of her. It was all she had of him. It was dog-eared, worn out with a mother's caresses and troubled conversations. Beaten dull by the pain absorbed from her fingers. It was the center of her world.

Jason studied the picture. He saw the baby. It felt like a baby but not necessarily his baby. "Nathaniel," he told her, "is a beautiful name."

"I named him for my grandfather."

"A very good name," he repeated. He was angry and he didn't know why.

Lizzie had watched him when she told him what had happened. She watched his eyes when he examined the picture and she saw no horror fill them, no tears spill from them. She couldn't understand how this thing that was the ordeal of her life, the central affliction of her being, could leave him untouched. A single tear would have done. An angry howl. A whimper, even that. But all she got from him was that Nathaniel was a good name. That and some comfort, but she'd survived with nothing but her own comforting for so long that it hardly seemed necessary. What she needed was his grief and he showed her none.

It filled her with desperation and terror, and she could only pray that it was the words, only the words that left him empty.

"I have to take you somewhere," she announced. "There's something you have to see."

He reached out to touch her hand and she pulled away.

She sat back against the cliffs, feeling alone for the first time since he'd returned.

NINETEEN

When the orderly at Bayshore Hospital failed to wake from his coma and died, it added considerable weight to the case against Jason Ondine, but the way Malcolm Brae got the news did nothing for his reputation. It was early morning, half an hour before his shift began. The TV was on at the precinct because there was a rumor that the commissioner was going to be on, talking about the new over-time policies, but instead of that they led with Malcolm's case. "Good morning. Top of the news today, we have late-breaking developments in the Ondine affair."

"Jesus, Brae," Adachi complained, aborting his trip to the can. "You the new media breakfast special or something?"

"It's not about me, Cap."

"It's your case, no?

"I don't write the news."

"According to our exclusive sources," the newscaster was saying, "Brian Arcata died at 6:04 this morning. The young orderly, coma-tose since being brutally beaten by—"

Adachi erupted. "This is our case, my department, and this is how I learn about it, on the goddam tube!" He was glaring at Malcolm.

The case had started becoming an issue with some of the senior officers the day Jason took Lizzie from White Meadows. Before that it had been a case they were happy to hand to a rookie; it was just cheap tabloid stuff at best—lunatic rapes a patient, cripples an orderly—another ugly urban incident with few of the requisite resonant chords to bolster careers. But when Lizzie moved to center stage, they began to sense that the story was moving toward critical media mass. A few of the older guys had already lobbied Adachi to get on the case, but he wouldn't hear of it. "It belongs to Brae," he told them in a display of confidence they wished they'd get for themselves once in a while, "right to the end."

Now, watching the news, Adachi wasn't feeling so generous. He was pissed. Jason Ondine was now a homicidal maniac—TV-certified—and it was getting worse. Before the piece was done, the news-spitter was talking about murder charges to go along with the kidnapping. "Now they issue warrants too!" Adachi fumed.

And then they cut to a live interview with Dr. Wayne Elliot. "Without an autopsy it would be premature to announce an official cause of death. On the other hand, regardless of the specifics, it certainly looks like he died as a direct result of the injuries he sustained."

"That would make his death a murder, would it not?"

"Well I'm no lawyer," Elliot answered, "but I would assume so."

"You better get your ass over to the hospital and shut this Elliot guy up," Adachi told Malcolm. "He's killing your case."

Sipping his coffee, Adachi started back to his office, muttering, "Goddam newspricks."

—

Elliot was in the hospital basement, back to his quest for the key to Jason Ondine. On the surface he continued to be the good doctor that everyone knew and sucked up to. He made his rounds, saw his patients, diagnosed disease, and prescribed treatments. All as flawlessly as ever. On the inside he was obsessed, however, and all too conscious of it. He knew what was happening to him, but he couldn't stop himself. Sometimes he took responsibility for it. Sometimes he denied it. Sometimes he regretted ever taking Taryn Stream-Cleaner out for that damn cup of coffee.

In fact, Taryn had said very little, only that her grandmother had told her a story about a white boy named Jason Ondine who was given spirit powers and was condemned to live out eternity as a sea lion. She believed that one day he would return, and no one knew if it would be for good or evil.

The seed was planted and Elliot couldn't shake it. It wasn't superstitions or Taryn's native legends that had him in their clutch, it was, he assured himself, science. He saw with his own eyes how the wounds had healed, and while that by itself was proof of nothing, it couldn't be ignored. He saw in Jason secrets that could unlock some of the most stifling paradigms of biological science, magic that could change the very essence of life on the planet. To harvest it, he spent every spare moment in his small lab. From his perspective the problem wasn't that he was unreasonably consumed with the hunt for the holy Ondine grail, it was that he only had a few cc's of Jason's blood to work with. So single-minded was his focus that he was profoundly startled when Malcolm Brae burst into his lab.

"What the hell is the matter with you!" Malcolm hollered.

Elliot almost dropped the test tube.

"You medical mound of camel shit! Just what do you think you're doing?"

"Calm down, Detective."

In fact, Malcolm had already calmed down considerably since he heard Elliot's interview. "Exactly what the hell did you think you were going to accomplish by telling some dumb-ass reporter—"

"Ah," Elliot relaxed, knowing now what this was about. "In the first place, I didn't invite them here, they just showed up asking questions. In the second place, at the time they showed up here, this was still a free country, and in the third place, you raise your voice in my lab again and I'll make so much trouble for you you'll be lucky to get work directing traffic on an escalator."

It was a quick reminder to Malcolm that he was dealing with a formidable adversary. Strong. Smart. Maybe a little crazy. An adversary who could be a real challenge, and he hated that. He was trying to solve crimes not play games. On the other hand, once you're in it, you're in it.

"Don't you ever—*ever*—threaten me," Malcolm threatened, making sure to raise his voice just enough so that Elliot couldn't be sure if the line had been crossed or not.

He won. He could tell because Elliot didn't respond. Now Malcolm wouldn't have to resort to babble about obstruction and intimidation, which always, always weakened one's hand. It was, Malcolm believed, what distinguished cops from attorneys. "Do you have any idea what you've done here?" he pressured, softening his tone considerably.

"I made the announcement because I was the only one here. Look, I apologize. I wasn't thinking about you and I sure wasn't trying to make it harder for you."

The moment Malcolm heard that, he realized it was exactly what Elliot had in mind, and he could relax. Now he knew the lay of the land. "I appreciate that," Malcolm responded, "but you got to understand, making a public announcement like that before we get a chance to figure out how to handle it, that gives Ondine a couple of hours of lead time that just might make the difference between catching him and not."

"Oh jeez, no, I guess I wasn't thinking."

"Hearing something like that on the tube could just push him right over the edge. I'm thinking about the woman here, you understand?"

"I said I was sorry," Elliot persisted, delighted.

"Are we going to keep up this bullshit all day or what?"

Elliot liked Brae, as much as it was possible to like someone who was stalking you, or maybe it was just because he hadn't slept for days, but he didn't want to fight anymore. "Alright, here it is. I don't want to see Jason Ondine hunted down like a rabid dog over the likes of Brian Arcata."

"Don't tell me you believe Ondine's story," Malcolm asked.

"I knew Arcata. He was a mean sonuvabitch. He'd have raped a pincushion if he thought he could make it whimper in pain."

Malcolm didn't know why Elliot would suddenly break rank with the hospital and open up like this. He knew that in the same way that cops don't turn on cops, these people don't turn on each other. Elliot had to have another agenda and Malcolm figured he could wait him out.

Elliot took a little time to reflect. His chief worry was that Jason would get gunned down . . . and heal, and then everyone would see Jason's magic—what Elliot now thought of as "the Elliot Factor"—and the glory would go to someone else. As he sat there looking at Malcolm, it occurred to him for the first time that perhaps his scientific inquiry should in fact have been pursued not in miserly secrecy but in the bright light of public oversight.

Godammit. When he stumbled on Jason, he should just have announced and claimed it right then. What the hell was he thinking? "I should have told you this before," he told Malcolm.

"It's never too late," Malcolm assured him.

Elliot was not entirely assured but it was all he had. Can one cite a police officer as valid precedent in a scientific journal? He wasn't sure, but staking a claim was the issue of the moment, not footnotes. "alright . . ." Elliot decided.

"Yes?"

"Alright . . ." he hesitated again.

"Yes?"

"Look, this is going to sound crazy . . ."

Malcolm already figured that from the way Elliot's eyes were darting in and out of focus like a man chasing lottery numbers in a daydream.

"Jason Ondine," Elliot went on, "is over two hundred years old."

"Ah."

"Now, I can't prove it, but I think it's true."

"Uh-huh."

"I don't have any scientific confirmation yet, but I have what you could call . . . anecdotal evidence."

"Okay. Two hundred years," Malcolm said.

"At least."

"And you heard this from who, his grandfather?"

"I knew it. I knew you were going to make a joke, but I'm not joking and I don't care if you understand it or not, I just want to make sure you put this in your report."

"You want me to write in my official report that a distinguished doctor thinks that a murderer-kidnapper currently on the loose is really some poor misunderstood two-hundred-year-old?

"Exactly."

"You might want to think about this," Malcolm counseled Elliot.

"I already thought about it."

"I'm not going to do it. Maybe you don't care about your reputation, but I'm not going to do this to mine."

"All you have to do is quote me. It's on me, not on you," pleaded Elliot.

"Jesus Christ, don't you understand what you've done! You're gonna get his brains blown out. Maybe the woman too."

"I gave him a chance to save his ass!"

"Save him!" Not even close, thought Malcolm.

"What you've done is sign his death warrant. Wake up, Doc. You're a country sheriff or Highway Patrol and you spot this guy. You know he's a killer and a lunatic 'cause you watch the news and Dr. Wayne Elliot told you so. So you tell me, you gonna walk up and ask for his license or you gonna come out shooting?"

"I'm going to follow procedure," Elliot hoped.

"Bullshit. Even if you do and you call for backup, backup's gonna come out shooting."

TWENTY

There is a kind of primordial darkness that takes over every so often. It requires a combination of very specific atmospheric conditions and a certain deep-seated personal alienation, sometimes of the soul, sometimes of the psyche. This time, however, Jason and Lizzie were swallowed by a disaffection that was mechanical and circumstantial, not personal. They were doing the speed limit and a bit more in an old Jeep Cherokee station wagon, just keeping up with traffic, and they were both scared. Jason, who had never driven a car, was not driving. Lizzie, who hadn't driven one in twenty-five years, was.

"Oh, Jesus. Oh, Jesus," she kept saying, which inspired little confidence in either Jason or herself. "Oh, Jesus."

"You can do it," he encouraged, but there wasn't a lot of conviction in his voice. "You can do it."

"I think we should just ditch the damn thing and walk."

"Ditch?"

"Get rid of it."

"Oh," he said. "No." Now that he knew where they were going, he didn't want to waste any time getting there. For his own sake as much as hers.

"You do want to see your son?" she checked again.

"Yes," he said. "Yes."

"You're sure? I mean with everybody after you and everything?"

"Yes. I want to see my son." It would only be the grave, of course, but that was better than nothing.

For Lizzie, just to hear him say "my son" was thrilling and it took a serious effort to keep the tears that were welling up in her from flowing. This was his moment, she had to remind herself. This was for him. That he was willing to set aside his fear of her driving—his appropriate fear, she figured—she took as a good sign. In the two hours since they left the coffee shop with the car, they had covered more ground than on the previous nine days walking. She couldn't decide whether speed or fear was the more overrated. She was still glad she'd spoken up.

—

They had been at the edge of forest, in sight of the restaurant, and the scented waves of roasting meat and baked sugar were beyond seductive. For the first time since leaving White Meadows Lizzie wondered what the hell she was doing out in the wilderness scraping by on romance and berries. *Oh God,* she thought, *take me out of the asylum and I sound like my mother.* "There are other ways of handling things," she said to Jason.

He could smell the change come over her. He could see it too, a determination in her eyes that was not directed at him. "What do you mean?"

"I have money. Lots of it. There are more comfortable ways of hiding out. Better ways of getting what we want." While it was true that the Bennett trustees allowed her to make very generous charitable donations from her trust funds, it wasn't true that it all went to charity. Enough of it did, but half of it was channeled to private foundations that she herself owned and controlled. She'd always had a knack for making money, it came with the genes. Riding the phones and the early high-tech start-ups, Lizzie had gathered a small fortune quite out of the family's reach. "It might take some time to convert it to cash," she explained, worrying only slightly that reaching for the money she might catch a cop, "but it's there."

"And will this make you feel better about Nathaniel?"

Fuck you, she wanted to scream at him, *how could clean sheets and hot water make me feel better about Nathaniel?* But the obviously earnest nature of Jason's query made it clear that he wasn't accusing her of being like her mother, she was. "No," Lizzie answered, "but a clean plate might make me feel better about me. The keyword here is clean. I think I'm more addicted to showers than I knew."

"You're right," Jason agreed. "A hot meal is just what you need."

The SUMMER SPRINGS COF EE SH used to be on the main highway. Then the freeway came through. The town didn't get an exit, and Annie Melacroni's thriving little business turned into a place that couldn't afford to repair the missing letters. People took to calling it the SH. Annie hated it but there never was, nor will there ever be, a way to buck the tides of language. Once a thing got a name, especially a name that lent itself to easy scatologies, it was doomed until another tide moved through. There wasn't a thing Annie's protests could do about it.

Annie was a full-blooded Bella Coola from way up north of the Queen Charlotte Strait. She still had family up there and she talked to them by radio every now and then and dreamed about going back someday.

It was an unusually good day. The weekend was coming up and folks always spent a little more on paydays. A sure sign that her customers were feeling good was that they weren't crowded around under the old TV hanging in the corner. They only did that when they were down and didn't feel much like talking but did feel like hanging around, or there was a game on. Not only were her regulars going for that extra beer or two, but she'd sold out both of the apple pies and half the shortcake. On top of that, it seemed like several travelers had found their way off the interstate and were stopping in for a taste of old-fashioned.

For Jason and Lizzie it was the first food they'd eaten from a plate in nine days. Jason was on his fourth cheeseburger reveling in the grilled fat.

"It's not good for you," Lizzie complained.

"What do you mean? It's delicious," he explained. It reminded him of the great feasts in the village, where gobs of cooked fat were the primary delicacy, and he was unable to grasp her concern.

"She's right," Annie weighed in, delivering two more burgers. "All that fat, it's just not good."

"It's true," Jason agreed, "it's not like what I'm used to but it's better than raw, and a lot better than no fat at all."

Annie just smiled. She picked up the old plates and brought them back to the kitchen. As soon as she was out of earshot, Lizzie resumed a pressing conversation. "Did you think about it? You said you'd think about it."

"There's nothing to think about. He can't help."

Lizzie was talking about Cottie Prusch, the boy Jason had saved at the hospital. "But if he just came out and told the truth," Lizzie pleaded, "it would change everything."

"He can't," Jason tried to explain. "He must be in terrible pain."

"I'm glad you understand him," Lizzie said, making no effort to disguise her anger, "because I certainly don't, and I don't want to hear any psychobabble about it either."

"He ate the boy's spirit."

"Excuse me?"

"The man who attacked him . . . he ate his spirit."

"I heard you, I just don't know what that means."

"It means he's terrified," explained Jason. "Too terrified to talk about it. Without his spirit, how can he speak out?"

"Great," she said, getting even more pissed off. "Will he ever get it back, his spirit?"

"When he speaks out," Jason assured her, making it sound obvious.

"Oh my god!" Lizzie suddenly cried out sharply. She had just caught a glimpse of her parents on the TV.

—

"Please," Marianne begged her husband, "don't do this."

Robert Bennett stood in front of the bedroom mirror adjusting his tie. He loosened it. Not quite. A little more. No. He tried proper again and that just didn't feel right. A man in distress ought to look a little distressed. He pulled the knot and let the tie hang like dead silk tails from his open collar. That seemed to do it. It had just the right sense of desperation and exhaustion without giving up control—or hope—entirely.

"You want her back, don't you?" he finally answered. It was one of the things he did best—choose his words carefully—and she hated him for it. Yes, of course she wanted her daughter back, but not the way he meant. Not confined back in that horrible warehouse for wealthy psychotics. What she wanted back was the Lizzie she had destroyed. The Lizzie who sang from the treetops when she was happy and wept from the heart when she wasn't. The free Lizzie, the Deer Heart, the Lizzie she had robbed of a life.

"I just don't want her to hate me," Marianne admitted.

"We are talking about a woman who has run off with a guy who thinks he's a fish. She's not exactly playing with a full cookie."

Full deck, Marianne thought, careful not to think it out loud. Any time she ever corrected him he found a way to turn it around and make her feel like a moron. Correcting full cookie wasn't worth the price. Actually, he wasn't worth the price, something she'd only come to realize recently. In the old days a revelation like that would have destroyed her, thrown her into paroxysms of denial and self-flagellation. These days it was a welcome liberation.

"Spin, my dear Marianne. It's all about spin."

"You'd risk your daughter's life for . . . for a few points on the market!"

"Lizzie's life is hardly at risk. The police may think she's a hostage, some poor innocent victim, but you and I both know she went willingly with him. More than willing I would bet."

"No, you miss the point. I don't want my daughter turned into an entry in the corporate ledger."

"If the stockholders start seeing me as a bad guy, the bad guy, you're going to see some pretty significant shrinkage in your own portfolio. Is *spin* such a dirty word that you're willing to risk that?"

She didn't answer and felt worse for it. He gave her some time, then started for the door. "They're waiting," he said as he left.

Outside the house a dozen reporters gathered for the statement. The Bennetts faced them with the studied dignity of well-rehearsed breeding. Only the necktie betrayed the family's deep private pain. The media crush was unpleasant and rude. The questions came at them fast and frivolous, Bennett thought. He wasn't used to being treated so cavalierly, wasn't used to anyone questioning him directly, especially about personal issues. He refused to say anything until some decency settled into the assembly, and then he read what he said was a prepared statement. In fact, it was off the top of his head. The paper he held in front of him and pretended to read was a notice from AT&T about a sale on international calls, late nights and weekends.

"This statement is addressed to the man who kidnapped our daughter. Sir, please understand that Elizabeth is very fragile and delicate. She requires constant nursing attention and hospital care. We love our daughter very much and are prepared to do anything, anything to secure her safe return. Please, call us or the police or any intermediary of your choice. There will be no recriminations. We will press no charges. We will meet any demands. We will pay any ransom." He folded the AT&T letter and put it back in his breast pocket. He was very good at this.

"Mr. Bennett! Mr. Bennett!" reporters screamed.

He ignored them and turned to Marianne. He took her arm and they went back inside. She hesitated. Stopped for half a step to turn back and say something real, but then hurried to follow her husband inside just like she was supposed to.

Detective Malcolm Brae then stepped out from the crowd and walked toward the house.

—

Annie slipped into the booth beside Lizzie, facing Jason. "Mind if I join you for a minute?"

"We're just leaving," Lizzie panicked.

"I know who you are."

"You're making a mistake."

"Oh no, Darlin', no mistake. You guys are moving pretty quick to the top of the pop parade. Seen you on the news two or three times already. They treat you like you're the Virgin Mary, and you," she smiled at Jason, "they talk about you like you're the worst thing to happen to bad guys since Charlie Manson."

Jason shrugged. "Charlie Manson?"

"Don't matter, Darlin'. All you need to know is you don't want anybody talking about you and him in the same sentence."

Lizzie was feeling very hemmed in. She began to suspect that the police were already on their way.

Annie caught it. "Aw, shit," Annie said. "I'm sorry. You're on the run and I'm scaring you. I didn't mean to scare you.

"If you recognize us, everybody—"

"No. It's not like that. The picture they got of you must be twenty years old and all they got of him are drawings and they don't look nothing like him. You guys are still pretty invisible, the only reason I figured you is I seen you coming out of the woods, skittish, like hunted deer."

Jason finished eating and finally turned unblinking to Annie, as though he'd been paying attention all along. "So," he said in the way he remembered old Dzarilaw saying it when he wanted answers to unasked questions.

And Annie, Bella Coola that she was, seemed to understand it. "It's a long story," she said. "First off, my Grandpa was named Jason, so I got sort of a soft spot for it."

Lizzie nodded. She liked that. Connections. She liked that.

"'Course he was named after some Kwakiutl walrus or something," Annie laughed. "Anyway, way you walked in here, I could see right away you were no kidnapper, and if they were lying about that they were probably lying about the hospital stuff too. One look at you and I saw love, and boy, am I a sucker for that. Married four times myself looking for it."

"So you haven't called the police?" Lizzie asked directly.

"Hell no! I just came over to say if there's anything I could do for you, anything at all . . . "

Lizzie wasn't prepared for such generosity. Having just seen her parents lying on the news, she felt as if she'd taken a galloping hoof to the belly. It shattered a lifetime's worth of deceit. She always knew that they hadn't locked her up at White Meadows "for her own good," but she feigned that it was so to preserve the family by preserving the family lie. Somehow she managed to convince herself that it was an act of love. But when she saw Bennett looking into the TV camera and pretending that he was afraid that Jason would hurt her, pretending that he believed she was in danger, the house of cards, the basic frame of domestic dysfunction collapsed, and she was reeling.

"I got an old car I don't use much," Annie offered.

Lizzie, inspired by the generosity, accepted. What she was really accepting was not faster transportation, but a sort of turbo-charged perspective on her life. Which is how Jason and Lizzie got to be driving down the highway scaring the hell out of themselves in an old Jeep Cherokee wagon.

TWENTY-ONE

Something about her father looking out at her from a television set with Marianne standing beside him acting strong had brought it all to a head for Lizzie. Bearing for the cemetery at this speed was her answer. Tonight was the night. Tonight it would either all come together or . . . or she could vaporize herself and disappear into the ether once and for all.

"What is vaporize?" Jason wondered.

"Did I say that out loud?"

"No. I don't think so."

"You can read my mind?"

"Sometimes. I sort of hear it."

"Jesus."

"Sometimes. Just sometimes."

It was close to midnight when they found the cemetery. Lizzie parked not very far from what she believed was the right entrance, but the walk was longer than she expected it to be and much spookier. She hated graveyards in the daytime, but this, with nothing moving but shadows and wind, was much worse. Jason took her hand and made the shadows shadows and the wind wind, and she realized that it was the mission, not the environment, that was oppressive.

They moved slowly along the walkway as Lizzie searched for something familiar. There was enough moonlight to read the markers, and finally she came to one she remembered: CHAMBERS. I. N. REST IN PEACE. It was a normal sized tombstone but it seemed dwarfed by the large brass angel affixed to it, no doubt to carry Chambers—coffin, stone, and all—heavenward. Lizzie remembered thinking, the first time she was here, that with all that weight, Mr. Chambers shouldn't be surprised to find himself sinking straight into hell. It was what she thought now, seeing it again.

Judging from outward appearances, Mr. Chambers seemed to be resting comfortably, having neither ascended yet to frolic with the angels nor plunged deep enough to consort with demons. It was a boon for Lizzie because the brass angel snapped everything into sharp focus. She knew where she was, exactly.

The grave was up the hill to the far corner of the cemetery. It had been fairly isolated and there was an expansive view of the valley back then. Now the wide lawns were crowded with graves, and the open view of the valley was obscured by a large development of bungalows and small apartments, but she knew exactly where to find Nathaniel's grave.

They started up a branching gravel path when a big angry dog came straight for them, snarling. Lizzie grabbed Jason's arm.

Jason turned to the dog and snarled back. In a split second everything that was wild and ferocious about Jason occupied this human form.

Lizzie sensed it and felt immediately protected. It was a glimpse of living in the sea and swimming with its king. The dog sensed it. His growls sputtered and choked in his throat. He stumbled all over himself trying to stop and was scrambling backwards even as his momentum carried him closer—too close—to Jason.

Snarling, Jason lunged for the dog.

The dog whined. It pissed all over itself and fled whimpering. It would never recover enough to be much of a guard dog again.

"Jason?"

He was slow turning back to her, slow because he knew what he would see in her eyes, and it was there. Awe. Fright. Separation.

She knew it was in him. She knew from the very beginning that the beast was in there, but she had never seen it. She had certainly never imagined that it could erupt in him like that, so completely. So suddenly. The only thing that didn't change in that instant was the body, but everything else about him was the Jason of the seas.

"I'm sorry," he said.

"No, don't . . . uh . . . you . . ." she stumbled.

He understood. He touched her hand. It was enough for Lizzie. Not for him. What had happened represented everything Jason hated about himself. All he wanted of his life was to be a man, to become a human being, to live like a man, to love like a man, to die like one. When the Spirit took him over like that, it reminded him that his dreams were impossible. It taunted him with the curse he bore, that he could never have himself back. He could never live a simple life.

They walked in silence to the grave. It had a very plain headstone: NATHANIEL BENNETT. No dates. No comments. No commentary. There were flowers. Fresh flowers. "I have new flowers brought here every week," Lizzie explained.

Jason couldn't answer. His voice caught in his throat. He kept reading the small stone. Nathaniel. Nathaniel. Nathaniel. He tried to say it out loud and couldn't. Nathaniel, my son.

The sorrow began in his belly. It spread through him like some clawing colossal hungry weight burying his body inside itself. It rose like a howl from deep inside. He stared at this mound of earth and its flowers and he felt the tears welling in him. For two hundred years Jason Ondine had not cried, could not cry, and now it was drowning him. Consuming him.

"Nathaniel," he cried out, finally finding voice. "Nathaniel, my son."

Nathaniel. Jason stared, feeling as if all that was truly human about him, all that was possible, lay in that ground.

Nathaniel, my son.

He turned to Lizzie. She had no words for him. No comfort.

"Nathaniel," he bellowed. Two hundred years of dream lay in the ground before him. Two hundred years of sorrow erupted. Lizzie went to him and held his head against her belly. His sobbing body shook them both.

"Oh God, Lizzie."

He turned from her and fell onto the grave, his arms spread as though to embrace his son by embracing the earth.

Suddenly he stopped crying. He caught his breath and the sobbing ended. He got back up on his knees and touched the grave with his hands. His mind raced, swirling. He was confused.

On his knees he moved to the grave on the left. TONY COLLINS, it was engraved. He placed his hand on Tony Collins's grave.

"Jason, what? What are you doing?"

He couldn't answer, it was in his heart not his words. He moved to the next grave and placed his hands on it.

And then the next. He was excited. He beckoned to her and asked her to put her hands on the grave. She did. He took her to another and she touched that one too.

He took her back to Nathaniel's grave and placed her hands in the earth. "Do you feel it?"

She could feel his excitement but not whatever it was he wanted her to feel in the ground. He told her to wait and left her there. When he got back, he had a shovel and without a moment's hesitation he started digging up Nathaniel's grave.

"Jason!"

"It's alright."

"No, it's not. You can't do this."

She tried to stop him but he wouldn't be stopped. The more he dug, the more excited he got. By the time his shovel first hit the coffin, he was practically laughing. He cleared away the dirt and lifted the coffin out of the grave and laid it on the ground. It was lacquered maple and small. So pathetically small. Lizzie had to hold onto the tombstone to keep from falling over.

"Lizzie, no, it's alright."

She turned away. "No!" The shadows had become terrifying again. The wind spoke.

"I'm going to open it," he told her.

She rushed toward him, to stop him, but it was too late. She screamed as he lifted the lid, and she froze in her tracks and stared.

"I knew it!" he announced triumphantly.

There was nothing in the coffin. No bones. No remains. Jason knew this is what he'd find. Nathaniel's grave had radiated nothing. He sniffed the box to make sure. There was no spirit there. Nothing. Never had been.

"What does this mean?" her voice trembled, hardly daring to think what she thought. "What does this mean?"

He dared not answer her. He was just as afraid.

She could barely get the words out. "Nathaniel is alive?"

TWENTY-TWO

The two uniformed officers kept circling around it, as though by circling they would make sense of it. In the plain light of unadorned day, the little maple coffin was even more pathetic.

"What kind of sick sonuvabitch does something like that?" the stockier one asked, meaning it as an accusation, not a question.

"I seen some sick shit on the job," the young cop answered in the spirit of the thing, "but I never seen nothing like this."

"You ain't seen shit."

"What do you mean?" the younger demanded, sensing there was less camaraderie going on than he had assumed.

"You been wearing the badge three months, you ain't seen nothing. When you been around long as me, then we'll talk."

"I'm just saying, what kind of sick sonuvabitch digs up a baby's grave?"

"Exactly," the stockier one agreed, not noticing that it was himself he was agreeing with. "I know we're supposed to do this innocent-before-proven-guilty bullshit, but lemme tell you, Malcolm Brae's alone when he finds this cocksucker, Ondine'll never make it to a courtroom. You know what I'm saying?"

"Yeah, I'm saying the same thing."

"You can bet your mother's ass Brae's got a very clean .32 in his back pocket for just such a situation. Pow! It's done." His voice trailed off when he noticed Malcolm finish up on the cell phone and turn his attention back to them.

"Pelletier," Malcolm said to the stockier of the two, "if you're finished dusting, take it downtown and log it in."

"Yeah, we got good prints. Very clear."

Malcolm had the feeling that no matter how clear the prints were, they weren't going to help. "Well, run 'em and see what comes up."

"Uh . . . " Pelletier hesitated.

"What?"

"They look kind of weird."

"What do you mean weird?" Malcolm asked.

"They're like . . . I dunno . . . they're too perfect, you know?"

"No."

"It's like they hardly ever been used. There's no wear on the prints, like you'd expect. It's like the guy never touched anything in his life, or if he ever did he was wearing gloves. No wear, you know what I mean?"

"You sound like you're saying too good to be true," Malcolm pressed.

"Exactly. I don't trust 'em. I don't think they're gonna show up in the base."

"Run 'em anyway. What the hell, right?" Malcolm figured that even if they couldn't make the prints, the fact that he'd opened a file for them might come in handy.

"Mr. Brae . . . Detective." It was Sammy Sanchez, the cemetery's chief on-site administrator and caretaker, wheezing as he made his way over as fast as his well-pressed funereal legs would carry him.

"Sammy," Malcolm greeted him. He'd learned early that you always got better cooperation when you remembered names. "Sammy, that was quick. What'd we get?"

"I got what you asked."

"Good. That's good."

"Well, not exactly what you asked. I pulled the files. Nothing. I made the calls. Nothing. No death certificate. No autopsy report. No release from the hospital. Nothing."

"Then just what did you get me, Mr. Sanchez?"

"I got you the address. Mr. and Mrs. Robert Bennett. They're the grandparents." He handed a slip of paper to Malcolm.

"I know where they live."

"I did what I could."

There was no point being pissed off at Sanchez and Malcolm eased off, gave him a little cop-ly pat on the ego. "Yeah, you did what you could. I appreciate it."

"Thanks."

"They've been notified, the Bennetts?"

"Absolutely. Something like this happens . . . you want to say something right away. People got a right to know," Sanchez said.

"What'd they say?"

"Nothing much. I spoke to Mrs. Bennett and she didn't say anything much. She just cried. A lot. She cried a lot."

"Pelletier, I want this run through every goddam test the lab can come up with," Malcolm ordered.

"Looking for what?"

"C'mon, you saw how clean that thing is. I want to see if the white-coats can find a drop of blood, some shed cells, body fluid stains, embalming fluid. Anything. Anything at all that says there was ever a body in there."

"I think you may be right," Sanchez agreed.

Malcolm's mind was racing. It wasn't just coincidence that Lizzie gets kidnapped and then her baby's grave gets dug up. The old puzzle was unraveling and a new one was falling into place. There must have been something hidden in that grave, and Ondine needed Lizzie Bennett to find it. Jewels. Gold. Something really valuable. Special. Malcolm decided that if Ondine waited twenty-five years to come after the treasure, whatever it was, it could only mean that he couldn't get to it sooner. Maybe prison.

Loony bin. Out of the country, way out of the country.

It also meant that if Ondine now had what he was looking for, he no longer needed Lizzie. Jesus. Malcolm picked up the shovel and started poking around in the open grave, dreading the prospect that he'd find her body in there. When he didn't, he felt a wave of relief. It would be an awful thing to have to live with if she died just because he was too slow finding her. He lay the shovel down against the tombstone and studied the name. NATHANIEL BENNETT. He wondered if there were clues in that.

"Mr. Sanchez . . ."

"Detective?"

"About an hour from now the media will find out about this and they'll be all over you."

"Don't worry about it," Sanchez assured him. "In this business you learn discretion early."

Malcolm put his hand on Sanchez's shoulder. "I owe you," he told him.

Sanchez was touched. Hardly anybody ever really appreciated him. This was nice.

"By the way," Malcolm said in a way that Sanchez knew this was no idle by-the-way, "when you spoke to Mrs. Bennett, you didn't happen to mention that I was coming out there?"

"Discretion, Detective. No. No, I didn't say anything about you."

"Good. I want to do that myself." Malcolm was grateful and nervous. Something had been gnawing at him from the moment he saw the despoiled grave and it wouldn't go away.

—

Marianne Bennett had been scared before, but nothing had ever quite shaken her up like the call from Sammy Sanchez. For twenty-five years she had been waiting for her life to unravel. Although she had imagined a thousand paranoid scenarios, she didn't know how it was going to happen until Sanchez called.

She cried for a long time after she got off the phone and then she felt better. Much better. Relieved, in fact. Although the guillotine hadn't yet sliced through her neck, she felt a great weight lifted from her shoulders.

When Detective Brae called to say that he was coming over to discuss this latest development, Marianne put on a light jacket and went out to the greenhouse. It was a good place to gather herself and she could trim a bonsai or two by the time Brae arrived. The bonsai were always in need of trimming.

The greenhouse felt cold. Too cold, she thought, but the plants didn't seem to mind. Back in the days when she was still enamored of tropical orchids, the cold was deadly. Now it was only she who minded. She had set up her bonsai worktable way at the back because of the shade provided there by the big trees that lined the woods on that side of the property, and because it was private. Nobody ever bothered her when she worked back there.

On her way down the west aisle, she stopped twice. Once to try to talk a drooping *Dieffenbachia picta* into better posture and once to tickle the sensuously heavy leaves on an odd little violet that had not bloomed in the six years she had so far been tending it.

When she looked up, she gasped. "Oh my god!" Hardly audible. Almost a whisper. She thought she must be hallucinating. The brandy last night, she'd had too much of it. Or a stroke maybe. In any case, it so startled her that she dropped her basket of bonsai pruning tools. "Oh my god, Lizzie!"

It was a fairly gray day but occasional fingers of sun reached through the branches into the greenhouse and fell on Lizzie with almost gracious commendation, almost formal welcome. The light made her glow. "I knew if we waited here you'd come," Lizzie said. "I couldn't imagine you going an entire day without spending at least some time in here." She didn't smile when she said it and it made her heart ache.

With every fiber of her being Marianne wanted to grab Lizzie up in her arms, envelop her, hold her tight. Hold her. Hold her. She started toward her and Lizzie stopped her. Held up a hand warning her to come no closer.

"Oh God, Lizzie."

"Hello, Mother."

"You shouldn't be here!"

"Thank you. I missed you too.

"No, I mean the police are on their way."

"Mother, this is Jason."

Marianne had worked very hard at avoiding Jason's eyes but could now no longer put it off. Drawn in, she wondered how different everything might have been had she seen him all those years ago. She couldn't bring herself to speak to him directly. Pulling free of his gaze, she turned back to Lizzie. "I'm serious, Deer Heart, the police really are on their way."

Jason stepped forward. "What happened to our son?"

"Your son?"

"Mother, I spent twenty-five years mourning in an insane asylum for my dead son and—"

"White Meadows is hardly an asylum."

"Mother, help us."

Marianne was trembling. She seemed so old, and aging by the second. So fragile. So frightened. "I can't."

Jason went to Marianne and took her hands in his. His eyes fixed on hers and she could not escape them. "Everything before this moment," he told her, "is as distant and irretrievable as a dream, but everything from this moment on is our lives. Don't deny us. Whatever happened . . ."

"It was not my fault."

"What, Mother? What wasn't your fault?"

Jason persisted. "Is our son alive?"

"Oh God . . . I don't know. I don't know."

"You don't know!" Lizzie screamed. "You know! Goddam you, Mother, you know!"

Turning her back to the bonsai table, Marianne closed her eyes. "Your father never saw the baby," she began, barely able to get her quivering voice above a whisper.

"Nathaniel, Mother. He has a name."

"He never saw Nathaniel," Marianne corrected. Nathaniel,

Nathaniel. She said it to herself a thousand times a day. Still. He was her grandson. Her first grandchild. It left a hole in her too, but it was not something she was willing to engage.

"What are you talking about?" Lizzie protested. "Every time Dad came into the room he would say something about seeing Nathaniel in the nursery, about what a beautiful baby he was. I remember that. I can still hear him."

"It wasn't true. He never once went to the nursery, and if you recall everything else so well you'll remember that he never came into the room when the baby . . . when Nathaniel was there."

It was true. It surprised Lizzie to remember it, but it was true.

Robert Bennett never laid eyes on Nathaniel because he never accepted him as his grandson. Long before the child was ever born, Bennett had excised him from the family. The last thing in the world Bennett wanted was to have to deal with the illegitimate son of a lunatic child making hereditary claims on the family fortune. The only way to insure against it was for the child to be dead, and for his purposes not carrying the family name was dead enough. His scheme was a simple one. He had dispatched the child to a convent as a foundling, along with a comfortable anonymous donation.

Lizzie couldn't believe she was hearing this. She held onto Jason for support. "But he came into my room. He told me himself. He said Nathaniel was dead! I was at the funeral!"

For Marianne the unburdening was getting harder, not easier. It weighed more, squeezed tighter. "It was for show. For public consumption. It was for you, for your sake, he said. Because if you knew that Nathaniel had been given up for adoption, you would have gone looking for him."

"And you knew? All along you knew? What kind of monsters are you!"

Lizzie lunged at her mother but Jason swept her into his arms and kept himself between them. "She didn't know, Lizzie. Look at her."

Marianne was blank. Drained. "I did," she admitted, "I knew."

Lizzie expected to be consumed with hatred and rage, but all of a sudden, she felt strangely released. Relieved.

Jason felt the change immediately and released his hold on her. Like Lizzie his mind was already racing elsewhere. They had a son out there somewhere. The moment seemed to go on forever. All of them silent, each of them quiet. Captured in universal inertia, they might have remained locked in the instant forever without an outside force to restore motion.

It came in the form of Detective Malcolm Brae calling from the patio. "Mrs. Bennett? Mrs. Bennett . . . Malcolm Brae. Would you like me to come down there?"

Suddenly Marianne was reanimated. "That's the police," she announced. She hurried to the door.

"Mother, don't!"

Marianne opened the door and stuck her head out. "I'll be right up," she called to him. "I'll meet you in the library, go on and make yourself comfortable."

"I thought you were going to tell him," Lizzie admitted when Marianne returned.

"Turn you in?" Marianne was disappointed but not surprised. "I guess I deserve that."

Lizzie said nothing.

"Is there another way out of here?" Jason asked.

Marianne was so focused on Lizzie that it took a moment for the question to register, another to form an answer. "No. No, there isn't. The best thing to do is just hide in here and I'll give you the all-clear when he leaves."

Jason took that to mean that when they got the signal, they could escape. Lizzie understood it better. Lizzie knew exactly what her mother meant. "My God! You're about to invite us to stay for dinner!"

Marianne was not about to admit that Lizzie took the words right out of her mouth, and feigned surprise. "Dinner? Well, why not? We do have so much to talk about."

For a moment, less than that, Lizzie teetered between rage and regret, and then she started laughing. She couldn't help it. She laughed because even in the face of everything else that had happened, even against the specter of a lifetime stolen from her, she saw in Marianne, her mother. She saw in her the bonds formed by a lifetime of familiar gestures and responses, by countless conversations around the dinner table, and by the sheer indomitable power of proximity. She might never forgive her, but she couldn't help but love her. With her heart breaking and healing all at once, she took the several steps to Marianne and put her arms around her and held her.

Marianne burst into tears. "Thank you." Over and over, thank you thank you until Lizzie touched her lips to remind her that this was not about gratitude.

The door burst open and Malcolm Brae raced in holding his gun in two hands and pointing it at Jason's chest. He was screaming at the top of his lungs. "Don't move! Don't you fucking move!" Moving quickly. Straight for Jason. "Move away from the women. Do it! Do it now!"

Lizzie screamed. "No! No!"

"Detective! Don't!" Marianne screamed, her voice joining the pandemonium. "It's okay!"

Inside the greenhouse every sound was magnified, every noise echoed, and everybody's adrenalin cascaded in one continuous flush.

"Do it or I'll blow you to pieces where you stand." Moving closer. Holding the gun so tightly even the tremble disappeared.

Every fiber of Jason's being responded to the threat. Every cell in his body coiled as if to spring. His heart was racing but his mind was still and focused.

Lizzie saw it, the thing she had seen with the dog, but now it was much more intense. More volatile. Much more dangerous. "Jason, no!" she screamed. "He has a gun!"

Lizzie and Marianne were both screaming and Malcolm was hollering louder, but for Jason the world had become silent. He launched himself at the closing detective, hurtling his body with massive force.

Malcolm fired. The bullet entered Jason's body on the left side, just below the ribs. His blood sprayed in front of him and behind him.

Jason's flying body collided with Malcolm before the detective could get another shot off. The gun was jolted free as they hit the ground. Grabbing the stunned detective's throat in his hand, Jason began to squeeze until he could see the life slipping from Malcolm's eyes.

There was a loud, startling screech. It returned the world to Jason. The sounds came back. Natural motion restored itself. He could hear Lizzie again, and Marianne, screaming. He heard the screech again and looked up. A raven had landed on the roof of the greenhouse and was screeching hysterically. Then Lizzie was on his back, pounding him. "Don't hurt him! Jason, let go! Let go!"

Jason looked in Malcolm's eyes, took a deep breath, and let go. Malcolm coughed and spluttered, wheezed to get his breath back.

Jason handcuffed Malcolm to the table with his own cuffs and gagged him with some strips of cloth from the rag box. "I am not your enemy," he said. "Do not come after me or you will make it so."

Lizzie apologized and tied Marianne to the table. "I'm sorry to have to do this to you."

"No," Marianne told her, "I understand."

Lizzie kissed Marianne on the lips and then began to cover her mother's mouth with a rag but changed her mind. "I love you," she said, and tossed the rag back into the box. Marianne understood the gesture and she was very grateful. She said so, and then Jason and Lizzie slipped out of the greenhouse and made their way back to the woods from where they had come.

The raven remained behind on the greenhouse roof.

TWENTY-THREE

Watching Jason heal was almost more upsetting to Lizzie than seeing him get shot. The outcome was much better but the process was certainly as disorienting. "You frighten me," she said sharply. It wasn't that he healed like a god, or that his existence was a total denial of everything she believed the nature of life to be, it was that they would never grow old together.

All these years she waited for him and this had never crossed her mind. There are a million ways to say it—My soul is your soul, my life your life; When the moon hits your eyes like a big pizza pie, that's amore; Let me count the ways; and so on—but really it all boiled down to this most sublime of human accomplishments: growing old together, where growing is the operative phenomenon and true love its highest and grandest reward.

They could wish it, dream it, will it, scheme it, pray for it, but they could never have it. They could never grow old together.

—

It wouldn't be long before reliable composites of Jason started circulating in the papers and on the evening news. It was going to be much more difficult to get around. Doors would close, avenues would shut down. They had to find Nathaniel quickly and Jason insisted the old ways were the only ways they could rely on. "I need a shaman," he told Lizzie. "I need to find a shaman who can see."

"A shaman!" It upset her. "We're not going on a deer hunt. This is our son we're looking for!"

He heard the contempt in her voice and put it down to fear. He understood it, he forgave it. She believed in a different magic, a modern magic of electrons and bits and bytes, and there is a limit to just how much invisible stuff one has room to believe in. She had hers, he had his.

"And if we find one and he tells you to go look in Kansas City or Timbuktu, will you go?" she asked him.

"If I believe he is a shaman with vision, how can I not? How can we not?"

"We? This is not a we question. Dammit, Jason, what if he tells you Nathaniel is dead?"

It stung. "It would be better to hear it from a holy man than an undertaker or a clerk."

The search to find the shaman wasn't hard, but it was distressing. Lizzie had a throbbing headache, nothing like the migraines she used to get but still relentless. Not knowing exactly where to look, she took him to the bars and back alleys of the old city, where the dispirited and the downtrodden assembled and wandered, the invisible paths to which so many tribal expatriates had been discarded. Jason was appalled by what he saw. Drunks staggering in the street. Bums sleeping in doorways and dumpsters. Sick and empty. Toothless women sucking their way from one gulp of bad whiskey to another.

He could scarcely believe that these sons and daughters of people he had known some generations back as proud hunters and carvers, mothers and warriors, fishers and storytellers had come to this.

Kwakiutl. Bella Coola. Tsimshian. Niska. They were all here. Aimless. Broken. Cut off from their Spirits.

Jason thought this must be hell, that they must have all somehow succumbed, become Christians and fallen into it. If it was so, he reasoned, others must be in heaven. It hardly seemed fair, but he remembered the Jesuit telling him that the world wasn't fair, it was a test.

"No wonder you're upset," he said to Lizzie, "but this is not who they are, this is an illusion, a veil they wear because they abandoned their shamans. This is not who they are."

The first man they spoke to was a diabetic Tlingit, drowsy with bad memories, scratching open wounds on his leg.

"I need to find a shaman," Jason said to him.

"I'm no damn shaman," the Tlingit answered, with much less hostility than his tone implied. "You got a drink?"

Jason had no drink and the Tlingit turned back to the sores on his leg.

It was late and most of the people they passed in the streets hurried away, and most of those they found in the alleys were in stupors or asleep. Eventually they found a Nootka sitting on a bench in a bus stop kiosk. He was stooped with a sadness permanently carved into him by too much loneliness for much too long. It was a loneliness so thoroughly dispiriting that he pushed anyone away who tried to breach it.

The only reason he spoke to Jason was that Jason came to him speaking Nootka. Jason knew the language only a little, but enough to make some headway. His grammar wasn't good and his vocabulary was extremely limited, but his accent was perfect. That turned out to be enough.

"What the hell is that?" the Nootka demanded.

"You're Nootka, are you not?" Jason answered in English.

"Yeah, sure. Sure, but Christ, I don't speak it. We're Christians now. Even my mother couldn't speak it."

"But you recognize it?"

"My grandfather. He used to sit outside in the middle of the night talking it to my grandmother. That's where I heard it."

"I don't speak it real good," Jason apologized.

"One Christload better'n me. I tell you, I loved the old man."

"Ask him, Jason," Lizzie hurried him. Being here troubled her. It was a world she didn't want to deal with. It pulled too much at her heart. "Ask him."

"I lost something," Jason explained to the Nootka, "and I need a shaman to help me find it."

"Ah," the Nootka understood. "You want Mike." He sent them several blocks uptown where he said they would find a formidable gray stone building, a museum of some kind. If they went another block past, there they'd find an alley with a Chinese restaurant on this side and a locksmith shop on the other. "If he's not in the restaurant, he's in the alley."

Jason thanked him. In Nootka. Three ways.

The man was very grateful. "I miss him," the Nootka said, tears rising in his eyes. "The old man, I miss him."

They found the museum building and the Chinese restaurant, closed. As they turned to go down the alley, the sound of police sirens exploded everywhere.

Two cars came racing down the street.

A third came up the alley at them. They turned to run, and the cop cars raced on by. They had other business.

From the alley came a new sound, a wheezing, coughing, booming laugh. From deep in the belly. "Damn near scared the shit out of me," the laugher laughed. "I was sound asleep."

The man was forty or fifty, hard to tell because they were obviously all heavily used years. He was a wreck. He was blind, his eyeballs missing and his lids sewn shut. He smelled. "Scare you too?" still laughing as he made his way toward them.

"We're looking for Mike," Jason answered.

"Jason, he's blind," Lizzie whispered urgently.

"I know I am, you don't gotta whisper about it."

"Sorry."

"You're not sorry."

"She is afraid it would make your heart blind," Jason explained.

"Brown eyes," Mike announced. "She has brown eyes, yes?"

Jason was impressed. Lizzie shrugged it off. "Gimme a break, how many guesses are there? You say brown around here you're going to be right nine times out of ten."

"Five foot eight," he added, "and you, Jason, your hair is short, it comes only to your shoulders."

Jason was delighted, but Lizzie just thought it was a trick and looked away.

Mike walked right up to her and put his hand on her breast. She started to protest but Jason stopped her. Mike caressed her breast for a moment. "Nice tits," he said, and burst out laughing. That same laugh, from the belly.

Jason laughed too but Lizzie was pissed off. "I don't know about you, but I'm going."

"Aw, pretty lady, don't go."

"I'm not interested in your stupid games and little parlor tricks."

"What about your son? Don't you want to ask me about your son?"

That took her breath away. Jason too. "She means no disrespect. She—"

"No, she's right. Cheap parlor tricks, all of it. I've been listening to the news, that's all. You can't listen without hearing about Jason Ondine and Lizzie Bennett. You put two and two together—you know, the grave, Ondine—and some white people show up looking for a shaman . . . it's just not hard to figure. In fact, I been expecting you."

Somehow the admission of fakery relieved Lizzie. It wasn't because she could now dismiss him, exactly the opposite. She now saw him as a human being, maybe with some insight, maybe not, but at least he wasn't some imaginary creation out of Jason's world. "Do you know where my son is?" she asked without hesitation.

"Lizzie, you can't—"

"It's okay," Mike said, putting a hand on Jason's arm to calm him, to reassure him. To Lizzie he said, "Yes. Yes I do."

"Well, where—"

"First," he stopped her, "you must bring me the third egg of an

African quail clutch. Then I'll need the fresh-cut balls of a mountain goat, and after that—"

"What!" Lizzie stopped him. "What!"

Mike burst out laughing again. "I'm just joking around. You know, you live in an alley you don't get to joke around all that much."

She was furious. "You are the single most aggravating asshole I have ever met."

"She's right," Jason agreed.

"Okay, okay, I'll be serious."

"Good-bye," Lizzie answered.

"We can't go," Jason told her.

"You said yourself he's an asshole."

"But he's also a great shaman. Very holy."

"How can you say that!"

"Sometimes they're like that, they act crazy with people so they can be calm when they're with the Spirits. Can't you feel him? He has very big . . . what's the word . . . ?"

"Ego," Lizzie replied.

"Soul. Very big soul. You can feel it in him, almost overflowing. Can't you feel it?"

She was furious. Her stomach was in knots. Her head was pounding and she felt the pain all the way down her neck into her back. She felt nothing about Mike except disgust. He was a mean and nasty man preying on her most awful agonies.

"Let me apologize," he said to her.

All she really wanted was to go, so she said fine, thinking that was the apology but it wasn't. This was: He touched his fingers to her temple. She felt a bolt of energy go through her body unlike anything she had ever known. She trembled. *Oh God.* It was orgasmic. Skipped the body and went straight to her soul. *Yes.* The headache went away immediately. Her shoulders relaxed and the knots in her stomach unraveled. She laughed. A deep laugh from the belly, just like Mike's, and he laughed too.

"Is Nathaniel alive?" Jason asked.

"Yes," Mike assured him.

Lizzie gasped and said oh God again and sank into Jason's arms.

"Can I find him?" Jason asked.

"No. First, do what you must do, and he will come to you."

The words pierced Jason with the same electrical intensity that had been visited on Lizzie. For Jason the words unlocked two hundred years of psychic knots and aches. For two hundred years Jason had asked the question, over and over: Why me, for what purpose?

In the beginning he had asked it over and over, whining to the cosmos. Why me? Why am I made to suffer such a fate? What did I do to deserve this? Why am I singled out? Why am I cursed? Eventually he grew beyond the whining and complaint to a more serious consideration. What did it mean? What is required of me? What is the purpose? What is my purpose? To what end this blessing?

And then, for a hundred years he let it go. He didn't ponder it or chew on it. He didn't think about it at all, but nevertheless it gnawed at him continuously like some underground creek raging silently through the core of his being. Now, without warning or preparation, Mike was going to give him the answer. The irony wasn't lost on Jason that it was in search of one issue that he would find the answer to another. It wasn't lost on him that the search for his son had brought him face to face with the discovery of himself.

"You know what it is I'm supposed to do?" Jason asked. Timidly. He heard in his voice himself as a young boy. He felt in his heart the wonder of his boyhood. He felt Dzarilaw in his heart even before Mike said the name.

"Your village, the great gathering of Dzarilaw, is no more. It has been sacked and destroyed. Its treasure plundered and Dzarilaw's bones unearthed and carried away. It is for you to bring them back."

It cut like a hot steel fork through Jason's gut. "The Yupik!" he announced. "I never trusted the Yupik."

Mike smiled. "No, Jason Ondine, it was your people," he explained, "white people who could speak nothing but their own words and believed in nothing but their own gods. And her people— a man called Crazy Jack." Mike told Jason and Lizzie the story of the raid and how the village was destroyed and the last of its people dispersed to places far away and full of Jesus.

Having a purpose changed everything. It made the universe new, and comprehensible, and Jason accepted his charge with a singing, soaring heart.

"What about my son?" Jason asked before he took leave of Mike. Mike hesitated, then told the truth. "He will kill you."

"That's crazy!" Lizzie shot back. "You're being crazy again!"

"This son will kill him. The People sing of it."

Jason thought for a moment. "Finally, doesn't every father die for his son?"

"Jason," Lizzie tugged, "don't listen to him."

"I would die gladly for even a glimpse of my son."

—

Soon after Jason and Lizzie left him, Mike made his way down to the back end of the alley. It got darker and darker—a matter of no concern to a blind man—until he spread his arms and flew away, transformed into a raven. The Raven.

It was of course Hanging Hair and she flew with majestic strokes of her powerful wings. Now that Jason was out of the sea and back on land, he was her charge, and she was pleased with him. Pleased with her own stewardship. It was going well, she thought, as she flew across the night sky to a rocky beach and landed as the old woman with the shiny long, black, young woman's hair.

Two other old women waited for her. Sedna the Orca, Mother of the Sea, the sister who had breathed the spirit into Jason in the first place, stood on a rock, her long long silver-white hair sparkling in the moonlight. Adee, Ruler of the Sky and most cynical of the sisters, hopped about, her feathered hair bouncing with every step.

"What did he say?" Adee demanded before Hanging Hair had even settled in.

"He said that he would do it."

"He will return the bones?" Sedna ventured nervously.

"Yes," Hanging Hair confirmed. "He will."

"I knew it!" Sedna crowed, hesitation evaporated.

"You knew nothing," Adee snapped back.

"I picked him, didn't I? I breathed into him, didn't I? Don't tell me what I know!"

"It was a lucky guess," Adee insisted. "You knew nothing, you just got lucky."

"Oh go back in the sky and fart some clouds, you old hag!"

"Do we have to do this?" Hanging Hair interrupted. "The lost city of Dzarilaw is going to be restored. Do we have to fight about it?"

"It is a task," Adee harped, "that should go to the People, not to some pink-skinned noisy-tongued—"

"There is not another human being on the earth who knows where the village was or where the bones need to be buried," Hanging Hair pointed out.

"You call that a human being!"

"What is the matter with you, Adee? Probably too few storms for you lately," Sedna jumped in, seizing yet another opportunity to stick it to her sister.

"I still say he should have been left to die in the first place," Adee trumped, ignoring Sedna.

"Then Dzarilaw would be lost forever," Hanging Hair reminded her.

"That's why I breathed spirit into him."

"Liar."

"Do we have to fight about everything! He's going to turn the world around, isn't that enough?"

For Adee it was clearly not. "I should destroy him. That would be enough."

"You can't," Sedna challenged, "he's mine."

Adee screeched a screech so loud and piercing it hurt even Sedna's ears, and then she turned into a cloud and disappeared back into the night sky.

"You smell like a wet bear!" Sedna screamed after her. Adee answered with ground-shaking thunder and lightning bolts aimed straight at Sedna, who scrambled back into the safety of the sea.

"He is our future," Hanging Hair shouted at both the sea and the sky. Only Adee answered. She sent the rain down in sheets of fury.

Hanging Hair flew into the forest and took shelter in the trees, thinking nothing's easy when you're a god.

TWENTY-FOUR

In the summer of 1903, half a dozen young Indians went on a tear in a mining town just east of the Okanagan Range. Most of them were from coastal tribes, but there was a Nez Perce up from Idaho and a Shawnee who was so young when he was abandoned in this part of the country that he couldn't remember if he was from Chicago or Missouri, or if there was a difference. They were celebrating the news that a rail spur was going in to the north. With the clearing and the blasting even before they began laying tracks, that probably meant a couple of years' worth of decent jobs for strong backs and hard hands, and that was them.

There was nothing extraordinary about the revelry, nothing even particularly loud for a mining town, until the six left Cora's Baths, a low-rent flophouse, bar, and whoring palace, and crossed the street to Crazy Jack's, the finest bar and hardware store in the territory. (Jack also owned the seed shop and part-time bar to the east of him, and Leathers—shoes, harnesses, saddles, gloves, and sometime bar—to the west.)

The six gathered at the far end of Crazy Jack's bar. They ordered three whiskeys to share between them. They nursed them and they were quiet, which was their way, particularly around white men, and not bothering anybody when Samuel Findley, a Montana drifter fairly new to mining sidled up to the bar next to the six and elbowed one of them to make a little more room for himself, not that there wasn't plenty of room to his right.

"Jesus, Jack," Findley announced loudly, "I didn't hear that you'd opened the place up to aboriginals."

"Place is open to anyone can afford the price of a glass," Jack answered certainly.

"Yeah, you can tell by the smell."

After his first drink Findley sort of settled down to ignoring the six, and they continued to ignore him, until it came time for him to order up and pay for his second drink. He reached into the buck-skin wallet that hung from a thong around his neck and screamed. "My money's gone! Two gold pieces!" Findley turned and scanned the room. "Goddam injun stole my money," he yelled, turning to the Nez Perce.

The Nez Perce could scarcely comprehend the accusation. It was so far beneath him that he hardly believed a response was required until he looked around and everyone was staring at him. He turned to Jack behind the bar. "It is not true," he said. Of course it wasn't true. Nobody stole any money from Samuel Findley because he had no money to begin with.

"Now you calling me a liar, you two-faced savage?" Findley challenged. Findley was the liar, the kind who got immediately attached to the lies he told, so to have someone doubt him was just too much. Defending his honor—and still hoping for that second drink—he reared back and threw his best punch at the Nez Perce.

The young Indian took the blow to the face and gave not an inch. He hit back with a wallop to the belly so fierce that it had Findley chucking his dinner up all over himself. "I took nothing," the Nez Perce announced to everyone. Determined to avoid any more trouble, the six left, following the tallest of them, who seemed to be their natural leader, a handsome young man named Kitimat for the town where his mother was born.

Thinking Crazy Jack's was behind them and determined to continue honoring the rail spur unhampered, the six made their way up the block to the Okanagan Barbershop and Bar where, word had it, you could buy the coldest beer this side of the top of the world.

Before they made it into the Okanagan, Findley came running across the street after them in a blind fury. "Goddam savages. Redskin rat-eaters. I'll kill you all." He went straight at the Nez Perce and buried his hunting knife into the young Indian's shoulder. He was aiming for the heart, but the Nez Perce had just enough time to turn his shoulder to the knife and save himself.

Findley pulled the knife out to strike again, but Kitimat stepped up to stop him.

"Kill you too, injun bastard," Findley screamed. He struck for Kitimat's throat but the younger man blocked the blow and grabbed Findley's hand to disarm him. They struggled for the knife and fell to the street. Rolling for position, the knife cut deep into Findley's chest, slicing up from his diaphragm until it drove into his heart.

By the time Kitimat could break free, Findley was dead.

The six ran. The Nez Perce was bleeding profusely and they had to carry him. He said they should just leave him and go, but they would not.

The miners were outraged. A posse formed quickly to track down the murderous savages. Crazy Jack took it upon himself to outfit the operation. He gave a rifle to every man who needed one and paid for the cook and his gear out of his own pocket. Twenty men strong when they left town the next morning, the posse picked up support along the way. By the end of the week forty-four heavily armed men were on the trail of the six young Indians. Actually only five by the end of the week. The Nez Perce died, bled to death because they couldn't stop the bleeding from his stab wound. Even with the vigilantes on their tails, they took the time to bury the Nez Perce and sing prayers to comfort him throughout the first night of his death.

In the morning, having lost considerable ground to their pursuers, the surviving five of the six decided to split up and find their own respective routes to wherever they were going.

The two Bella Coolas were caught first, exactly two weeks from the day that Findley died. They were brutally beaten and when they were delirious with fear and agony, they confessed the name of Kitimat and said that he lived in the village of his great-great-great-great-grandfather's grandfather, Dzarilaw. The Bella Coolas were hanged together from the same branch of a twisted old tree, and left dangling to feed the coyotes and whatever other scavengers happened by.

Word of the event spread quickly. The posse lost the trail of the Nootka and never picked it up again, and the Shawnee, who was hiding out in Port Hope on the Olympic Peninsula when he heard the reports, was so scared that he swam out into the Straits and drowned himself to escape. So once the posse had dispatched the Bella Coolas, there was only Kitimat. The vigilantes went after him with a singular determination. Fire in their blood stoked every step they took. The anger in their bellies was fueled by thoughts of Findley and by a longing to get home.

By the time they got to Dzarilaw's Village, they were nothing more than enraged marauders riding their fury. They'd been away from home too long, they were getting on each other's nerves, and the simple act of catching someone was clearly not going to satisfy the sum total of the efforts these men had expended. They were, even they knew, a disaster in the making.

The village itself had become fairly nondescript over the years. It was no longer the magnificent crossroads it had been in the days of Dzarilaw, no longer a fertile beacon for other villages and tribes along the coast. It had never really recovered from the smallpox and had become just another ramshackle fishing village with little or no reflection of its glorious past.

The vigilante posse attacked in late afternoon. Except for a short-lived war over a bear several hundred years ago, this village had never experienced a hostile attack. Certainly no one was expecting this ambush, and no one knew what to do. The raid was as mean and ugly an episode as ever took place on the West Coast between European settlers and native inhabitants.

The battle cry was "Give us Kitimat," and it was shouted over and between the blasts of gunfire.

Give us Kitimat.

Give us Kitimat. Terrified villagers displayed their crucifixes like tokens of peace, to show the raiders that they too were Christians and whatever this was about was a mistake and this could all be settled in the spirit of Jesus. Christian to Christian.

Give us Kitimat. They held their crucifixes out in front of them like overfed French royals—who had sent the Jesuits to them in the first place—warding off vampires. To no avail, this posse was even less vampire than it was Christian.

The first to die were two boys, teenagers, young even for that, who stood up to the onrushing attack with their hunting knives drawn and ready.

"Give us Kitimat!" the raiders cried and cut down the two boys in a hail of bullets so awesome that it left their bodies shredded and scattered.

At the time of the raid fourteen families lived in the village. Eighty-six people, mostly women and children. Sixteen men were killed, eighteen if you count the two boys as men. Twenty-six women died, most of them trying to protect their children. Eleven children. The rest escaped. Some to the sea in their canoes. Some into the forests. Some across the river.

The last villager they caught was a fifty-year-old grandfather named Joseph. He took the name when he converted to Christianity. He had wanted to take the name Mary, but the missionaries convinced him that it was a name for women only and he reluctantly gave it up for her husband's name. Joseph was a carver and when they found him hiding in the woods behind his workshop, he had an impressive collection of carving knives. The knives marked him and it wasn't long before everyone agreed that they had in fact caught Kitimat.

"Admit it! You're Kitimat."

"My name is Joseph." Someone slapped him and he began praying, almost silently, all the words he had been taught. They kept hitting him, demanding that he admit his true identity. He was frightened and would have admitted to just about anything, except that the idea of admitting to being someone else was so foreign to him he just couldn't do it. The notion—I am not me; I am someone else—was impossible. It just didn't work in his own language, so he couldn't construct a way to say it in English.

The cook took over the interrogation. Mario Botorez was Crazy Jack's personal representative on this crusade and so considered it his personal responsibility to settle the matter. He had them tie Joseph to a tree. "You will say it," he told the terrified captive. "I am Kitimat. You will say it."

"I am not."

"When it was six of you attacking an innocent man, you were a big warrior but now you're not so brave."

"I am not Kitimat."

"Alright, we'll do it the Indian way," Botorez threatened, his mind racing through projections, entirely imaginary, of what sadistic savages might subject each other to. He began by making the necessary incisions with his butchering knife and then ripped a strip of flesh from Joseph's chest. Joseph prayed.

"Cut his lying damn injun eyes out," one of the miners encouraged, sitting by the fire in a laudanum stupor.

Botorez didn't hesitate. He grabbed a fork and stuck it in Joseph's eye. To staunch the bleeding, Botorez shoved a glowing coal into the eye.

"Holy Mother of God," Joseph screamed before he passed out.

When they revived him, he said yes, "Yes I am Kitimat." In the morning he was executed, killed with a bullet to the brain.

Botorez then instructed the posse to remember that Crazy Jack wanted souvenirs. It was here that Botorez's real role in all this grew clear. He was the appraiser, the collector. The raiders seized bounty. Anything left in the village that they thought might fetch a price on the outside was collected and offered to Botorez for approval. Furs. Tools. Decorations. Blankets. Religious masks and other carvings. And when they learned where the great Dzarilaw's grave was, they dug up his bones and took those too.

Everything of value was carried back in gratitude to Crazy Jack Bennett.

TWENTY-FIVE

Lizzie woke with a terrible sense of foreboding and loss, and although she kept telling herself that there was nothing in the world that could ever make her leave Jason, she kept hearing it running around her mind like a persistent interview. They had talked for hours last night before she fell asleep and got nowhere. She had money. Resources. They could hire experts to conduct a professional search for Nathaniel, people who were more adept at the game. She was not going to let her dreams fall prey to some drunk in an alley. "I just can't believe you're going to do this."

"Maybe you're right, maybe finally we will have to do it your way, all I'm asking is that we try this. If it doesn't work—"

"No. I just know that if we do this, if you go after the bones . . . they'll kill you."

"What will they do, shoot me again?"

"I don't know, I just know I saw death in that man." She was right of course to see death in the shaman. It was there. It always was.

Lizzie believed, fervently, that Jason was allowing himself to get sidetracked, and if he went after Dzarilaw's bones they'd lose whatever chance they may have had to find Nathaniel. Jason, with all his heart, free of suspicion or doubt, knew that he had no choice but to do what the shaman had prescribed, that it was the only direct line to his son. She'd tossed and turned all night. Now with the sun streaming in through the half-drawn shades, she sat on the edge of the bed, hardly able to get herself up.

"Is something wrong?" he asked her. He was in the bathroom brushing his teeth and he poked his head out to ask.

"Nothing. No," she assured. "I guess I just don't like the idea of going to the museum." Her family had been important benefactors, and she'd spent considerable time there as a child. She tried to dismiss the discomfort she was feeling as having something to do with the proximity of Bennett influences, and although she knew it wasn't true, it was enough to get her out of bed.

"We won't stay long," he promised. It wasn't going to be easy liberating what he wanted from the museum, but he was operating on faith, certain that a decent scouting trip would point the way.

—

It was a busy day at the Pacific History Museum—school trips, tourists, time killers, and regulars. By the time Lizzie and Jason got there, his sense of mission was so intense that she decided that the only way to deal with it was in good faith, and pray that by the time they finished their scouting tour he would see the light. So confident was she that this would happen that she even allowed herself to get caught up in the excitement of it.

They went through several wings before they found what they were looking for. The first sign that they were getting close was a wide arched doorway guarded by a large wooden carving of the Thunderbird, a mythical creature who was believed to have an extra head in its abdomen.

"His wingbeats sound like thunder," Jason explained when Lizzie stopped to admire it, "and lightning flashes from his beak."

"You know him?" she laughed, teasing.

It was the first time all day either of them had laughed. "I knew the man who carved him," he explained. It was a Haida Thunderbird, easy to recognize by its big bold shapes and colors. Even now, after all this time and years of fading, the colors still felt bright.

"It's the first thing I've seen here that looks familiar," Lizzie announced, "the first thing I remember from when I was a kid."

They came at last to the exhibition hall they were looking for. Two small totem poles—which Jason recognized immediately as Kwakiutl—marked the way. On each side of the entrance an identical plaque introduced the collection.

In the summer of 1903 a band of six renegade Indians raided a small mining town called Bennett's Camp, known today as Campbelton.

The band was led by Kitimat, a maverick great-grandson of the legendary Chief Dzarilaw. In the raid, believed to be launched in retaliation for the confiscation of Indian lands by the railroad, the band robbed and killed Samuel Findley, a miner from Montana who had no connection whatsoever to the railways.

The murder of Samuel Findley led to the formation of the now famous Bennett Camp Posse, a group of miners who dedicated themselves to bringing the renegades to justice.

The hunt took four months and all six were ultimately brought to justice. Kitimat himself was the last one captured. He was found hiding in the Village of Dzarilaw, where he was tried and executed. No one knows anymore exactly where the village was located, and it is believed to be the fabled "Lost City" of Indian legend somewhere on the North Pacific Coast.

All the artifacts in this collection were gathered by the Bennett Camp Posse in 1903 and were donated to the Museum Society in 1921 by Jonathan "Jack" Bennett.

When Jason was finished reading he turned to Lizzie. That the outrage of the Posse could be turned into a story of lofty heroism was simply preposterous, one more crack in the rapidly flaking veneer of cultural civility. It was an outrage born of a deeper malaise than simple pride. "Jonathan Bennett? Is this the one the shaman called Crazy Jack?"

Lizzie wondered how it was that when worlds crumbled they crumbled so quickly. None of what was happening could be an accident. Not her meeting Jason, not his coming back. Nothing. The circles were getting too small for any of it to have been by chance. She knew it the minute the shaman mentioned Crazy Jack. "He was my father's grandfather."

Jason touched her face so she would know he did not hold her responsible. He loved her. "It's a sign," he said.

"I never knew him," she said, trying to free herself from the currents of personal history.

They walked through the giant portal beams into the Bennett wing with its Bennett Camp Posse collection. The first thing Jason saw was such a shock to him he thought he could hear his heart stopping. He certainly heard himself gasp. There in the middle of the room, on a black lucite pedestal was an eight-foot-tall totem carving. It showed the crouching figure of a man. His face was painted, as was the intricately carved bear's-head hat he was wearing. Many teeth were carved into the bear's mouth, all painted a very bright white.

"What?" Lizzie demanded, grabbing Jason's arm when she saw his whole body tense. "What?"

"It's the marker from Dzarilaw's grave."

She let go of his arm.

Jason approached the wooden statue full of awe and trepidation. He seemed almost afraid of it, and curiously drawn by some tenacious grip reaching into his soul and dragging him closer. Lizzie watched him moving forward and thought he was moving like a boy. Tentative and uncertain, both cocky and confused. He circled the pedestal, sometimes looking at the carving, sometimes looking away.

Jason circled twice. He felt his heart racing and he was as disturbed and lonely as he had ever been in those days in the village. He felt the spirit of Dzarilaw trying to comfort him. It frightened him.

Girding all his considerable courage—and it felt to him like this was his defining moment, that it was the bravest thing he had ever done—he walked up to the big wooden grave marker and put both his hands on it. Near the heart.

"My son," Dzarilaw said, "at last you have come for me."

Jason was stunned.

"You make an old man's heart soar," he continued.

Jason's mind raced to keep up with itself and could not. He looked around to see if anyone else had heard Dzarilaw speak. No one had and he was relieved. He caught his breath. He felt Dzarilaw fill his heart. He felt the tears come welling up from his belly and flood from his eyes. It was agony and it was joy.

"Excuse me, sir," a docent scolded, "but there is no touching."

Jason turned from the marker to find Lizzie. She saw the tears streaming down his face and took him in her arms.

Later she asked him, "Am I going to lose you?"

"Not in this lifetime," he answered without hesitation.

"It feels like you have already gone to something I can't understand."

—

They spent several more hours in the museum while Jason examined the exhibits, deciding which masks and artifacts he would take. Mostly he favored the masks and carvings, ritual figures of some significance if anyone ever potlatched again. And of course, the bones. Above all else, Dzarilaw's bones. They were in a clear lucite box in a large display case behind a picture window. The earth had done its work and there was little left of them. Fragments mostly. A small piece of the right thigh, and the left thigh almost intact. The skull was well-preserved. Beyond that, a section of the breastplate and half a hip. The rest was not much more than blanched shards. It sickened Jason to see it.

Behind the small case of bones was a cyclorama. On it was a painting of an old Tsimshian in full ritual garb, purporting to be Dzarilaw. Dzarilaw was not Tsimshian and the painting looked nothing like him anyway. Another illustration showed a warrior being buried. He was shown—correctly—being set into the ground in a sitting position.

Jason scouted entrances and exits. Windows and skylights. Ventilation shafts. When he was satisfied that he knew what he needed to know, and he and Lizzie were just about to leave, he noticed a small, somewhat hidden and almost embarrassed display. The card described the display as "jewelry stolen from European settlers." It contained a few irrelevant knickknacks and two important pieces: his father's ruby brooch and the Jesuit's silver cross.

He told Lizzie it was a lie, that they had been gifts, stupid gifts that almost got them all killed. He sounded angry, and she couldn't tell what he was thinking until he got quiet and said, with a faraway longing in his voice, "It was my grandmother's."

—

The museum was closing when they left. They went to a park nearby to wait for dark. Jason sat cross-legged on the grass and chanted, praying for the absolute focused clarity of purpose it would require to carry out his obligations.

Lizzie climbed up into a tree to be alone with her thoughts and forebodings. She could sense that he was already on his path and that the only light he was seeing was the one that blinded her. On this day and in this way her world was coming to an end. Neither she nor Jason spoke for a long time. They were afraid to. They waited until the sun went down and the night had taken firm hold before they could talk about it.

Jason took her hand. "Something terrible is happening to us," he said to her. "I can see it in your face."

What was happening to them was that their magical affair was running into mundane life and its swamps of endless ironies. The search for their son, which any dreamer would know was supposed to drive them deeper into each other's hearts, was instead wrenching them apart.

"I love you," she answered.

"And I you," he assured her, although she needed no assurance. It wasn't the love she was doubting, it was the possibility of living it.

When she was a young girl, dreaming endlessly of things romantic and impassioned, she dreamt wondrous dreams, inspired young visions. But never in the wildest of her imaginings could she have created anything approaching this magical lover with the unscarred spirit and the bold and boundless heart.

Now that she had him, now that she had given over all that was her self and bliss, she was about to lose him. "Jason . . ." she said, and then said no more because she was unable to speak of it. Neither one of them could believe they were having this conversation. *The* conversation. The universe that had taken all this time to allow Jason and Lizzie to find each other was now about to crush them. "Jason, please don't go back in there."

"I'm just going in for the bones," he said. "A few small things. I'll be gone before the police ever get close."

She was furious. "I can't let you do this. I won't."

"I have no choice," he answered.

"Then you and me are . . . you and me . . . no. No, I won't be part of this."

"I need you, Lizzie."

It was true and she didn't want to hear it. There was a place inside her where she accepted the nature of his duty and dreams that called him to the bones, but she could not tolerate his risking their opportunity to find Nathaniel.

Jason trusted what the shaman had told them in the alley, that if he attended to the bones, Nathaniel would come. "You felt his power," Jason tried to reason with her. "You know it's real."

"I don't know what I felt, I just know that this is crazy. How can you choose some old bones over our son!"

"I'm doing it for him," he told her.

"You walk into that museum," she told him, "and you walk out of my life."

"Lizzie—"

"I will. I will leave you." Now that she'd said it, she realized it had been coming all day. The ultimatum had been lingering nearby, hovering just shy of the tongue, and yet it still sounded so foreign and frightening when it was finally spoken out loud. Just saying it made her feel like some cosmic hand had reached through her belly and was pulling her insides out.

"We are meant to be together," he said.

"We're only what we make of it," she answered sadly.

"If I don't return the bones, we will never find Nathaniel."

It was intolerable.

"I will never forgive you," she said. She turned and walked away. In a matter of steps she disappeared into the dark, dissolved into it.

"Lizzie!" he called out. "I have to do this."

Two hundred years, he thought, and he was still no good at endings. He blamed his father for that. "Lizzie."

She was everything to him. All things. More than she could know. His heart cried out for her to stop and come back, but his voice was still. He understood that it was his destiny standing between him and the words he would need to say to bring her back.

In the silence she kept walking, crushing her own heart with each step.

TWENTY-SIX

Malcolm Brae had fallen asleep in the late afternoon. When he woke up, the killer headache hadn't gone away and the phone was ringing. A fourth ring. A fifth. He still made no move to pick it up. *Rrrrrrrnnng* again.

He'd said it was a migraine from too much coffee, but he knew, as did everyone down at the precinct, that it was the humiliation. Getting manacled with your own handcuffs is hardly the kind of thing a young detective wants to hear about himself in the halls. And of course he wasn't being paranoid, people really were smiling at him.

Rrrrrrrnnng.

So now, home alone at night, driving around in the car, or taking a crap, almost any time his mind had a chance to wander, he found himself thinking that the only solution was to kill the sonuvabitch.

That's what gave him the headache. A personal vendetta to pop someone is not exactly the hallmark of a good cop. Not exactly the kind of thing that would make Malcolm Sr. proud, he thought, but then he's not the one who has to face everybody every day, and it was right around then that his head started throbbing.

Rrrrrrrnnng.

He gave in. He answered the phone. It was Adachi. "Jesus fucking Christ, Brae!" Adachi hollered.

"Captain?" It sounded garbled, his throat still full of sleep.

"How the hell did you think you could keep something like that from me!"

"Keep what?" he said, clearing his throat this time, trying to sort out whether it was the phone or the dream that woke him.

Malcolm almost never remembered the dreams, but he'd had this one for several days now and couldn't get it out of his head. He was walking down a country road alone and his feet hurt. A bear appeared in the road. It stood up on its hind legs and roared. It must have been twelve feet tall. A second bear, and then a third, joined him. Malcolm's impulse was to run, climb a tree, materialize a car, or turn himself into an even bigger bear, but despite the fact that this was his dream, he could make none of those things happen. In spite of himself, he kept walking toward the bears, and the closer he walked the more his feet hurt.

More and more animals came out of the woods and fell in on the road behind the bears, and Malcolm kept walking. Coyotes. Deer. Muskrat. Beaver. Birds—crows or ravens, he couldn't tell the difference. A wolf, and then the rest of his pack. And a fox. And caribou. "No wonder your feet hurt," a voice said. "You can't be out here in shoes like that." It was his mother's voice. Not the mother who raised him, not the one whose face he saw when he thought Mother, she had a different voice, a Midwest voice. No, this voice was mother.

"They are the only shoes I have," he answered.

"No," she said, "your feet are the only ones you've got. Shoes are a dime a dozen." And then the pain moved up from his legs into his skull, and he woke up to his brain throbbing and the phone ringing.

"Get your goddam ass down here now! We're waiting for you. Jesus fucking Christ!"

—

Jason climbed a tree, moving higher and higher through its branches with a grace and ease that surprised him. Arm over arm, he pulled himself up almost effortlessly. He followed the route he had sighted earlier in the day, including the branch that waved itself toward the third-story balcony. As he made his way onto the limb, it seemed to him somewhat less sturdy than it had appeared from the ground. It began to groan under his weight. He edged farther out onto the branch. It was a long way down. He could feel the branch begin to crack, and then he heard it start to go.

He leapt. He sailed through the air in the general direction of a small balcony, one of several that decorated this side of the building. The leap was exhilarating. It took only a split second but it felt like flying. The wind rushed by and almost seemed to float him on its currents. In flight he looked down. It had seemed high up when he was on the branch and it seemed much higher now without it. And then he landed, exactly where he had hoped to.

The window was unlocked, just as he had left it, and he climbed through. All he had to do now was follow the hallway to the next wing and go down the fire stairs, which would put him just steps from the Camp Bennett Posse Collection.

It seemed almost too easy, and of course it was. Although he heard nothing, the electronic alarms had already been triggered. He made his way quickly down the hall, and despite the light-footed silence of his gait, his every move was already under surveillance by the many remote videos, and the police had been automatically notified.

The two security guards in the main lobby were thrilled as they watched Jason on their several monitors, tracking him like an animated icon in a computer game.

"Two years I been here," Gelman said to Borshak, the senior guard, "and I was beginning to think nothing was ever going to happen." Gelman took out his gun and checked the chamber. He was good to go.

"Don't do anything stupid, let's just wait for the Man," Borshak said calmly.

"They can't do anything I can't do," Gelman announced and took off down the hall.

Borshak, with a mixture of alarm and concern, kept his eyes peeled on the monitors, finally getting a fairly close-up glimpse of Jason as he made his way into the Posse Collection gallery. It was the same fairly close-up shot that the media would show with numbing insistence.

Jason worked quickly and efficiently. He'd walked himself through it in his mind so many times, the doing of it felt almost automatic. Get fire extinguisher from corner. Go to first display. Shatter case. Get the whale mask, the small carved gull, the skinning knives, and the two harpoons.

Second display. Break case. Get the blankets, the buckskin pouch, and the shaman's rattle.

Third: Bear mask, Raven mask, the large duck body shield. A few of the small potlatch carvings, and two pieces he considered his own—the ruby brooch and the silver crucifix.

Finally, the bones, which he would place with loving care in the buckskin pouch.

Gelman arrived as Jason was about to break into the bone display. "Hold it right there, asshole!"

"Please," Jason answered, "I don't want to hurt you."

"Hurt me? I'm the one with the gun, jerkoff. Now drop everything and get down on the floor. Spread-eagle."

"Your bullets are useless against me. Please. Just go." Jason clutched the harpoon in his throwing arm. He felt sorry for Gelman. He knew from firsthand experience how painful the harpoon could be. A bullet enters the body with such explosive force that it is almost numbing. The pain is so generalized and body-wide it feels like getting swallowed by a scathing ache. The harpoon, however, cuts into you and stays local. It sears through the flesh and anchors there, throbbing. Every movement, every breath, tears more flesh and intensifies the agony.

He had been harpooned once, by a Yupik hunter, which is why he didn't like the Yupik. It was winter. He had gone north following a feeding trail. He was under the ice looking for a breathing hole when he saw the shaft of light shimmering down through the water. He figured it for a harp seal hole because it was small and looked so well-tended. He didn't see any around, for which he was grateful because they were so hyper and skittish and generally a pain in the ass.

He made his way to the hole to fetch some air. No sooner did he poke his nose through than he knew he'd made a mistake. Hovering above him on the ice, standing absolutely still, harpoon at the ready, was the Yupik hunter in his winter furs. Harp seal skins. Jason backed off with all the force he could muster in his tail and fins, but the Yupik was just as quick. The harpoon broke through the thin layer of ice and cut deep into his shoulder. The blade felt like fire slicing through his body.

The Yupik held fast to set the harpoon and most seals would have given up there, but Jason continued to back away and pulled himself free with a wrenching agony that flooded the area with his blood. The Yupik cursed him. Denounced him for not playing by the rules. The Yupik felt humiliated. He had danced, prayed, and followed all the ritual steps for preparing his weapons and choosing the breathing hole. He had stood motionless above the hole since before dawn, paying no mind to the ferocious aches that developed in his legs and back. He had done everything he had been taught, including offering a clean and powerful throw, and still, Jason swam away.

"Drop everything and hit the floor!" Gelman hollered.

Jason set everything down carefully but the harpoon.

"Drop it now!"

"You understand," Jason tried to explain, "I have to take all this back to where it belongs."

"Drop the spear. Now!"

Jason hesitated and Gelman fired. Three shots, all wide of the mark. All intercepted by Dzarilaw's grave marker in the middle of the room. Gelman took better aim and Jason loosed the harpoon with such awesome power it was barely visible as it streaked across the room. The harpoon hit Gelman hard through the right shoulder and pinned him to the wall with a shuddering thud.

Jason broke into the lucite case and gathered the bones. He placed them carefully, one by one, into the buckskin pouch. He was setting fragments when he first heard the sirens. He refused to allow either Gelman's cries or the imminent arrival of the police to interfere with his respectfully deliberate packing of the bones. He put the rest of the stuff on the duck shield and wrapped it with blankets. The sirens were closing, obviously pulling up to the building.

"You hear that? You're dead, motherfucker! You're dead!"

Jason gathered up his treasure and hurried out.

"I'm in agony, man, don't leave me like this," Gelman pleaded. Jason came back. "No. Don't kill me."

Jason didn't bother to answer. He grabbed the harpoon and pulled Gelman free of the wall.

—

When Malcolm got to the station, the museum story was still being handled locally and word hadn't reached downtown yet. Nonetheless, his head was still throbbing and he was anxious, like a schoolkid going to the principal's office.

"Jesus, Brae," Adachi greeted him, "what the hell you trying to pull?"

It was quite a welcoming committee. Malcolm took in the assembly in a single glance and knew it was serious. Adachi was all buttoned and neat. There was someone from Internal Affairs, a guy from the commissioner's office, and beside him, Sergeant L. Mallory from the union. These people represented a lot of grim signals, especially this time of night. Malcolm hadn't shot anybody or stolen anything, so whatever this was about must have to do with Dr. Wayne Elliot, who looked both frightened and defiant and very much out of place down at the end of the table.

"Captain?" Malcolm said, stalling to figure out what the hell was going on.

"Your badge," Adachi answered, "and your gun. On the desk."

"What's going on?"

"Just do it," Adachi said. "Just goddam do it."

It was clear Adachi wasn't there in his role as mentor, and he could see the old man was hurting about this. Not wanting to make it any harder for him, Malcolm looked to Mallory for support. Union guy. Had to be on his side. "Sarge?" he said to him.

"Do what he says, Brae," Mallory answered.

Malcolm put his gun on the desk first, then his shield. "Now will somebody tell me what's going on?"

"You're on suspension," the IA guy announced.

"I think I already figured that part out," Malcolm answered.

"This is no time to be a wiseass," Adachi warned him, hoping the tone conveyed the message that he hated being in this position but couldn't do anything about it. He had an ass of his own to cover.

"The review holds up," the IA went on, "and you're looking at charges. Accessory for sure. Murder one, maybe. Depends what we find."

"Not meaning to be a wiseass, sir," Malcolm shot back, "but what the hell are you talking about?"

"Jesus, Brae," Adachi complained, "why the hell didn't you say something, at least to me?"

"Captain, I still don't know what—"

"Cut the shit, Brae," IA ordered. "It's over. Let me put it on the line for you. Whatever else goes down, anything happens to this man," he said, indicating Elliot, "you answer to me personally. By which I do mean personally. Off-duty, one on one."

"Why would I—"

"When I say 'anything,' I'm talking not just the obvious, I'm talking he gets struck by lightning, or hit by a meteor, I'm coming after you."

Malcolm knew that Internal Affairs was a pretty political job and figured this guy was bucking for a promotion and a tough-ass attitude in front of the commissioner's rep couldn't hurt. "Understood," Malcolm assured him.

"That's better," IA told him and then looked over and nodded at Adachi, clearly a signal.

"Brae," Adachi began, "we know that Jason Ondine is your father!"

Malcolm laughed. "Do I look like a fucking comedian to you!" Adachi bellowed.

Malcolm thought he'd died and gone to hell. "Captain, that's nuts."

Adachi spoke to Elliot without turning to look at him. "Show him the file, Doc."

Elliot had figured it out quite by accident. He was running genetic bands, looking for Mendelian mutations and found himself two charts that on first glance looked almost identical. He got very pissed off because he thought for a minute that he'd done two tests on Jason's blood and he didn't have enough of it for that kind of experimental luxury. When he checked the samples, he discovered the first was indeed Jason, but the second had come from Malcolm. He immediately started on some pedigree charts and there it was. Clear as day: Jason Ondine was Malcolm Brae's father.

Elliot freaked. It didn't take long for him to suspect that he was into something way over his head. Father and son were up to something, and the more he thought about it, the more scared he was that he was somehow in their way. If they were willing to rape hospital patients and kill orderlies, they certainly weren't likely to stop at doctors. His first impulse was to hide, then it occurred to him that the only real chance he had of staying alive was to be visible.

"Go ahead," Adachi repeated, "give him the folder."

Elliot held it out. Malcolm hesitated and then took it. "Captain," he said, "you knew my father. And my mother. They were killed four years ago on the interstate by a drunk trucker."

"I'm sorry," Adachi said. It wasn't much more than a whisper.

"You knew them!" Malcolm insisted.

"We're talking biology," Adachi explained. He felt for Malcolm and wanted to say something nice, but he couldn't, not with the IA guy and the commissioner's rep there.

Malcolm had spent a lifetime wondering, wishing, but he could never imagine it would come to him like this. He was furious. He was elated. His head was raging. His heart was in tears. He was trying not to let any of it show, especially his fury, when the desk sergeant walked in and announced that they just heard from the Twenty-Second Precinct that they had Jason Ondine trapped.

TWENTY-SEVEN

Hanging Hair hadn't been this happy in a very, very long time. Almost everything was in place. She had her ducks—coyotes, foxes, salmon, and so on—all lined up, and it was a tribute to patience. Everything was in motion. All that was missing was the People, and she was working on that.

Neither Adee nor Sedna were likely to admit it, and scoffed at the notion whenever Hanging Hair brought it up, but they needed the People. It was lonely without them. Without people to tell their stories and sing the songs, without the carvers shaping totems out of trees, without the women bearing children and the hunters courting prey, the Spirits were nothing. They still had their magic and their powers, they could still contest the nature of the universe, but it meant so little. There was no substance to it, no memory without the stories handed down from one generation to the next.

"Without them," Hanging Hair told her sisters and all the Spirits who would listen, "we are little more than passing events. Incidents that come and go. Transient ideas with no consequence or meaning."

Some knew she was right. Others didn't care. In either case it was left to her to deal with it. And she did. From the day Jason first made his way back onto land, the day he first saw Lizzie, Hanging Hair was on the job. In large gatherings, in small groups, and in isolated encounters, she was there.

When the Mohawk at Oka fought to save sacred grounds from becoming a golf course, they took the bridge to the island and faced down the well-armed, trigger-happy Quebec Provincial Police. Hanging Hair was there as a young woman encouraging the warriors and standing up with them against the fury of the frustrated police. She was the one in the red plaid shirt, the one with the incredible long black hair and the Expos baseball cap. "Not now, not ever," she shouted back at the bullhorns demanding their surrender. It came at a time when everyone was tired and despairing. It came at the moment when spirits had waned and the protest seemed entirely hopeless. She climbed on top of a police car, raised a fist in the air, and shouted.

She had chosen her words very carefully and her time precisely. It was the only time she raised her voice in the entire stand-off. Not now, not ever. The others heard her and the fire was rekindled. *Not now, not ever. We will not give up our dreams, we will not give up our souls, we will not collapse in the face of your greed.*

At Traveler's Rest it was Hanging Hair who pointed out the burial grounds behind the mansion and helped begin the campaign to save and preserve the remains. At Wounded Knee she came as an elder to mourn. The Cascade Riots in Oregon were led by Hanging Hair. She showed up there as a fire-eyed revolutionary, a young warrior demanding dignity and honor for a People too long denied. The People heard her and remembered themselves. At the Mid-Tennessee Pow Wow, the Copper Mountain Council, the Salish meetings, the Restoration Hearings in Washington, Hanging Hair, in one form or another, was there.

Whatever role she took in public, her private mission was always more important. Person by person, she delivered the same message: "Go home. Return to the home in your heart."

Mostly she was dismissed as just another crazy Indian, but every now and then she'd actually reach somebody and she could feel it. She didn't have to reach every Indian, just a few, just enough to get things moving when the time came.

And the time had come. While the media feasted on Jason Ondine, Hanging Hair prowled the bars and alleys, the trailer parks and suburbs, hotels, condos, ranches and farms, hospitals and colleges, courts, jails, movie theaters and record stores, high-rise offices, military bases, construction sites, and anywhere else she thought she might find an Indian.

Her mission was not to return everyone to the village or the reservation, it was a call to roots and memory. It was an invitation to make a pilgrimage back to their own souls and then return more whole to their carpentering or doctoring, fathering or mothering, taxi-driving or poetry. She talked to Taryn Stream-Cleaner in a dream and to Annie the Bella Coola in a song. She was gathering the People. To each and every one she found, she brought the same message: Jason Ondine is bringing Dzarilaw's bones back to the Lost City.

Like all the messages brought by gods and spirits, most were ignored. She expected that. She planned for that. Spirit or not, Hanging Hair had always been a realist. If it took ten encounters to reach one person, that was simply what it took. Or a hundred. Or a thousand. It took whatever it took and she was prepared to pay the price.

She was exhausted. She had done her work, but she wasn't confident. She figured all they needed to make the village come back to life was a dozen People or so. They would be the seed, and the forests that followed would grow on their own. First the Lost City of Dzarilaw, a few families, a beacon. More would join them, and the other villages would rise as well.

The last thing Hanging Hair had to attend to before she left for Eulakon was the suicide of Dr. Wayne Elliot.

When Elliot looked back to survey the landscape of his recent past, he simply couldn't bear it. There were no signs of the young idealist who had become a doctor because he had the magic of healing and wanted to help. All he could see of himself now was the monster who would indeed have killed Jason Ondine to advance his career. His mirror reflected nothing but his ego, separate and free-standing. He was truly ashamed and plunged into a despair from which he knew there was no escape. He drew a hot bath, swallowed a bottle of Ativan, and drank a last scotch. Then he sat in the water, trembling in dread until he fell asleep.

Raven sat in the tree outside his window thinking about it, thinking she had enough to do without letting this too become her problem. But had it not been for her and her sisters, Elliot would never have crossed paths with Jason and would never have climbed so far up his own ass—or whatever it was that white people said. What the hell, she thought, as long as she was tidying up, she might as well give him another chance.

"Oh my god! Help! Help!" the old man across the street started screaming. "Help me! The baby! Help me!"

The terror in the old man's voice reached right through Elliot's dying stupor and woke him. That was Hanging Hair's gift. The rest was up to him and the cry stirred not Elliot the rich doctor, not the hunter in search of immortality and other prizes, but Elliot the healer. Hanging Hair had lifted the veil.

The old man was baby-sitting his grandchild and she had stopped breathing. Elliot, Doctor Wayne Elliot, heard the call. He grabbed his robe and his soul and rushed out to save the child.

Hanging Hair didn't wait around to see if the child would also save the man. That was something they'd have to work out on their own. Chuckling to herself, pleased, she flew away because she had other worlds to tend to, and destiny to meet.

—

Within minutes of arriving at the museum, the first investigating officer on the scene was looking at the security videotapes while several uniforms attended to Gelman, keeping him calm while they waited for the ambulance. As soon as they got to the close-up of Jason on the tape, the detective yelled, "Freeze it."

Borshak, not good with pressure, fumbled with the buttons.

"Freeze it! Freeze it! Can't you freeze the goddam tape! Jesus!"

Borshak hit several buttons and finally got the right one. He had to rewind a little but managed to stop it again on exactly the right frame. It was even the same angle as the most recent sketch the department had been circulating.

"Just hold it there," the detective said. Pulling a sketch from his pocket, he held it up beside the monitor.

"Jesus!" The security guard examined one and then the other. The resemblance was uncanny.

"Jesus!" the detective repeated. Instead of a simple burglary, he was now point man for a manhunt, a responsibility he wanted to be relieved of as quickly as possible. In the meantime he handled it by recalling his days on traffic. He spread the arriving cars around the block and within minutes had the beginnings of a solid perimeter. The rest was a matter of filling it in and making it tighter until some heavyweight from HQ showed up to take over. Hold the line, that's all he had to do.

When Jason got up to the roof of the museum, the world below was a circus. There must have been two dozen police cars on site and more arriving in a steady stream of wailing and lights. Because his heart was pounding, racing, the sirens were even more piercing and awesome, announcing in very direct terms that he was pretty much screwed.

Word had already hit the street that it was Jason Ondine trapped inside, and crowds gathered in the exhilarating anticipation of impending newsworthiness. Jason stood at the edge of the roof and looked down on the dissolute cacophony of the modern world, all of it gathered to remind him that it was from this he was saving Dzarilaw.

So there it was, clearly and certainly: He was going into battle. He hadn't really understood that before. He had thought just getting the bones and masks and trekking them across the mountains was all the test required of him. Now he knew there was more. It stilled his confusions and slowed his racing heart. All at once, the sirens were just sirens, not assaults. The gathering forces below were puzzles, not avengers. In a single breath the warrior in him was wide awake. Every sense was focused, sharpened, even for him. Every cell, every fiber, every sentient possibility was poised and prepared.

Scouting, he raced along the edge of the roof, quickly, so quickly that if anyone from below caught a glimpse, it would look like nothing more than a fleeting shadow, a gust of wind disturbing the night air. He found the spot he wanted, above a clear patch in the wooded parkland across the street, eclipsed from bystanders on the ground by trees and circumstance. It was a perfect landing place not yet occupied by the cops or the curious. It was, however, a good sixty or seventy feet away with a four-story fall to carry him there. He had no idea in fact how far he could jump, but this seemed an awful long way, both down and across.

Jason cradled the buckskin pouch in his arms as he knelt beside the treasures of his bundled mission and spoke to Dzarilaw. "The journey begins again, Old Man," he said with the greatest respect, knowing that he himself was now many years older than Dzarilaw ever got to be. "Pray for us."

He hung the pouch around his neck and secured it. Then he tied the bundle to his back, and stood. He was ready. Absolutely ready. He raced to the edge of the roof. In three steps he was at full speed. He leapt up to the top of the parapet and, with all the spring he could muster, lifted off.

With that one step he crossed from the world of the mundane to a universe of essentials, from the edge of his life to the center. Jason was in full flight, soaring through the night. Over the heads of police and spectators, parked cars and barricades. Four stories from the sky to the ground, and not a single heartbeat came with any doubts. Carrying seventy-five pounds on his back, he sank like a hard rock-candy treat for the monster of gravity, but it felt like floating. It felt like he was simply settling down from the pleasures of heaven to the duties of earth.

No one saw him. Even the landing was silent. The Warrior was on his way. He moved swiftly to the heart of the park, deeper into the trees. The trek had begun.

TWENTY-EIGHT

Malcolm was a wreck, tied up in knots. Churning. He pulled up to Lock-It and Leave-It, knowing it was a long shot, but maybe his only shot. He keyed in the access code and waited while the old metal gate began slowly rolling open.

When he was a kid he used to have fantasies about his biological parents, fantasies molded by whatever predicament his life happened to be in at the moment. Usual stuff. His mother was a great princess disowned for her illegitimate pregnancy who killed herself soon after Malcolm was born, and sometimes she was a teenage beauty so pure, but poor, oh so poor, that she had no choice but to give him up, and so on. When Malcolm was into role-playing adventures, his father was a daring fighter pilot who gave his own life to save the Air Force. When Malcolm was charged with that car theft, and Malcolm Sr. had little more to say than, "You know, Boy, the world doesn't need another loose cannon," Malcolm imagined that his real father was the world's greatest criminal lawyer and he was going to come charging up the court steps on his blazing Harley and save the fucking day.

He never took any of it really seriously. They were daydreams and he was comfortable with that. But he never ever imagined, nor could he accept now, that his father was a vicious killer and his mother a certified lunatic. It couldn't be. He wouldn't let it be and he was praying that somewhere in those trunks, he would find what he needed to prove to Adachi and Elliot and the whole damn world that he was falsely accused.

It felt like it took forever, but the old gate finally opened enough for him to pull through and park. He hated storage. Not so much having it or paying the bills, but visiting it. Rows and rows of padlocked storerooms. Four-by-eight. Eight-by-ten. Ten-by-twelve. Whatever your former needs, there was place for it here.

He hated everything about it, from having to remember the access code for the security gates to the fluorescent lights on the timers. The hollow sound of his steps echoing through the cavernous warehouse put him on edge, and the temperature always pissed him off. On cold days it was too cold and on hot days . . . etc.

Mostly it upset him because it was a repository of broken dreams. People stored possessions here because something in their lives hadn't worked or wasn't working. They didn't have enough room at home, or they had no homes. Fires, floods, evictions, and foreclosures brought lots of furniture and boxes of mementos here. The accumulated cartons of peoples lives were abandoned here. Hopes on hold were carted here. Promises were stacked up in disarray.

In Malcolm's case, it was his parents neatly packed away. After the accident Malcolm sold their house and what he could of its accumulated contents. Much of it he gave away. He took a few small things back to his place, but that still left some pieces of prized furniture and a silver set he would never use but couldn't bring himself to discard, and several trunks of memories. It was for the trunks he came. He'd often wondered about his birth mother and biological father, who they were, what they were. His parents tried to help, but they had no answers either.

He spent six hours in the locker sorting and found himself inspired to some of the best and some of the worst moments over his dead parents that he had experienced since the accident. It was the closest he had come to them since they died and he felt deeply connected. Of course he never would have come here if it hadn't been for this threat of biological links to Jason Ondine and Lizzie, and so he was, reluctantly, oddly, grateful to them.

He spent the first two hours looking at photographs, cuff links, baubles. A pewter teapot. Newspaper clippings that meant little at the time and less now. Some books, including his mother's Bible. He leafed through that for clues like a family tree, but she had never written anything in her Bible. It would have seemed a sacrilege to her, even though she wasn't much of a churchgoer.

He found letters his parents had written to each other when one or the other was away, which wasn't very often. Although he was desperate for clues about himself, the letters were love letters, too personal to pursue. If the only clues to his early history were in the letters, he was never going to find them.

The trunks were full of photo albums, tchotchkes, and memorabilia that were pretty much all about Malcolm. There was a shoebox full of postcards from the drive they took to Disney World on his sixth birthday, about which the thing he remembered best was the seven-legged calf.

Some three hundred miles from Georgia they began seeing signs for a seven-legged calf. It was a challenge of comprehension and a thrill for any six-year-old. It was something not to be believed but evidently existed. They saw the sign three or four times until they were about a hundred and fifty miles from the goal and Malcolm noticed that the signs were appearing more frequently but now they advertised a six-legged calf.

"Did that say six?"

"Yes, it did, Dear."

They were about fifty miles from it when the signs started reading "Five-legged calf."

"Five?"

"Yes, Dear."

"We'll stop and get some hot dogs and a milk shake or something, Son."

"Okay, Dad, but what happened to the one with the seven legs?" The parents smiled—how cute—but Malcolm kept a sharp eye out the window. When they pulled up to a roadside canteen and tourist sinkhole called "The Four-Legged Calf," Malcolm was appalled. It was one of the great disappointments of his childhood. It even made the experience at Disney World seem not quite right. Somehow suspect. What if Mickey Mouse wasn't real either?

He'd been filling a duffel bag with stuff to take home from storage and he added the postcards. Maybe it was the postcards, maybe the calf, maybe it was the fact that in an entire lifetime he never once got an unadulterated you're-a-good-kid pat on the back from Senior, one of those you're-mine-and-I-love-you-no-matter-what-Son embraces, and maybe that was because Senior wasn't good at that kind of stuff. Maybe it was because he resented the fact that Malcolm wasn't really his blood, but whatever it was, sitting there on the cold concrete floor, Malcolm suddenly exploded.

He let out a baleful scream of anguish and started throwing things. Whatever he got his hands on: a bound bundle of Classic Comics, a baseball glove, a small ceramic black panther that he had won in some Wolf Cubs competition, a lamp. Most of it he hurled at the wall of the adjoining locker, and everything that could break did. A set of dishes smashed the loudest.

In the locker next door, the smashing dishes must have sounded like the world exploding because it brought the occupant out of hiding. "Okay, okay, I give up," he said as he opened the door of the locker and stuck his head out. "I give up." The man was an old Indian who'd been living in the locker for several months. Not that old, actually, maybe fifty, but he looked much older. He was a Choctaw, a long way from home, living on a military disability pension.

Scaring him made Malcolm feel like shit. "I'm sorry," he said, "I didn't know anyone was there."

The old Choctaw was relieved. "So you're not going to turn me in?"

"What?"

"I got nowhere else to go." It was illegal of course to be living there, and Malcolm was in fact a police officer, so it wasn't like he had a lot of choice, officially, but sometimes a little choice is all you need.

"No, I'm not going to turn you in," Malcolm assured him, thinking it shouldn't be a crime to do the best you can.

The Choctaw shook his head. He believed him and he was grateful, but even so, he sure as hell didn't want to hang around him. "I'm going to go get me something to eat. I'll come back after you leave."

"You don't have to go," Malcolm tried to convince him. "Really."

"Uh . . . that's okay," he mumbled as he shuffled off. Halfway down the long hall, he stopped for a second. "You know," he called back to Malcolm, "getting crazy ain't going to help you find what you need."

"Yeah, thanks," Malcolm said because he was still feeling bad about scaring the shit out of the guy.

He turned his attention back to filling the duffel bag, quickly because now he just wanted to get the hell out of there. He dumped a couple of small photo albums in, a file folder of legal papers, and then he reached into the bottom of one of the trunks and found the small blanket. He'd seen it often enough before but never paid much attention.

"It was your swaddling cloth, Malcolm," he'd been told. Not something an eight-year-old cares to hear or a sixteen-year-old would listen to. He had come to the Braes wrapped in it. For the first time in his life it meant something. Written across it, essentially invisible to him all these years, were the words: "Secord-Wells Maternity Hospital."

It screamed at him like it was flashing in neon. A chill clamped his body right down to the marrow. He didn't remember ever hearing about Secord-Wells as a child, and if he had, it certainly never took hold. What he did remember, however, was much scarier.

When Jason had shackled Malcolm and Marianne to the table in the greenhouse, there wasn't much for him to do but listen to Marianne talk. She began with irrelevant asides but got serious when Malcolm made it clear, even through the cloth still tightly bound across his mouth, that he was going to get Jason Ondine and put an end to him.

"All they want is their baby," Marianne tried to explain. "That's really what all this is about you know, their baby." Malcolm had answered something cold about grave robbing, and that's when she told him that their son Nathaniel wasn't dead. It was just a cover-up. She had said, "Those first two days at Secord-Wells were like heaven for me. It was the happiest two days Lizzie and I ever had together. You're too young, you probably don't remember the old Secord-Wells. It was strictly a maternity hospital. It was a wonderful place."

Those were the words that stuck in Malcolm's belly now. Secord-Wells. Secord-Wells. Secord-Wells.

It felt like the air was going out of his world.

—

Lizzie had never felt this alone, even during her worst days at White Meadows. She had lost the love of her life and this time it wasn't possible to hang onto the dream that she might somehow see him again. She found a nice hotel room and stayed pretty much to herself trying to figure out what next. She knew she had to remain undercover if Jason was to have any chance at all. If the authorities realized that he didn't have his hostage, no telling how they might proceed.

She found herself watching a lot of TV news and their ubiquitous hunt-for-Jason-Ondine spots, which were ascending to ephemeral dominion over the usual hysteria. One station was even doing weather-style maps speculating on the course of Jason's escape route, complete with sweeping arrows, clumsy circles, and front-style squiggles. Lizzie's own projections were just as bizarre: He's been struck by lightning or run over by a truck or he's fallen down some giant gopher hole and was now forever entombed in the bowels of the earth. "No," she scolded, catching up to herself, "that's ridiculous."

She'd had enough. The news was just getting her pissed and she wanted to turn it off, but couldn't bring herself to do it. She felt like a sports fan trying not to jinx her team. Screwing up her courage, she decided what the hell and changed channels. A talking head named Ted Mishawahara was addressing other pundits, massaging his theory about Jason and the artifacts. "I'm with the police on this," he was saying. "Look at the facts."

"Facts," Lizzie hissed. "What does he know about the facts!"

"In the first place," he went on, "he told the security guard—before he tried to kill him—that he was taking these artifacts back where they belong. If we knew where this Lost City was we could just go there and wait. Unfortunately we don't."

"I guess that's why they call it the Lost City," one of the other guests chimed in. Everybody chuckled a little, not because it was witty or clever or insightful, but because if you didn't chuckle for other panelists, they wouldn't chuckle for you.

"What about the rumor," the host interrupted, taking the chuckling for a sign to move on, "that the original detective on the case may be implicated, and in fact, may be Jason Ondine's son?"

Lizzie's coffee mug fell out of her hand and she didn't even notice. "What! What did you say?"

"Doesn't that lend some credence," the host pressed, "to the idea that this was all about financial gain, and Ondine is not looking for any Lost City but is in fact, as NBC is saying, taking the artifacts to market?"

They put up a picture of Detective Malcolm Brae and Lizzie stared at it, thinking no, it can't possibly be. But it was clear to her that Malcolm did in fact look like Jason around the eyes. Especially around the eyes. She was surprised she hadn't noticed it back in Marianne's greenhouse, but she could see it now. Clearly. Around the eyes. Out loud, she said to herself, "Oh my god, he's got Grandfather's mouth."

When they dropped the picture and Ted Mishawahara came back on the screen, Lizzie gasped, startled, feeling like her son had once again been snatched from her.

—

She knew it was risky but she couldn't help herself, she had to go. In several ways throughout the course of the rest of the afternoon, she tried to talk herself out of going, but she wouldn't be dissuaded. "I'll be very careful," she promised herself. It took enormous restraint, but she managed to wait until after dark. She was going to see her son and every moment delayed was an agony. The excitement she felt, the surges of sheer terror or flights of ecstatic anticipation were overwhelming. She spent the afternoon laughing and crying and pacing and chewing her fingernails.

Malcolm's address was broadcast by a rabid radio talk guy riding the fever. He kept saying things like they ought to be scalped, both him and his father, and even he was astonished by how many calls he got from listeners agreeing that, yeah, the damn Indians get too many breaks from the government as it is.

When Lizzie got to Malcolm's block the street was crowded with media reporters and their crews, along with the burgeoning standard-issue curiosity brigade. She moved freely through the crowd, and despite the pictures of her that had been running on television, no one recognized her. Hiding in plain sight was easily accomplished as long as she didn't act like she was hiding.

She was pushed and bumped as she made her way through the crowd, and it was soon clear to her that even if Malcolm were in his apartment, there was no way she could get to him under these conditions. She turned to leave, fighting the press of the crowd, and was getting nowhere. She started feeling anxious. Claustrophobic. She was beginning to panic when she heard the voice. "Hello, pretty lady." It was Mike. She had no idea how a blind shaman could pick her out in a crowd, or how the hell he even got himself there, but she was calmed by the sight of him.

"What are you doing here?" she wanted to know.

"Same as you," he told her, "just out for an evening stroll."

"I think you're in the wrong alley."

He laughed. "Well, maybe you can get me out of here." He extended his arm and she took it. She stayed close to him and a path seemed to open as they made their way from the center of the bustle back to quieter streets.

"You know, don't you?" she said, both puzzled and resigned.

"I know?" Mike dangled.

"About Malcolm Brae . . . Nathaniel."

"Only what I read in the papers," he chuckled.

It made her smile.

"That's better," he said. "Sometimes that's all there is . . . to smile."

"I have to see him," she pleaded, as though she now believed that Mike had some measure of control.

"Go home," he said.

"No. I can't. I've got to find a way to get to him."

"Go home," he said again.

"You don't understand."

"Go home!"

She finally got it. Of course. Like any lost child, Malcolm would want to get as close to the bosom of his family as he could manage. "Of course."

She wanted to ask about Jason, but Mike stopped her. He reached out and touched her face, so gentle, and he heard her sigh. "Just go home," he said.

—

Lizzie spent almost an hour pacing around outside the gates of her parents' estate. The high walls, old trees, and manicured lawns that were so protective and comforting when she was a child were now formidable obstacles. It was once home, and now for the first time in her life, she got to see it as the rest of the world did, imposing and forbidding.

All she had to do was press a button and identify herself and the gates would open. She wondered for a moment if they would only welcome her in order to pack her back off to White Meadows, but she quickly set that thought aside. Too much had happened for that. They could never send her back now, and she would never go.

What stopped her was Nathaniel. Detective Brae. She had no idea what to call him although she knew perfectly well how she thought of him. She knew he was in there, she'd seen him go by the window twice while she was watching. She tried to imagine what he was saying, what Marianne was saying to him. He must hate her, Lizzie thought. Especially now. She wanted to go in to explain that this wasn't what she had intended, that this wasn't how it was supposed to be, that she never knew he'd been stolen from her.

Everything she thought made her intrusion into his life feel wrong. She fought with herself until she could no longer, and then turned and walked away, knowing with whatever conviction she could muster, that he was better off without her. Her journey was done. All was lost and there was no point adding to anyone's upset. Roads had seemed dark before, but none ever so bleak as this one tonight as she walked away.

"Elizabeth?" Marianne called, as she stepped through the gate. "Deer Heart, is that you?"

Lizzie stopped. It took tremendous will to turn herself around.

"Come back," Marianne pleaded, knowing that her apologies were pointless and she certainly couldn't make up for what she'd done in the past. Marianne understood that she had nothing to offer but her heart. "Please, don't go."

Lizzie saw her without rancor, she saw her for a woman who simply loved too much and too poorly in too many directions, another woman—another human being—crushed by fear. Lizzie held her ground, searching for words, when the universe interceded. She stood both daunted and entranced as Nathaniel emerged from the gates behind Marianne.

He walked straight to Lizzie, no falter in his step, no hesitation in his eyes. He was proud and sure. It almost made her dizzy to see him. So handsome, she kept thinking. So tall.

He walked right up, stopped so close to her that she could almost reach out and touch him, and she would have except her bones had turned to jelly and she couldn't move anything. She didn't know what to say and even if she did, she was sure she couldn't speak anyway. She was paralyzed with joy and frozen with fear.

"Hello, Mother," he said.

Her mind froze. She was trembling, overwhelmed, but she opened her arms to him and, without hesitation, Nathaniel took her into his. She held on saying his name. Nathaniel. Nathaniel.

"It's alright, Mother," he said as she began to sob. "It's alright."

TWENTY-NINE

The hunt for Jason Ondine had by now developed enough momentum to stimulate a spreading net of police jurisdictions and media appetites. A lethal combination. Every day new police sketches of Jason were faxed across the country, and every day new stories materialized on TV, assembled from less than whole cloth.

The current conventional wisdom had Jason pegged as a murderous desperado who'd scam his own mother for a freelance nickel. He was probably armed and certainly dangerous. The cop who caught him was going to win himself a big-time bump up the ladder, so there were a lot of uniforms out there hoping that Jason would come their way.

—

He didn't know where he had come by them, but Jason's instincts were unerring. He followed trails he had never seen before—most of which had no human scents—and floated rivers whenever the opportunity arose. Moving, moving, moving. He hardly ever slept, he had no maps, he couldn't read the stars, but he knew he was taking the most direct manageable line to the village.

Up here in the high mountains along the northern coast, little had changed in all the years he'd been away. The trees still reached into the sky, and the peaks even higher. The ocean below still broke in waves of froth, still silent from up here, and though he hadn't seen them, he assumed the deer still ran below the crests. He sat on a great granite ledge looking out at the world. He ate roots and fruits and wild vegetables he collected along the way, and although he didn't know the names of any of the plants, he liked the smells and that was enough.

He knew the police would stay on his trail, growing angrier and more vengeful with each failed day, so he stayed away from the farms and villages, away from the temptation for human contact which, it surprised him to discover, had become so precious to him, so hard to give up. Some days out he crossed a dirt fire road that snaked through a valley between two minor ranges. There was a small wooden shack and a one-horse corral, a way station for rangers, down near the creek. He just couldn't pass it up. More than ever now, he seemed to need to touch things human. It was a dangerous notion, he knew that, but he was willing to risk it, willing to risk his entire mission for what? Walls?

He waited until midmorning when the ranger finally came out and saddled up. By the time Jason made it down to the valley floor, the ranger was long gone, but he'd left half a loaf of bread and a still warm pot of tea. Jason savored both with an urgent, mystical appreciation. At this lonely, lonely moment nothing could speak more directly to him than cooked food. Warm tea, baked bread. Two hundred years in the sea had left him with a permanent awe of the majestic mastery of fired food.

It made him sad. Here he was, the White Man's conscience incarnate, returning to the People what belongs to the People and he was stealing someone's bread, not because he needed it but because he missed it.

The bones of the old chief and the masks of long forgotten dances were only tokens, but if he brought them home, they would once more become transcendent symbols. Jason was bringing back an apology, some measure of honor and dignity, and the recognition that dances to the Spirits were no less sacred than hymns to Jesus.

It was harder than he remembered, this business of being a human being. It was hard to feel worthy. It was easier in the sea. There, you were just who you were. Honor among sea lions was automatic. You lied to prey perhaps, and you lied to those for whom you would be prey, but you never lied to each other. He wondered if the answer, or at least the lesson, was somehow in that stone he threw so long ago that killed the deer. It was an accident, a happenstance, a coincidence in a universe with no coincidences. It was the blink of an eye and it changed the course of his life and the histories that sprang from it. As far as he could tell, the only lesson he had learned was that every instant mattered.

He finished the bread and the tea and lay down on the bed to rest. It was a comfortable bed, not quite as embracing as the pine needles and earth he'd been sleeping on, but comfortable enough, and he soon drifted off. Several hours later he was awakened by the hysterical screeching of a raven on the roof of the shack. It was apparent that the bird was warning him and Jason assumed, correctly, that the ranger must be returning. Grateful to Raven, he gathered up his things and when he came outside, the bird was already flying away.

"Hanging Hair," he called after her, "wait!"

Raven shrieked, just once, and then she was gone, flying for the sun. Jason watched her go and then hurried up the slopes to the next mountain.

City cops, local cops, highway patrols, and Feds had all joined the hunt at one time or another. Some officially, some as volunteers. Day by day, some came, some went, so that the corps was always swelling and shrinking. Ebb and flow. In many ways it began to take on the feel and complexion of the Bennett Camp Posse of a hundred years earlier. They even spoke of the Posse, in admiration, on the trails and around campfires.

Their trails were the highways and paved roads because they weren't really equipped for the back country. So while Jason stayed to the feeding paths and migration trails in the high mountains and sheltered valleys, his pursuers stayed in their cars, guessing. The campfires were more often than not motel restaurants or roadside gas dispensaries. Apart from that, they considered themselves the true heirs to the Bennett Camp Posse, and rightfully so.

The artifacts may have come from a now Lost City, but the one thing they knew for sure was that it had to be somewhere on the trail followed by the Posse. The problem was that nobody knew exactly where on the trail, which was several hundred miles long. It wasn't like they could just go to the end of the trail and wait—although a small squad had been sent to do just that, if they could find the end of the trail, which according to the latest reports they had been unable to do—because Ondine might be headed for the middle of the trail.

So they traversed the roads near the Posse trail relying on input from locals. A hunter saw him on the ridge. Some campers heard him singing somewhere. A couple of truckers claimed to have given him a ride, not knowing it was him until too late and then they were lucky to escape with their lives. None of it was true, but it kept Jason's pursuers on their toes. "Damn," one of them said, "sometimes I think I can feel him breathing down the back of our necks."

They were gathered for the night, courtesy of the army, in Fort Eulakon at the headwaters of the river. Some twenty-five or thirty cops, the main body of the posse. The rest of it, not more than a handful, was scattered through the mountains.

It had been a slow day racing up and down the roads in pursuit of air. One of the cars saw a bear and took potshots at it. Never even nicked it. So all the talk at dinner was about a guy named Bernie Pollard from Spokane. He was on loan to the posse for "however long it takes." He was maybe the finest hot marksman in the business—hot—meaning that under pressure he was unflappable. Hot also meaning he was a little trigger happy, although no one ever said that to his face.

They were flying him up, and just after dinner the helicopter swooped in off the river and settled *thwaka thwaka thwaka* onto the clearing in the middle of the camp. Everyone came out to get a look at him.

He wasn't much at first sight. Sort of medium by every measure, except for a droopy paunch too large for his frame and, when you got close to him, his eyes. Scary, scary eyes. Disturbed. This was not a guy strangers were prompted to say hello to on the street. This was a guy whose brash audacity was at the core of his skills, and Hanging Hair had come to fix that. Perfect was not what she wanted from him. She had followed the helicopter, a black raven in the dark of night, invisible because no bird could fly that fast and people only saw that which they believed with their own eyes.

Hanging Hair settled on a branch of the Japanese maple planted out in front of the canteen. She cawed several times so that when she took flight, no one would be surprised.

Pollard stood around basking in the adulation, shaking hands and establishing himself as The Man. He wasn't getting any arguments from anyone there and was feeling so good about it that he was thinking of opening the case and showing off his rifle, when Hanging Hair took action. She sprang from her branch, circled slowly, cawing once or twice, then flew by two feet over Pollard's head and shat on him.

A lot of people wanted to laugh, but no one dared. Hanging Hair made a lot of noise cawing and chuckling as she flew back to her branch and waited.

Pollard went pro, as she expected. He opened the case and assembled his rifle. Thirty-one seconds, he was on one knee and drawing a bead. He set the raven's head in the crosshairs. The red laser dot appeared right between Hanging Hair's eyes,

"Bye bye Blackbird," Pollard announced and squeezed the trigger.

Hanging Hair watched the bullet coming out of the barrel, and then she stopped time. Everything, including the bullet, froze exactly where it was, and Hanging Hair dropped down from the branch, the old woman with the young woman's long black hair. She didn't have long to wait before Sedna and Adee arrived. "What the hell are you doing?" Sedna demanded.

"That's the one," Hanging Hair told her sisters. "That's the one who will kill Jason Ondine."

"It's a very nice idea," Adee almost sneered, "but Ondine will never agree."

"I'm working on it," Hanging Hair answered, "and if the two of you will just go about your business, I've got things to do."

They left as quickly as they had come, and Hanging Hair walked over to the bullet suspended in mid-flight and nudged it ever so slightly to the left. Then she got back on the branch, exactly where she had been, and restored time.

The bullet whizzed by, several inches from the raven. Nobody could believe it. Hell, most of them could have picked off the bird with a sidearm at that distance.

Pollard himself was in shock.

This time, when the raven flew off, somebody did laugh, and Pollard didn't even turn to see who it was.

THIRTY

The mouth of the Eulakon River not only marks an area of great beauty but one of very old magic as well. A bounteous sea beckons on one side, fruitful mountains on the other, and in between the sky reaches all the way down to the ground. In the old days Dzarilaw lived here. Not the Dzarilaw who built and ruled over what is now the Lost City, but Dzarilaw, the first. Dzarilaw the Great Bear, the Prince of Bears. He came here in the summers for the fish and the berries, but mostly, it is said, because it reminded him of what the Other World must look like in its grandest glories. There was no better place for a city than the south bank of the river, where Dzarilaw—great, great . . . great-grandson of the Bear—built his. That so many different people came to it in peace was a tribute to a fountain of magic that people believed fed the Eulakon from under the mountains.

It was from here that the Spirits sprang or it was here that they came to visit, and it was impossible not to feel their presence. It was often here that the Gods showed their mercies and it was from one such demonstration that the river Eulakon got its name.

Many years ago, long before Dzarilaw built his city, there was a small village on these shores. About two hundred people. They had been prosperous, so prosperous that they grew careless. They wasted food. They were unkind to animals and often to each other. And worst of all, they failed to return to the sea the souls of those they had hunted. It was not long before a summer passed with hardly a catch, neither from the sea nor from the hills. Fall came fast and hard, and the winter was longer and colder than anyone could remember. The People were sick and starving, dying of disease and hunger and fear. They began to pray. They sang to the Spirits. They chanted promises to amend their ways, and they wept in shame.

Hanging Hair was the first to hear them and she took pity and told their plight to other Spirits. Not everyone wanted to forgive them or trusted that they had seen the light and would change their ways, but finally everyone agreed. Negafok, the Yupik spirit of cold weather, withdrew, and Sedna, Mother of the Seas, sent out the eulakon. The eulakon, a small fish, eight or ten inches long, swam straight to the mouth of the river and were harvested by the starving People. It was the most delicious fish they had ever eaten, very oily and described in modern times as tasting like big sardines without the cans. From that day on the river was called Eulakon—which means Savior Fish—and every spring great schools returned to feed the village.

When Jason stood on that final peak and looked down at the Eulakon basin, his heart soared so high he could almost feel his body flying with it. How he wished that he could fly, could float right down into the village, but he couldn't. It was still at least a full day's walk away, even for him. He took it slowly, savoring the end of the trek, inhaling the vistas and panoramas he had not seen for two hundred years, sampling berries he had only dreamed of for all that time and matching tastes he had never forgotten.

He slept that night in a clearing several hundred feet above the ocean, only a few miles south of the village. From here he could see the rocks out in the mouth of the river where he used to lounge with seals and lions and otters and other creatures of the coastal seas. He couldn't see the spot where the Jesuit was killed, except in his mind, and there he saw every detail and remembered every scream. He couldn't see Dzarilaw's burial place, though he could see a section of the path that led to it. The village itself was around the bend and it was better that he couldn't see it yet.

He lay back and watched the stars and listened to the waves breaking against the shore, tugging at him with old memories. Waves break differently at every shore, so their sounds are unique and special. He learned in his years in the sea that he could navigate by the echo of the waves, that he could find his way home by listening for familiar lines, songs returned by the rocks and sand. He was coming home and remembered only the soaring and not the pain. He could accept it all, except for the emptiness his father had left in him. Now that he himself had sired a child, he wondered if it would all be joined, if he would find his father when he found his son.

"Lizzie, Lizzie, you would love it here." He closed his eyes and tried to whistle the melody he had heard her playing that first day in Calder Cove. He could hear it in his head, but he was no better at reproducing it now than he was then. He drifted off listening to the waves.

—

"I think he's asleep," Johnny Oatmeal whispered into his walkie-talkie. He was watching Jason through binoculars from his own perch several hundred yards away and talking to someone down in the village.

"That means he's not coming down tonight," they answered.

Oatmeal agreed. "I figure we'll see him maybe an hour or two after the sun."

"Sounds right."

"Want me to stay up here or what?"

"Yeah, we don't want to spook him. You better stay put."

—

By the middle of the next morning Jason had made his way down to the village, so shocked by what he saw that he was completely unaware of all the hidden eyes watching him from the woods at the periphery of the site. He stood in what was once the center of the village, and there was nothing there. All the houses and lodges were gone, most razed by the Bennett Posse, some simply crumbled by weather and time. There used to be totem poles everywhere. Cormorant clan. Bear clans. Wolf. White Bear too. Thunderbird for Adee. Orca for Sedna. Now there were none. He looked for smokehouses and drying sheds, for spinners. Nothing. Nothing but a few broken pots, a couple of axe handles, some arrowheads, a broken shield-shaped plate that he cleaned the dirt from to yield a ceremonial copper.

Johnny Oatmeal joined the others in the woods, waiting for their moment. They were poised, they were ready. They had waited a long time for this. They watched.

Jason untied the large parcel and let it slip from his back to the ground. He sat cross-legged beside it and kept the pouch of Dzarilaw's bones close to his chest. He began to sing. It was a song of mourning that he had heard around the fires after Dzarilaw had died. It was very sad and very slow. There were few words, just the sounds of tears and longing. The sounds rose in sorrow from his heart. "Ay yi yi kwakwaka'wakw."

The sounds rose into the sky like the haunted lament of an arctic loon, and he waited for the silence to close in before he began again. "Ay yi yi kwakwaka'wakw." A tear fell from his eye and washed across his face. "Ay yi yi kwakwaka'wakw."

From behind his tree Johnny Oatmeal responded. "Ay yi yi kwak-waka'wakw."

Yes, Jason thought. He was home. He sang. "Ay yi yi kwak-waka'wakw."

This time Johnny Oatmeal stepped into the clearing to sing back. "Ay yi yi kwakwaka'wakw."

Jason's heart filled. "Ay yi yi kwakwaka'wakw."

Three more came men out of the woods. They joined Johnny Oatmeal and their voices now also mourned with Jason. "Ay yi yi kwakwaka'wakw."

And then the first woman's voice. Taryn Stream-Cleaner, tears of paradise in her eyes. "Ay yi yi kwakwaka'wakw."

And the rest emerged. Almost forty. Kwakiutl mostly, but Tsimshian and Salish, Nootka, Tlingit. Two Yupik. Even a Cherokee who said he had come to stand with his brothers, and a toothless would-be warrior who had never thought of himself as Indian until the other day when he met some blind old shaman in an alley who told him this was his destiny and he'd better get there if he cared anything at all for his soul.

"Ay yi yi kwakwaka'wakw."

Taryn led the others to Jason's side. He touched her hand and it made her strong, and she sat beside him as a measure of her gratitude. "I didn't think I was ever coming home," she told him, feeling whole.

It was a song of sadness and loss for the proud Kwakiutl Nation, but those from all the other Nations mourned with Jason and sang with him, abandoning tribal jealousies, just as it had been in this place in the days of Dzarilaw.

"Ay yi yi kwakwaka'wakw. Ay yi yi Dzarilaw." They mourned for several hours and then Jason led them to the path to Dzarilaw's grave, and they dug it open and set the bones to rest.

Jason spoke the only words. "Grandfather," he said, "it is as you wish." They covered his bones with the earth he had loved, and they sang to him. "Ay yi yi kwakwaka'wakw."

So it was that the gathering up had begun. It was exactly as Hanging Hair had imagined, including the small plane that flew by that night when they gathered in the center of what was once the village and would now be again. They sat all around Jason, and he told them of Dzarilaw's dream, about the visit with the Thunderbird and the promise of the bones. As he told them more stories of the old ways, his own heart began to open: There is no pack without a wolf, and there is no wolf without the pack.

—

The plane banked to circle for a second look. It was an old Cessna with some new fittings, as reliable a bush plane as there was around these parts, which was, after all, not saying very much. The pilot knew there wasn't supposed to be anything down there, so he was checking his maps not to confirm his suspicions but to double-check his coordinates. He came down low over the village, nodding happily to himself at the sight of the fires. He had found it. Dzarilaw's Lost City was lost no more, and he'd lay waffles to wing nuts that Jason Ondine was down there.

He didn't know if there was a reward or a bonus involved, but he was damn sure he'd make the papers. He radioed back to Fort Eulakon and made no effort to keep the excitement out of his voice. "Load up for bear," he said, "I found your boy."

THIRTY-ONE

The last three days with Lizzie had changed Malcolm's life, permanently and irrevocably and while he wasn't sure it was for the better, staying at the Bennett estate turned out to be an inspired escape from the world. Although the reporters continued to hound the Bennetts, it was sporadic. They'd come by regularly but they never camped out for very long and even when they did stay, they couldn't get beyond the compound walls without an invitation.

Malcolm loved being there. His thirst for the roots he hadn't even been aware of turned out to be unquenchable, and Lizzie's need to fill him in was every bit as strong. Robert Bennett, unable to face either of them, stayed away from the house. Malcolm was shown family albums, public histories of Bennett commercial triumphs, coats of arms, old family skeletons, legends, boats, and traditions. He absorbed it all and was fascinated, but his father still eluded him. While he devoured the rest, he still couldn't accept Jason.

Lizzie told him stories about that first day she saw Jason on the beach and gave him an almost day-by-day account of their whirlwind courtship and its unhappy conclusion at that dinky little motel on the northern California coast.

"So what are you telling me," he challenged her, very agitated, "that he's a freak? My father is a freak!"

"Nathaniel, don't say—"

"Malcolm," he corrected. "My name is Malcolm."

"I'm sorry. I've always thought of you as . . . fine, okay . . . Malcolm. You're father is not a freak."

"Either that or you're completely loony tunes."

"Is that what you think?"

"Somebody told you your father was a two-hundred-year-old fish, what would you—"

"Sea lion," Lizzie corrected.

"Whatever, what would you think? Or you put a bullet through him and he doesn't even react. Yes, I think that's all pretty damn freaky."

"Okay, fine, I'm a lunatic!"

"That's not what I said."

"Listen, I can't explain any of this to you, I can't even explain it to myself, but it's true, and I can't change it just because it doesn't make sense to you." It wasn't really understanding she was pleading for, or compassion or empathy, it was Jason's life. There was no one else to take his side, no one to stand up for him, no one to slow the inexorable march of the killing machine closing in on him. There was only Malcolm, and he wasn't buying into the notion that Jason was an innocent man falsely accused. He couldn't.

"They're going to kill him!" Lizzie shouted.

"The asshole should have thought of that before he took down that orderly," Malcolm shot back out of sheer helpless frustration.

Lizzie slapped him. Hard across the face. It made an almost ringing sound. "Don't you ever talk about your father like that!"

Stunned, Malcolm turned and started to the door.

"You ought to know what you're talking about before you shoot off your mouth." Had she been more mindful of the old curse, that Jason would die at the hand of his son, she would not have pressed so hard. She would not have pressed at all.

Malcolm did not turn back.

"Your father saved that boy's life. It was the orderly that attacked that boy, not Jason."

"Nathaniel!" Lizzie screamed, as he walked out, and then remembered. "Malcooooolm!"

He left seething.

—

This was the suburbs. Blossom Estates. Mostly three bedrooms, a den, a two-car garage, and a spectacular vista of all the other three-and-a-den neighbors. It was obviously some sort of camouflage. If people couldn't change their skin tones to blend into the background and escape their enemies, the least they could do is build all their homes to look alike and confuse the predators. The sales pitch was about enjoying an easier way of life, but the reality was about hiding. From the good guys as well as the bad guys. From others. From yourself. For kids life here was lived in backyards, until they could escape to the mall and shop on their own. It was the social equivalent of lead in the water.

Cottie Prusch was one such kid, but ever since the trouble at the hospital, he'd stayed pretty much to his room and avoided family, friends, school, and mall. "He's just embarrassed, and who can blame him," the school psychologist explained, trying to be helpful and being anything but. In his current seclusion, watching a lot of TV, the burden for Cottie kept growing heavier. He felt like the newscasts were broadcasting his humiliation, raping him anew, every time they mentioned Jason Ondine. So it was not a welcome intrusion when his mother knocked on his door and announced that Detective Brae was there to see him.

Malcolm bristled with anger and urgency, and it scared the hell out of Cottie to be left alone with him. The boy cowered to the farthest corner of the bed while Malcolm paced, taking in everything. Posters. CDs. A picture of Cottie in his junior high baseball uniform. It was some time before anyone spoke. Cottie broke the silence. "Did you come here to kill me?"

Malcolm, examining the baseball picture, didn't answer, didn't cut him any slack.

"Because he's your father, I mean," Cottie pressed.

Malcolm turned to face him. "Shortstop?"

"What?"

"The picture, you're sort of standing like a shortstop."

"Second base. I wanted short but my arm wasn't good enough."

"Me too," Malcolm admitted.

Cottie stared at him. "Is it true then, what they say on TV," Cottie asked after a long silence, "that he's your father?"

"Hey! I ask the fucking questions here." It really rankled Malcolm to think that something so private had already become so public.

"What do you want?" Cottie demanded, trying to act tough from the corner of his bed.

"I want to know what the hell happened."

"Read the newspapers," Cottie shot back, beginning to find his courage.

Malcolm grabbed him by the shirt and lifted him off the bed. "A man risked his life to save you and this is how you thank him! Where the hell's your heart!"

"Fuck you!" Cottie screamed, surprising both of them.

"They're going to run him down and kill him because you're a lying little shit!"

"Fuck you!" Cottie hollered again, shaking with a fury he could find no other words for. "Fuck you! Fuck you!" The tears were streaming down his face. "Fuck you! Fuck you!" And for the first time since that night in the hospital, he felt the terror and the shame lifting. He felt light coming back into his life. "It wasn't my fault."

Later, he told Malcolm the whole story and the humiliation went away. By way of apology, Cottie wrote out a short version and signed it. His mother witnessed. "I'm sorry," Cottie said. "I know it's not enough after what he did for me, but I'm sorry."

Before he left, Malcolm said, "Yes, he's my father." He was surprised that it was so easy to say to Cottie Prusch and so hard to admit to Lizzie.

Malcolm went out to the car to catch his breath, to try to still the welling sorrow in his chest. Knowing the truth made him feel closer to Jason and more scared for him. He said the words aloud: "My father." For the first time, it felt proud, and he meant it in his heart.

He dialed up on his cell phone and got through to Adachi without much trouble. It surprised him. "Captain?"

"You got something for me, Brae?"

"Captain . . . Jason Ondine is no killer."

"Right. He's a terrific Dad and—"

"Listen to me. I just spoke to the Prusch kid and he says it was the orderly, and Ondine was trying to stop him. Self-defense, Captain. I got it, signed."

"Gimme a break, Brae. You think I was born yesterday!"

"You have to do something!"

"It's out of my hands now, Brae, and it sure as hell is out of yours."

THIRTY-TWO

Jason sat near the fire telling every story he knew, answering every question he could. He recognized his own awakening and began to understand at last that there was purpose to all those years he had been isolated in the sea. It had kept him from contamination. His memories were clean and clear. The stories, the legends and rituals, the wisdom he had taken from Dzarilaw and the village, he could now return to the People uncorrupted.

The irony of an outcast white man as a vessel of sacred knowledge did not escape him. But it had long been said that someday Dzarilaw would return, and the People would know the gift of the Grandfathers. It was a promise originally made in hope, and then remembered in despair, so when Jason appeared, the People recognized that the message he brought was true and real and the shape of the messenger was irrelevant.

"When it seemed that all was lost . . . Muskrat surfaced. His mouth was so full of ground that he couldn't talk or even breathe," Jason explained. He loved the story of Wolverine and the creation of the world. He loved it when he was a child and he loved it more now, hearing Dzarilaw in his ears. He looked around and the tension was unbearable, just like it was when Dzarilaw told it. "Wolverine put his lips to Muskrat's ass and blew as hard as he could until the ground poured out of Muskrat's mouth, more and more ground seemingly without end. And more and more."

People cheered, some just for the pleasure of it and others, who knew the story, cheered in anticipation just like the children had with Dzarilaw. "And that ground," Jason told them, "is the very earth we walk on."

They screamed with delight. Jason laughed as hard as any.

For two days and two nights Jason spoke without pause. With every story he told, he felt lighter, emptying himself of old burdens. He spoke constantly because he knew his time was short. Throughout the two days and two nights, the People arrived almost continuously so that by the middle of the second day they were almost two hundred. It was said that no matter how close to Jason one sat, or how far away, his words were just as clear.

Some came from nearby villages, some from far away. Now that Jason was on the news all the time, everybody knew what was going on. For the authorities—the police, the courts, the media, the scholars and the psychics, for all the world out there—the Lost City was a place that couldn't, until now, be found.

For the People it never meant that at all. "Lost" meant only that it was gone. What had been was no more. The People, the ideas, the community—that was what was lost. The place itself was where it always was, at the mouth of the Eulakon.

It was wonderful that more and more kept coming, except for the news they brought. Fresh from their TV sets and radios, they all brought the same pressing warning: The police are closing in.

"Although it may be true that Wolverine made the world," Jason announced solemnly, looking at the spectacular glittering sky, "it is also true that he once tried to get rid of it."

"And did he do it," someone yelled out, "or are we still living on piles of shit?"

"You decide," Jason laughed with him. "It was winter and it was very cold. Wolverine didn't have any wood so he was burning bones for their fat, until he ran out of bones too. So Wolverine thought, well, maybe I can find some sort of female who'll keep me warm. A little later a pretty young girl showed up at his camp, and Wolverine thought, I'll get under her dress tonight. So he invited her to share some caribou hearts with him."

"It takes more than that these days," someone shouted to the general pleasure of all.

"It took more than that back then too," Jason assured him. "She was hungry and she looked forward to the delicacy, but 'Only if you cook them,' she told him."

People laughed. So did Jason. "'But I have no wood, or bones either,' Wolverine told her. And she answered, 'Well, if you won't cook them, I won't eat them.' And off she went on her snowshoes."

"Happens to me all the time," a young man called out.

"Me too," a woman answered. Everybody cheered.

"Well, Wolverine was so angry," Jason went on, "that he began tearing up the earth, grabbing it and throwing pieces into the sky. Most of these pieces just came back down again . . . and became the mountains. But some stayed up there . . . forever, and that's the Milky Way."

Jason looked up to the sky and everyone looked with him. There it was, the cloud of stars stretching across the sky. It had never looked so awesome to any of them as it did at that moment.

They all watched the sky in reverent silence. A shadow streaked by high above them and obscured the heavens for the blink of an eye. The shadow made a terrible loud shrieking sound and then was gone, settling somewhere in the woods beyond the village. Some thought that it must be Adee, arriving as the Thunderbird, and several noticed the appearance some short time later of an old woman with short feathery silver hair.

Only Jason could see that it was a helicopter, and only Jason knew that the loud shriek and the high fleet shadow radiating from it was the end of time, coming for him. Before returning to its base the scout chopper made two more passes, both very high so as not to spook the gathering.

—

It was three o'clock in the morning before Malcolm returned to the Bennett estate. Mostly he'd been sitting in his car just down the road listening to crickets and wind. He was angry and relieved, and he sat quietly, allowing his father to be born in him. Finally, in the dark he saw Jason's face and in it his own, and he wept for the sheer overwhelming loneliness of it.

Suddenly there was so much he needed to know, so much he needed to say, but it was all inside and the words wouldn't come, not even in his mind. "Father," was all he could manage. He could almost bring it to his lips, but not quite. It stayed in his heart. Father will you hold me? Father have you seen me? Father do you know me? Father.

Lizzie was still awake when he got there, battling a night of terrible loneliness and crushing guilt. It was the guilt that she was afraid would never heal. She knew now, too late, that Jason had been right, that the shaman could indeed see. If only she had believed. If only she had been able to see more clearly. If only her soul had not been in pieces, and she had not walked away, she might still have Jason. Or was the price that Nathaniel would never have been found?

"It's going to be alright," Malcolm soothed.

"Yes," she said.

"First thing in the morning," he promised, showing her the paper, "I'll take this to court and we'll get them to call off the hounds."

"Malcolm," she whispered as she touched his face. "Thank you."

"It's going to be alright," he assured her again.

Beginnings are sacred and this was Lizzie's. The promise opened her heart. It filled her with Jason, full as the very first time she saw him. When lovers meet, there is nothing more important than the chance to behold oneself anew, to tell the other about visions and stories, attitudes and dreams, perspectives that redefine oneself in the light of the fire. "The first story I ever told your father," she began, sitting on the sofa with Malcolm, "was of a visit I had taken to some Mayan ruins deep in the jungles of Central America."

She was fifteen and had a raging appetite for the world.

"We came up on the ruins really suddenly. We were surrounded by all this vegetation and I thought we were never going to see daylight again, and then there it was. A small clearing opened in the jungle and we could see broken temples and ancient storage bins, but most of all it was a crumbled village, with some chickens and goats that belonged to the one family that still lived there."

Lizzie had hated intruding on the family and insisted on leaving at once. On the way back she asked their Mayan guide how long the ruins had been there.

"The ruins?" he checked. It seemed such a preposterous question that he had to make sure he'd heard right.

"How long have they been there?" she repeated.

"They've always been there," he assured her.

Lizzie loved his response. It was about a way of seeing. A way of being. For the Mayan guide the world is as it has always been and people just come along to inhabit its dreams or challenge its terrors. The ruins have always been ruins. For the girl it was a deeply magnificent perspective. For the woman she had grown into, it was only half an answer.

"Which half?" Malcolm teased.

She smiled and touched his hand. "The one that lets us know that the world doesn't exist without us and that each of us is born to invent it all over again."

"And the other half is?"

"What joins us. The other half is love. How we give it. How we receive it." In the end, when the essential matters have been addressed, when the inventory of a lifetime turns to ash, when all the desperation for another moment, another vision, another hope fades away, and all that's left is life and death, it is only the details that separate one from another.

Just then Marianne came racing into the library, breathless. "They found him!" she screamed. Lizzie froze. Malcolm took her hand. "Well not exactly found him yet, but they know where he is." She looked ashamed.

"What?"

Marianne couldn't say it.

"Mother, what?"

"Your father just called, Deer Heart. He said the police are closing in on Jason and . . . and he told them that you were home."

"He didn't!"

"Safe and sound."

"Jesus," Malcolm growled. "If they don't think Lizzie's with him they'll . . . they'll shred him! Jesus Christ!" He couldn't let this happen. He couldn't. "Did they say where?"

Marianne didn't know.

Lizzie did. "He went to his village." She got the atlas down from the shelf and the book fell open to the right page—it had had much practice. Lizzie showed him the Eulakon and a picture of the south shore of the river's mouth, where the village had once stood.

There was no time to waste. Lizzie went out to the car to say good-bye. "He loved you," she told him.

He shrugged. She embraced him and patted down his hair.

"I'm too old for you to fix my hair," he told her.

"Malcolm, you will never be too old for me to—"

"Nathaniel," he corrected.

"Nathaniel." It sounded perfect and whole to her, so she said it again. "Nathaniel."

THIRTY-THREE

There was enormous excitement at the camp and lots of activity—loading gear, inspecting weapons, studying maps, and kicking tires in anticipation of a hard road trip. Now that they knew where Jason was, the rest was just a matter of execution. The sun was coming up and they were going to get him.

It had become very military, organized and efficient, which is often what human beings substitute for understanding in an effort to compensate for a lack of the intuitive cohesion displayed by most hunting packs. When wolves set off after prey, they move out with no wasted flailing and no committee meetings. When it's time, the alpha hunter stands and moves out. Everybody else takes their proper places. Nobody says you go here, and you go there, and you sneak around the other side. They move as a single organism with several bodies, and when they target the quarry—an aging elk, a caribou too well fed to run far enough, a deer culled from its herd—the chase begins. Again, no one needs to say anything. The entire pack runs, each one dreaming that he or she alone will make the kill, but knowing full well that it will be the alpha, as it always is.

A posse is like a pack. Stirs like a pack. Hunts like a pack. But unlike a natural pack, the posse had to be told what to do, where to park, when to go. How to howl. And while every man in this pack dreamed of taking Jason down, they all knew it would fall to their alpha hunter: Bernie Pollard alone would make the kill.

In keeping with his status, Pollard remained absolutely cool and detached. He had kept pretty much to himself since he had missed the raven. He'd been spending most of his time at practice. Practice. And more practice. Almost a thousand rounds at a dime-sized target from a hundred yards. A thousand rounds and not a single miss.

The guys still joked about what they now called "that shifty crow," but truth was Pollard had earned back whatever respect he'd lost. His dedication, the intensity of his practice, the focus . . . it was all levels above what any of the rest of them had ever attempted or were even capable of, and they knew it. "He's okay," they ended up saying. Very high praise for a guy from so far away.

Up in the chopper Pollard selected his ammunition—two bullets he kept in a small brass case. They were ugly bullets. Big. Hollow point. Scored. "You could take down an elephant with one of those," the pilot observed.

—

The dawning sun brought a not entirely welcome clarity. Jason felt like he had barely started and his time was already done. He had told stories of the creation and of the end of the world. He told stories about whales and bears and coyotes, about Wolverine and Raven. About the shaman's rattle he kept with him throughout, he told them only that he remembered one like it from a long time ago. It was carved in the shape of a long-necked oyster-catcher, carrying babies in a cradle on its back, and every time he rattled it, he remembered more stories.

He taught them the details of the seal hunt, including the personal purification rituals that made it possible to invite the seals, and the essential ritual of returning the seal's soul encased in its bladder to the sea that it might live again. He told them all the hunting stories he could remember so they would know how to hunt, and fishing stories so they would know how to fish. For the hunters and fishers these stories were a guide to their trade. For the others they were still a guide to their souls.

"These are not easy days we live in," he said, and after a moment of quiet he rose calmly and told them that it was time for him to go. There were shouts of panic and protest. No, don't go.

"Make yourself whole," he urged, "and the world will become whole."

You can't go.

"Make your family whole . . ."

There was a rumbling through the woods, a terror coming to them in uniforms. "Make the People whole, and the world will be whole." They moved closer to him, emphatic about protecting him. They would stand with him, they would keep him from the hands that would destroy him.

He turned to say good-bye to Taryn Stream-Cleaner and realized he was standing on the very spot where his father had stood when he had said his last good-bye to the young Jason. All the years since their parting, Jason had felt only his own pain and never his father's. Now standing there, he felt it and it made the emptiness go away, and the anger with it. Standing there he felt recovered, restored to the bosom of his lost father.

Taryn saw the single tear and mistook it for sadness. "You don't have to leave," she told him. "We will stand with you."

He thanked her for wishing it, but it could not be allowed. He knew what had happened with the Bennett Camp Posse at this very place and how easily it could happen all over again. His mind railed at the vision of another slaughter.

"You must not interfere," he demanded. He would not have their blood on his hands. "This is not for you," he told them. "This is not for you."

—

Even in the best of circumstances Nathaniel didn't much like flying. Bouncing and swaying on this old Piper with the peeling pontoons and clattering motor, he hated it.

"You okay?" the pilot asked him.

"Uh," he answered, trying to make it sound like something affirmative. He was gripping the armrest so hard he was going to leave permanent marks in either his hands or the leatherette and maybe both. "Uh," he repeated with what he hoped passed for a smile.

"Well you sure don't look okay," the pilot told him.

"No, no, I'm okay."

"Then maybe you could let go of the armrests before you rip 'em out of the goddam chair."

"Just trying to keep the plane up," Nathaniel explained.

"Hey, you're paying me a lot of money to fly you up here, and I don't get to spend any of it unless I get back in one piece, so relax. I'm what you call highly motivated."

Nathaniel let go of the armrests and was a little surprised that the plane didn't suddenly plummet to the earth. "Okay," he said. "No problem."

Nathaniel had no idea what in hell he was going to do. Armed with a signed statement from Cottie Prusch, one unmarked illegal handgun, and a warning from Adachi that if he stuck his nose into this he was not only ending his police career but also going to jail for obstruction, he had cause to be concerned.

At about the same time that his plane set down on the Eulakon and taxied to the beach, the police had everything in order and launched their attack.

—

Without the dance, the Kwakiutl say, they are nothing. Jason was dancing the Atlakim, a sacred dance of return to the forests, when he was interrupted by the sound of heavy boots and breaking branches closing in from every side. Twenty-three troopers on the move, exactly the same number as the original Bennett Camp Posse.

All the People who were there that day went home with separate stories in their minds, distinct legends in their hearts, unique visions of their lives. But about this they all agreed: The Spirits had come.

The People also knew the story of the slaughter, yet despite their fear they remained absolutely willing to stand with Jason. Their fear was real and it was awesome, until the Spirits came.

They came in every form. Some you could see, some not. But the People felt them. Some only saw or felt a single Spirit and its power, others saw and felt more, but they all knew that God was there that day in a hundred different Spirits, all come to be with Jason Ondine.

The first to come were the Sisters of Creation. Gyhldeptis—Hanging Hair—arrived as giant Raven, entirely invisible until she turned herself into an old, old woman with a young woman's long shiny black hair. It was because of her that invading cops making their way through the forest bumped into tree limbs and tripped over roots, which made the People laugh. Sedna, Mother of the Sea, was just another old woman in the crowd except for her glowing silver hair. No one realized she was there until she turned the hillside to mud and the half-dozen officers coming up from the beach got mired in it. A helicopter came in low, but the winds started to swirl and blow and scared it off. On the ground it was clear to one and all that Adee the Thunderbird had created the turbulence by swooping through the skies, and the People cheered.

For some the ground shook and the People said this must be Dzelarhons the Volcano Woman rattling the world. No one said if it was because she was angry or just having fun. They say that Kannuck the Wolf Spirit raced through the woods howling and barking and frightening the police. And some saw Meitlikh the Lightning Snake, and others felt the monster Qagwaai, Killer of Dragons. The Bear People saw Bear spirits, and the Fox saw Fox. To each totem clan appeared their totem spirit. And they all felt touched and blessed, and they began to sing and dance.

When the wave of troopers arrived all fierce and full of fury, they encountered no resistance, just a celebration, and it stopped them cold. The People were inspired, in reverie, soaring beyond the expectations of their wildest dreams and visions, and nothing here could harm them.

For Jason, in the midst of all the noise and confusion, there was only quiet. For the People it was a dance of liberation, but he saw the Spirits disguised as people and he knew that they were there for him. He knew it was a dance of death. It made him angry because he had been promised his son. Now there was only this, and it was as if he could see every single pursuer coming for him in slow motion. He knew he had to leave the People before the bullets started flying, but he didn't know which way to go.

He turned in a circle until he saw old Dzarilaw standing on a path at the edge of the village.

"Come," Dzarilaw said quietly, his soft voice sliding its way through the tumult. "Come."

Jason went to join him, but as he got there Dzarilaw said, "Today you have become a great Spirit," and then he smiled and disappeared.

Jason looked back. The people were dancing—some with abandon, some in anger—and the cops were frustrated. The village was poised on the very hairline edge of an explosive disaster. This is what it must have felt like, he thought, in that split second before the Bennett Camp Posse unleashed its fury so many years ago. Jason would not let it happen again. He raised his arms and shouted out with all his voice: "I am here!"

Several heard him and the chase was on. "There he is! There he is!"

Jason took the path. It led to the high plateau and great cliffs overlooking the sea. He felt all his powers now as he climbed. He was faster than the wind, stronger than the biggest bear. He knew everything he had ever learned and he remembered every vision he had ever dreamed. He came to the plateau running and continued until he stood at the very edge of the cliff. He felt the sea breezes in his face and sucked in great gifts of air.

The dancing continued undisturbed down in the village. He had accomplished at least this, that on this night, no harm would come to anyone in the village. He waited at the cliff edge and listened for the army of lawmen chasing after him.

The first wave reached the plateau just as Bernie Pollard's helicopter returned and hovered over them, no longer buffeted by Adee's winds.

"Put down your weapons and lie face down on the ground," someone shouted at Jason through a bullhorn.

He had no weapon. All he carried was the shaman's rattle and he could not imagine that was what they were referring to. He was surrounded, everyone pointing guns at him. Too many to resist, but what choice did he have? He wouldn't give up the rattle and he would not lie down.

Hovering high, Bernie Pollard loaded the hollow-point elephant round into the chamber and took aim. A little red laser dot appeared in the center of Jason's chest.

"Put down your weapons and lie face down on the ground," the bullhorn shouted again.

Nathaniel finally made it to the village from the shore. He came upon them dancing, and beyond them, high over the plateau, he saw the chopper. He took the handful of troopers at the foot of the path as a clear marker and ran past them in a burst of speed and stamina that surprised even him. He was not quite to the plateau when he heard the bullhorn.

"This is your last warning. If you don't lay down your weapon and surrender by the count of five, we will be forced to open fire."

"Nooo!" Nathaniel screamed at the top of his lungs, to no avail. No one could hear him over the noise.

"One!" the bullhorn warned.

Running, racing, he didn't know if there was any faster in him, but he reached for it and found it. "Nooo!"

"Two!"

Faster. "Nooo!"

On "Three" Malcolm reached the plateau, waving Cottie Prusch's paper like a flag.

"Four!"

There before him, Nathaniel saw his father standing bathed in sunlight at the edge of the cliff. His father. Not Jason Ondine the fugitive. Not Jason the legend or the freak, not Jason teller of stories and keeper of magic. Not Jason the Spirit.

"Father," he called, running. If he could just get to him in time, make himself a shield, then they'd have to hold their fire and at least listen to him. He never even noticed Pollard's laser dot on Jason's chest.

Jason saw Nathaniel running to him, and he heard Nathaniel call him Father, heard it in his heart. "Return the bones," Jason said aloud to the heavens, "and your son will come to you."

"Five!"

By some miracle of endeavor, Nathaniel got himself into the line of fire just in time.

"Don't shoot! Hold your fire! Goddamit!" the bullhorn bellowed.

But up in the helicopter, Pollard wasn't listening to bullhorns. He had a clear shot and fair warning had been given. He didn't even see Nathaniel until he had squeezed the trigger and the red laser dot was intercepted, settling on the back of Nathaniel's head.

Jason saw the red dot and screamed.

And everything stopped.

The cops were immobilized. The helicopter fell silent. Nathaniel was halted in full flight.

Time had been seized, frozen by Hanging Hair. She appeared immediately, bringing Sedna and Adee with her.

Jason was furious and scared. "You stole my life and now you would take my son!"

"We are in the Spirit world now," Hanging Hair admonished. "Blame isn't going to resolve anything."

He got the message, the promise in it, and tried to relax. He couldn't. "He is my son, yes?"

"Yes," Hanging Hair confirmed. "You were promised."

"He looks a lot like Lizzie," Jason said, "when he's not trying to shoot me."

"He didn't know who you were."

"It wasn't an accusation."

"Actually, I think he looks more like you."

Jason circled around to the better view of Nathaniel, and his fatherly pride was shaken when he saw the laser dot again.

"Where the red dot lands," he told them, "the bullet follows."

"I've seen it work before," Hanging Hair answered. "It is a powerful weapon."

Jason circled around and around Nathaniel, as though by circling he could protect him, as though by circling he could keep time from ever coming back, at least for long enough to find a solution. "Nathaniel," he said again and again, "Nathaniel, my son."

His son was going to die before his eyes. His son was going to die for no reason but that he'd come to see his father. Jason cried out in agony and rage, he roared against his helplessness, and nothing changed. Nothing mattered.

If he had known that Lizzie was pregnant, maybe this would all be different. If he had known he had a son, he would never have returned to the sea. If he had known, if he had only known. He never would have thrown the stone that killed the deer, he never would have let his father leave him behind, if he had known.

When he spoke the words to Nathaniel, words meant to convey how much he loved his son, and how much better he would have done it if he were a better man, it was as if his own father were at the same time speaking the same words to him. "If I had known," he said, barely able to get the words out, "if only I had known."

Jason turned to the Sisters. Except for Hanging Hair there was no welcome on any face. "You can't let him die!" Jason pleaded.

"It's up to you," Adee announced.

"I don't have the power to—"

"I do," Hanging Hair promised. "We do."

Clearly they were preparing to propose a solution, but Jason didn't have the patience for the feelers. "Don't play games with me. He's my son. Whatever it is you want from me . . . is yours."

"Done." Sedna was happy to have it settled.

"No," Hanging Hair interceded, "he can't agree until he knows all that he will agree to."

"She's right," Adee agreed. "It has to be of his free will."

"Jason," Hanging Hair explained, "if we do nothing here this day, your son will die, but you will live for a thousand thousand generations. In time your powers will exceed ours, and you will hear the People sing your praise until beyond time."

"I choose my son," he said without hesitation. It was not as if he hadn't considered the blessings of immortality before. "I choose life for my son. What do you want from me? "

"You have to return the spirit Sedna breathed into you. You have to relinquish it and become mortal."

"It is all I have ever wanted."

"And it will be your life the red dot takes."

In his quest to recover his mortality he had never imagined that he would only find it at the moment of his death, but how else could he find out? How else could he know?

Everyone is in fact immortal until they are not. He imagined mortality would infuse his every breath with the recognition of how precious every moment really was. He thought it would inform a consciousness of life that left him in a permanent state of celebration, like normal people.

But it was not to be. For him the joys of mortal toil would arrive only at the moment of his death. "I choose my son."

"I knew you would," Hanging Hair smiled and she touched his arm. To her sisters she said, "I knew he would."

"Well, I don't understand it," Sedna said. She was glad, but it nonetheless confused her.

"Neither do I," Adee added. "It's about this love thing humans have, isn't it?"

"Yes it is," Hanging Hair agreed, very happy to see love from so close.

"He's my son," Jason explained.

"Is there anything you want?" Hanging Hair offered.

Yes. There was still treasure left and it was meant for his son. "I want him to understand that he is celebrated, that he is loved," Jason answered. "I want him to know my heart."

"It will be so," Hanging Hair promised.

The Sisters had no objection.

With a wave of her hand Hanging Hair moved Nathaniel's frozen body a little to the right and freed him from the laser dot. Then she nodded to Jason, and he took his place on the edge of the cliff where he had been. The red dot settled once more on his chest.

The sisters disappeared and time resumed.

"Nathaniel . . . " Jason said and then the bullet exploded through his chest, obliterating the red laser dot and everything that lay behind it.

The force of the bullet blew Jason backward as Nathaniel reached for him.

Jason almost grabbed his arm but real life happens too quickly. All they could manage was the touch of their fingers as their hands flew by each other, and it was electric and ferocious, a touch both brief and eternal. It was a moment, less, but they looked in each other's eyes and shared their hearts. It lasted forever and it was over before it began. Jason sailed from the cliff and fell to die on the crashing waves and rocks below.

—

The police sealed off the shore while they searched for the body, but they never found it. All they saw was a dead sea lion broken on the rocks. When the police left and the People found the sea lion, what they saw in him was Jason Ondine and they wept for him. They took him off the rocks and laid him on the sand, and one by one they passed by and touched him and said good-bye. Some thanked him for his stories, some for returning the bones and the masks, and some asked him to carry messages to their ancestors.

It fell to Johnny Oatmeal, an Island Kwakiutl, to slit the body open and remove the bladder. They washed it and cleaned it and filled it with air. Then all the People lined a path to the sea, and Johnny Oatmeal announced to one and all that this bladder held the soul of Jason Ondine.

He handed it to Nathaniel, who didn't know what to think or

what to believe, but he treated it with great respect and carried it into the water as he was instructed to do, and set it free.

Nathaniel wept as he watched it float out into the ocean. It tore at him from within and from without and finally he said good-bye. "Safe journey, Father," he called out.

He watched for a little while longer, and then he turned and came back ashore to the others and the embrace of the mourning song.

"Ay yi yi Jason Ondine. Ay yi yi."

—

Hanging Hair and her sisters were pleased to have the world back in order. Dzarilaw's Village, known once again as Eulakon, was in full renaissance. In less than four months two houses and a full-size lodge had been built. In front of each stood a great totem pole, donated by clan cousins from other villages. And a carver, a Nootka from down the Sound, carved a huge sea lion to set up on the plateau for Jason's burial pole.

Nathaniel stayed behind in Eulakon for the several weeks of mourning. He learned the stories they had learned from Jason, helped build the lodges, and made everyone laugh when he practiced the dances.

One year exactly from the day of his death, Jason came to Lizzie in a dream, and she embraced him. She held him through the night and filled her heart. The next morning she went out to Calder Cove and played her flute for him. She played the melody that had drawn him from the sea so long ago, and both the notes and her tears flowed freely.

When she was done, she announced calmly that her mourning had come to an end. When she said the words, a great orca leapt from the sea, rising in a spectacular arc before it fell back below the waves and disappeared.

A giant bird flew by. She had never seen anything like it except for those Thunderbirds on the totem poles and she wondered if it could be . . . and she thought, yes, yes.

Raven screamed and Lizzie turned to see it sitting on her roof. For an instant, and only that, Raven took the form of Mike the shaman and smiled at her. All at once Lizzie felt whole. She felt like the journey had resumed, and she said to Raven, thank you, thank you.

Thank you.

Raven sighed, and deeply touched and profoundly jealous, flew away without a word.